MORE RAVE REVIEWS FOR
KINSEY MILLHONE
AND
"D" IS FOR DEADBEAT

"One of the things that makes Sue Grafton's Kinsey Millhone series so unfailingly entertaining is Millhone's character. She's the last one to cultivate eccentricities in the Nero Wolfe manner, and her unsentimental, loner's-eye view of herself and the world keeps her feet on the ground. But her cases often get messy because she feels things strongly. This happens again, more satisfyingly than ever, in *"D" is for Deadbeat*."

—The Detroit News

"Kinsey Millhone has the characteristic persistence of the good private eye who won't be deterred from digging out the truth. With skill, Grafton keeps not only her appealing detective but her readers on edge to know more."

—Ms. magazine

"Taut prose and controlled plotting make Grafton an outstanding writer of hardboiled detective stories. Social awareness and human weakness play a great part in the Millhone books, which always manage to finish with a heart-stopping climax. Well done indeed."

—Library Journal

"D" is for Deadbeat

A Kinsey Millhone Mystery

SUE GRAFTON

BANTAM BOOKS
NEW YORK • TORONTO • LONDON • SYDNEY • AUCKLAND

"D" IS FOR DEADBEAT

*A Bantam Crime Line Book / published by arrangement with
Henry Holt and Company, Inc.*

PRINTING HISTORY
Henry Holt edition published May 1987
Bantam edition / June 1988

CRIME LINE *and the portrayal of a boxed "cl" are trademarks of Bantam Books, a division
of Bantam Doubleday Dell Publishing Group, Inc.*

ISBN 0-553-27163-6

Published simultaneously in the United States and Canada

**Bantam Books are published by Bantam Books, a division of Bantam Doubleday Dell
Publishing Group, Inc. Its trademark, consisting of the words "Bantam Books" and the
portrayal of a rooster, is Registered in U.S. Patent and Trademark Office and in other
countries. Marca Registrada. Bantam Books, 1540 Broadway, New York, New York 10036.**

PRINTED IN THE UNITED STATES OF AMERICA

OPM   24   23   22   21   20   19

For my sister, Ann,
and the memories of Maple Hill.

The author wishes to acknowledge the invaluable assistance of the following people: Steven Humphrey, Florence Clark, Joyce Mackewich, Steve Stafford, Bob Ericson, Ann Hunnicutt, Charles and Mary Pope of the Rescue Mission, Michael Thompson of the Santa Barbara Probation Department, Michelle Bores and Bob Brandenburg of the Santa Barbara Harbor Master's Office, Mary Louise Days of the Santa Barbara Building Department, and Gerald Dow, Crime Analyst, Santa Barbara Police Department.

"D" is for Deadbeat

1

Later, I found out his name was John Daggett, but that's not how he introduced himself the day he walked into my office. Even at the time, I sensed that something was off, but I couldn't figure out what it was. The job he hired me to do seemed simple enough, but then the bum tried to stiff me for my fee. When you're self-employed, you can't afford to let these things slide. Word gets out and first thing you know, everybody thinks you can be had. I went after him for the money and the next thing I knew, I was caught up in events I still haven't quite recovered from.

My name is Kinsey Millhone. I'm a private investigator, licensed by the state of California, operating a small office in Santa Teresa, which is where I've lived all my thirty-two years. I'm female, self-supporting, single now, having been married and divorced twice. I confess I'm sometimes testy, but for the most part I credit myself with an easygoing disposition, tempered (perhaps) by an exaggerated desire for independence. I'm also plagued with the sort of doggedness that makes private investigation a viable proposition for someone with a high school education, certification from the police academy, and a constitutional inability to work for anyone else. I pay my bills on time, obey most laws, and I feel that other people should do likewise . . . out of courtesy, if nothing else. I'm a purist when it comes to justice, but I'll lie at the drop of a hat. Inconsistency has never troubled me.

It was late October, the day before Halloween, and the weather was mimicking autumn in the Midwest—clear and sunny and cool. Driving into town, I could have sworn I smelled woodsmoke in the air and I half expected the leaves to be turning yellow and rust. All I actually saw were the same old palm trees, the same relentless green everywhere. The fires of summer had been contained and the rains hadn't started yet. It was a typical California *unseason*, but it *felt* like fall and I was responding with inordinate good cheer, thinking maybe I'd drive up the pass in the afternoon to the pistol range, which is what I do for laughs.

I'd come into the office that Saturday morning to take care of some bookkeeping chores—paying personal bills, getting out my statements for the month. I had my calculator out, a Redi-Receipt form in the typewriter, and four completed statements lined up, addressed and stamped, on the desk to my left. I was so intent on the task at hand that I didn't realize anyone was standing in the doorway until the man cleared his throat. I reacted with one of those little jumps you do when you open the evening paper and a spider runs out. He apparently found this amusing, but I was having to pat myself on the chest to get my heart rate down again.

"I'm Alvin Limardo," he said. "Sorry if I startled you."

"That's all right," I said, "I just had no idea you were standing there. Are you looking for me?"

"If you're Kinsey Millhone, I am."

I got up and shook hands with him across the desk and then suggested that he take a seat. My first fleeting impression had been that he was a derelict, but on second glance, I couldn't find anything in particular to support the idea.

He was in his fifties, too gaunt for good health. His face was long and narrow, his chin pronounced. His hair was an ash gray, clipped short, and he smelled of citrus cologne. His eyes were hazel, his gaze remote. The suit he wore was an odd shade of green. His hands seemed huge, fingers long and bony, the knuckles enlarged. The two inches of narrow wrist extending, cuffless, from his coat sleeves suggested shabbiness though his clothing didn't really look worn. He held a slip of paper which he'd folded twice, and he fiddled with that self-consciously.

"What can I do for you?" I asked.

"I'd like for you to deliver this." He smoothed out the piece of paper then and placed it on my desk. It was a cashier's check drawn on a Los Angeles bank, dated October 29, and made out to someone named Tony Gahan for twenty-five thousand dollars.

I tried not to appear as surprised as I felt. He didn't look like a man with money to spare. Maybe he'd borrowed the sum from Gahan and was paying it back. "You want to tell me what this is about?"

"He did me a favor. I want to say thanks. That's all it is."

"It must have been quite a favor," I said. "Do you mind if I ask what he did?"

"He showed me a kindness when I was down on my luck."

"What do you need me for?"

He smiled briefly. "An attorney would charge me a hundred and twenty dollars an hour to handle it. I'm assuming you'd charge considerably less."

"So would a messenger service," I said. "It's cheaper still if you do it yourself." I wasn't being a smart-mouth about it. I really didn't understand why he needed a private detective.

He cleared his throat. "I tried that, but I'm not entirely certain of Mr. Gahan's current address. At one

time, he lived on Stanley Place, but he's not there now. I
went by this morning and the house is empty. It looks
like it hasn't been lived in for a while. I want someone to
track him down and make sure he gets the money. If you
can estimate what that might run me, I'll pay you in
advance."

"That depends on how elusive Mr. Gahan turns out
to be. The credit bureau might have a current address,
or the DMV. A lot of inquiries can be done by phone, but
they still take time. At thirty bucks an hour, the fee does
mount up."

He took out a checkbook and began to write out a
check. "Two hundred dollars?"

"Let's make it four. I can always refund the balance
if the charges turn out to be less," I said. "In the
meantime, I've got a license to protect so this better be
on the up and up. I'd be happier if you'd tell me what's
going on."

This was where he hooked me, because what he said
was just offbeat enough to be convincing. Liar that I am,
it still didn't occur to me that there could be so much
falsehood mixed in with the truth.

"I got into trouble with the law awhile back and
served some time. Tony Gahan was helpful to me just
before I was arrested. He had no idea of my circum-
stances so he wasn't an accessory to anything, nor would
you be. I feel indebted."

"Why not take care of it yourself?"

He hesitated, almost shyly I thought. "It's sort of
like that Charles Dickens book, *Great Expectations*. He
might not like having a convicted felon for a benefactor.
People have strange ideas about ex-cons."

"What if he won't accept an anonymous donation?"

"You can return the check in that case and keep the
fee."

I shifted restlessly in my chair. What's wrong with

this picture, I asked myself. "Where'd you get the money if you've been in jail?"

"Santa Anita. I'm still on parole and I shouldn't be playing the ponies at all, but I find it hard to resist. That's why I'd like to pass the money on to you. I'm a gambling man. I can't have that kind of cash around or I'll piss it away, if you'll pardon my French." He closed his mouth then and looked at me, waiting to see what else I might ask. Clearly, he didn't want to volunteer more than was necessary to satisfy my qualms, but he seemed amazingly patient. I realized later, of course, that his tolerance was probably the function of his feeding me so much bullshit. He must have been entertained by the game he was playing. Lying is fun. I can do it all day myself.

"What was the felony?" I asked.

He dropped his gaze, addressing his reply to his oversized hands, which were folded in his lap. "I don't think that pertains. This money is clean and I came by it honestly. There's nothing illegal about the transaction if that's what's worrying you."

Of *course* it worried me, but I wondered if I was being too fastidious. There was nothing wrong with his request on the face of it. I chased the proposition around in my head with caution, wondering what Tony Gahan had done for Limardo that would net him this kind of payoff. None of my business, I supposed, as long as no laws had been broken in the process. Intuition was telling me to turn this guy down, but it happens that the rent on my apartment was due the next day. I had the money in my checking account, but it seemed providential to have a retainer drop in my lap unexpectedly. In any event, I didn't see a reason to refuse. "All right," I said.

He nodded once, pleased. "Good."

I sat and watched while he finished signing his name to the check. He tore it out and pushed it toward me, tucking the checkbook into the inner pocket of his suit coat. "My address and telephone number are on that in case you need to get in touch."

I pulled a standard contract form out of my desk drawer and took a few minutes to fill it in. I got his signature and then I made a note of Tony Gahan's last known address, a house in Colgate, the township just north of Santa Teresa. I was already feeling some low-level dread, wishing I hadn't agreed to do anything. Still, I'd committed myself, the contract was signed, and I figured I'd make the best of it. How much trouble could it be, thought I.

He stood up and I did too, moving with him as he walked toward the door. With both of us on our feet, I could see how much taller he was than I . . . maybe six-four to my five-foot-six. He paused with his hand on the knob, gazing down at me with the same remote stare.

"One other thing you might need to know about Tony Gahan," he said.

"What's that?"

"He's fifteen years old."

I stood there and watched Alvin Limardo move off down the hall. I should have called him back, folks. I should have known right then that it wasn't going to turn out well. Instead I closed the office door and returned to my desk. On impulse, I opened the French doors and went out on the balcony. I scanned the street below, but there was no sign of him. I shook my head, dissatisfied.

I locked the cashier's check in my file cabinet. When the bank opened on Monday, I'd put it in my safe deposit box until I located Tony Gahan and then turn it over to him. Fifteen?

At noon, I closed up the office and went down the back stairs to the parking lot, where I retrieved my VW, a decaying sedan with more rust than paint. This is not the sort of vehicle you'd choose for a car chase, but then most of what a P.I. does for a living isn't that exciting anyway. I'm sometimes reduced to serving process papers, which gets hairy now and then, but much of the time I do preemployment background checks, skip-tracing, or case-and-trial preparation for a couple of attorneys here in town. My office is provided by California Fidelity Insurance, a former employer of mine. The company headquarters is right next door and I still do sporadic investigations for them in exchange for a modest two rooms (one inner, one outer) with a separate entrance and a balcony overlooking State Street.

I went by the post office and dropped the mail in the box and then I stopped by the bank and deposited Alvin Limardo's four hundred dollars in my checking account.

Four business days later, on a Thursday, I got a letter from the bank, informing me that the check had bounced. According to their records, Alvin Limardo had closed out his account. In proof of this, I was presented with the check itself stamped across the face with the sort of officious looking purple ink that makes it clear the bank is displeased.

So was I.

My account had been debited the four hundred dollars and I was charged an additional three bucks, apparently to remind me, in the future, not to deal with deadbeats. I picked up the phone and called Alvin Limardo's number in Los Angeles. A disconnect. I'd been canny enough to ignore the search for Tony Gahan until the check cleared, so it wasn't as if I'd done any work to date. But how was I going to get the check replaced? And what was I going to do with the twenty-five grand in the meantime? By then, the cashier's check was tucked away in my safe deposit box, but it was useless to me and I didn't want to proceed with delivery until I knew I'd be paid. In theory, I could have dropped Alvin Limardo a note, but it might have come bouncing back at me with all the jauntiness of his rubber check, and then where would I be? Crap. I was going to have to drive down to L.A. One thing I've learned about collections—the faster you move, the better your chances are.

I looked up his street address in my *Thomas Guide to Los Angeles Streets*. Even on the map, it didn't look like a nice neighborhood. I checked my watch. It was then 10:15. It was going to take me ninety minutes to reach L.A., probably another hour to locate Limardo, chew him out, get the check replaced, and grab a bite of lunch. Then I'd have to drive ninety minutes back, which would put me in the office again at 3:30 or 4:00. Well, that wasn't too bad. It was tedious, but necessary, so I decided I might as well quit bellyaching and get on with it.

By 10:30, I'd gassed up my car and I was on the road.

2

I left the Ventura Freeway at Sherman Oaks, taking the San Diego Freeway south as far as Venice Boulevard. I exited, turning right at the bottom of the off-ramp. According to my calculations, the address I wanted was somewhere close. I doubled back toward Sawtelle, the street that hugs the freeway on a parallel route.

Once I saw the building, I realized that I'd spotted the rear of it from the freeway as I passed. It was painted the color of Pepto-Bismol and sported a sagging banner of Day-Glo orange that said NOW RENTING. The building was separated from the roadway by a concrete rain wash and protected from speeding vehicles by a ten-foot cinderblock wall sprayed with messages for passing motorists. Spiky weeds had sprung up along the base of the wall and trash had accumulated like hanging ornaments in the few hearty bushes that managed to survive the gas fumes. I had noted the building because it seemed so typical of L.A.: bald, cheaply constructed, badly defaced. There was something meanspirited about its backside, and the entrance turned out to be worse.

The street was largely made up of California "bungalows," small two-bedroom houses of wood and stucco with ragged yards and no trees. Most of them had been painted in pastel hues, odd shades of turquoise

9

and mauve, suggestive of discount paints that hadn't quite covered the color underneath. I found a parking space across the street and locked my car, then crossed to the apartment complex.

The building was beginning to disintegrate. The stucco looked mealy and dry, the aluminum window frames pitted and buckling. The wrought-iron gate near the front had been pulled straight out of the supporting wall, leaving holes large enough to stick a fist into. Two apartments at street level were boarded up. The management had thoughtfully provided a number of garbage bins near the stairs, without (apparently) paying for adequate trash removal services. A big yellow dog was scratching through this pile of refuse with enthusiasm, though all he seemed to net for his efforts was a quarter moon of pizza. He trotted off, the rim of crust clenched in his jaws like a bone.

I moved into the shelter of the stairs. Most of the mailboxes had been ripped out and mail was scattered in the foyer like so much trash. According to the address on the face of the check, Limardo lived in apartment 26, which I surmised was somewhere above. There were apparently forty units, only a few marked with the occupants' names. That seemed curious to me. In Santa Teresa, the post office won't even deliver junk mail unless a box is provided, clearly marked, and in good repair. I pictured the postman, emptying out his mail pouch like a wastepaper basket, escaping on foot then before the inhabitants of the building swarmed over him like bugs.

The apartments were arranged in tiers around a courtyard "garden" of loose gravel, pink paving stones, and nut grass. I picked my way up the cracked concrete steps.

At the second-floor landing, a black man was seated in a rickety metal folding chair, whittling with a knife on a bar of Ivory soap. There was a magazine open on his lap to catch the shavings. He was heavyset and shapeless, maybe fifty years old, his short-cropped frizzy hair showing gray around his ears. His eyes were a muddy brown, the lid of one pulled askew by a vibrant track of stitches that cut down along his cheek.

He took me in at a glance, turning his attention then to the sculpture taking form in his hands. "You must be looking for Alvin Limardo," he said.

"That's right," I said, startled. "How'd you guess?"

He flashed a smile at me, showing perfect teeth, as snowy as the soap he carved. He tilted his face up at me, the injured eye creating the illusion of a wink. "Baby, you ain't live here. I know ever'body live here. And from the look on your face, you ain't thinkin' to rent. If you knew where you were going, you'd be headed straight there. Instead, you be lookin' all around like somethin' might jump out on you, including me," he said and then paused to survey me. "I'd say you do social work, parole, something like that. Maybe welfare."

"Not bad," I said. "But why Limardo? What made you think I was looking for him?"

He smiled then, his gums showing pink. "We *all* Alvin Limardo 'round here. It's a joke we play. Just a name we take when we jivin' folk. I been Alvin Limardo myself lass week at the food stamp line. He get welfare checks, disability, AFDC. Somebody show up lass week wid a warrant on him. I tole 'em, 'Alvin Limardo's done leff. He gone. Ain't nobody here by that name about now.' The Alvin Limardo you want . . . he be white or black?"

"White," I said and then described the man who'd come into my office on Saturday. The black man started nodding about halfway through, his knife blade still smoothing the surface of the soap. It looked like he'd carved a sow lying on her side with a litter of piglets scrambling over her to nurse. The whole of it couldn't have been more than four inches long.

"That's John Daggett. Whooee. He bad. He the one you want, but he gone for sure."

"Do you have any idea where he went?"

"Santa Teresa, I heard."

"Well, I know he was up there last Saturday. That's where I ran into him," I said. "Has he been back since then?"

The man's mouth drooped with skepticism. "I seen him on Monday and then he gone off again. Only other peoples must want him too. He ack like a man who's runnin' and don't want to be caught. What you want wid him?"

"He wrote me a bum check."

He shot me a look of astonishment. "You take a check from a man like that? Lord God, girl! What's the matter wid you?"

I had to laugh. "I know. It's my own damn fault. I thought maybe I could catch him before he skipped out permanently."

He shook his head, unable to sympathize. "Don't take nothin' from the likes of him. That's your first mistake. Comin' 'round this place may be the next."

"Is there anybody here who might know how to get in touch with him?"

He pointed the blade of his knife toward an apartment two doors down. "Axe Lovella. She might know. Then again, she might not."

"She's a friend of his?"

"Not hardly. She's his wife."

I felt somewhat more hopeful as I knocked at apartment 26. I was afraid he'd moved out altogether. The door was a hollowcore with a hole kicked into the bottom about shin high. The sliding glass window was open six inches, a fold of drapery sticking out. A crack ran diagonally across the pane, held together by a wide band of electrician's tape. I could smell something cooking inside, kale or collard greens, with a whisper of vinegar and bacon grease.

The door opened and a woman peered out at me. Her upper lip was puffy, like the kind of scrape children get falling off bicycles when they first learn to ride. Her left eye had been blackened not long ago and it was streaked now with midnight blue, the surrounding tissue a rainbow of green and yellow and gray. Her hair was the color of hay, parted in the middle and snagged up over each ear with a bobby pin. I couldn't even guess how old she might be. Younger than I expected, given John Daggett's age, which had to be fifty plus.

"Lovella Daggett?"

"That's right." She seemed reluctant to admit that much.

"I'm Kinsey Millhone. I'm looking for John."

She licked uneasily at her upper lip as if she was still unfamiliar with its new shape and size. Some of the scraped area had formed a scab, which resembled nothing so much as half a moustache. "He's not here. I don't know where he's at. What'd you want him for?"

"He hired me to do some work, but he paid me with a bum check. I was hoping we could get it straightened out."

She studied me while she processed the information. "Hired you to do what?"

"Deliver something."

She didn't believe a bit of that. "You a cop?"

"No."

"What are you, then?"

I showed her the photostat of my license by way of reply. She turned and walked away from the door, leaving it open behind her. I gathered this was her method of inviting me in.

I stepped into the living room and closed the door behind me. The carpeting was that green cotton shag so admired by apartment owners everywhere. The only furniture in the room was a card table and two plain wooden chairs. A six-foot rectangle of lighter carpeting along one wall suggested that there'd once been a couch on the spot, and a pattern of indentations in the rug indicated the former presence of two heavy chairs and a coffee table, arranged in what decorators refer to as "a conversational grouping." Instead of conversation these days, Daggett apparently got right down to busting her chops, breaking anything else that came to hand. The one lamp I saw had been snapped off at the socket and the wires were hanging out like torn ligaments.

"Where'd the furniture go?"

"He hocked it all last week. Turns out he used the payments for his bar bill. The car went before that. It was a piece of junk, anyway, but I'd paid for it. You ought to see what I've got for a bed these days. Some peed-on old mattress he found out on the street."

There were two bar stools at the counter and I perched on one, watching as Lovella ambled into the small space that served as a kitchen. An aluminum saucepan sat on a gas flame on the stove, the water in it boiling furiously. On one of the other back burners, there was a battered aluminum kettle filled with simmering greens.

Lovella wore blue jeans and a plain white tee shirt wrong-side out, the Fruit of the Loom label visible at the back of her neck. The bottom of the shirt had been pulled tight and knotted to form a halter, leaving her midriff bare. "You want coffee? I was just fixing some."

"Yes, please," I said.

She rinsed a cup under the hot water faucet and gave it a quick swipe with a paper towel. She set it on the counter and spooned instant coffee into it and then used the same paper towel as a potholder when she reached for the saucepan. The water sputtered against the edge of the pan as she poured. She added water to a second cup, gave a quick stir to the contents, and pushed it toward me with the spoon still resting up against the rim.

"Daggett's a jerk. They should lock him up for life," she remarked, almost idly, I thought.

"Did he do that to you?" I asked, my gaze flicking across her bruised face.

She fixed a pair of dead gray eyes on me without bothering to reply. Up close, I could see that she wasn't much more than twenty-five. She leaned forward, resting her elbows on the counter, her coffee cup cradled in her hands. She wasn't wearing a bra and her breasts were big, as soft and droopy as balloons filled with water, her nipples pressing against the tee-shirt fabric like puckered knots. I wondered if she was a hooker. I'd known a few with the same careless sexuality—all surface, no feeling underneath.

"How long have you been married?"

"You care if I have a cigarette?"

"It's your place. You can do anything you want," I said.

That netted me a wan smile, the first I'd seen. She reached for a pack of Pall Mall 100s, flipped on the gas burner, and lit her cigarette from it, tilting her head so her hair wouldn't catch fire. She took a deep drag and exhaled it, blowing a cloud of smoke at me. "Six weeks," she said, answering my question belatedly. "We were pen pals after he got sent to San Luis. Wrote for a year and then I married him the minute he got out. Dumb? Jesus. Can you believe I did that?"

I shrugged noncommittally. She didn't really care if I believed it or not. "How'd you connect in the first place?"

"A buddy of his. Guy named Billy Polo I used to date. They'd sit and talk about women and my name came up. I guess Billy made me sound like real hot stuff, so Daggett got in touch."

I took a sip of my coffee. It had that flat, nearly sour

taste of instant, with tiny clumps of coffee powder floating at the edge. "Do you have any milk for this?"

"Oh, sure. Sorry," she said. She moved over to the refrigerator where she took out a small can of Carnation.

It wasn't quite what I had in mind, but I added some to my coffee, intrigued as evaporated milk rose to the surface in a series of white dots. I wondered if a fortune teller could read the pattern, like tea leaves. I thought I spied some indigestion in my future, but I wasn't sure.

"Daggett's a charmer when he wants," she said. "Give him a couple of drinks, though, and he's mean as a snake."

That was a story I'd heard before. "Why don't you leave?" said I, as I always do.

"Because he'd come after me is why," she said snappishly. "You don't know him. He'd kill me without giving it a second thought. Same thing if I called the cops. Talk back to that man and he'll punch your teeth down your throat. He hates women is what's the matter with him. Of course, when he sobers up, he can charm your socks off. Anyway, I'm hoping he's gone for good. He got a phone call Monday morning and he was out of here like a shot. I haven't heard from him since. Of course, the phone was disconnected yesterday so I don't know how he'd reach me even if he wanted to."

"Why don't you talk to his parole officer?"

"I guess I could," she said reluctantly. "He reports to the guy every time he turns around. For two days he had a job, but he quit that. Of course, he's not supposed to drink. I guess he tried to play by the rules at first, but it was too much."

"Why not get out while you have the chance?"

"And go where? I don't have a nickel to my name."

"There are shelters for battered women. Call the rape crisis center. They'll know."

She gestured dismissively. "Jesus, I love people like you. You ever had a guy punch you out?"

"Not one I was married to," I said. "I wouldn't put up with that shit."

"That's what I used to say, sister, but I'll tell you what. You don't get away as easy as all that. Not with a bastard like Daggett. He swears he'd follow me to the ends of the earth and he would."

"What was he in prison for?"

"He never said and I never asked. Which was also dumb. It didn't make any difference to me at first. He was fine for a couple weeks. Just like a kid, you know? And sweet? Lord, he trotted around after me like a puppy dog. We couldn't get enough of each other and it all seemed just like the letters we wrote. Then he got into the Jack Daniel's one night and the shit hit the fan."

"Did he ever mention the name Tony Gahan?"

"Nuh-uh. Who's he?"

"I'm not sure. Some kid he asked me to find."

"What'd he pay you with? Can I see the check?"

I took it out of my handbag and laid it on the counter. I thought it best not to mention the cashier's check. I didn't think she'd take kindly to his giving money away. "I understand Limardo is a fabricated name."

She studied the check. "Yeah, but Daggett did keep some money in this account. I think he cleaned it out just before he left." She took a drag of her cigarette as she handed back the check. I managed to turn my head before she blew smoke in my face again.

"That phone call he got Monday, what was it about? Do you know?"

"Beats me. I was off at the Laundromat. I got home and he was still on the phone, his face as gray as that dish rag. He hung up quick and then started shovin' stuff in a duffel. He turned the place upside down lookin' for his bank book. I was afraid he'd come after me, thinkin' I took it, but I guess he was too freaked out to worry about me."

"He told you that?"

"No, but he was cold sober and his hands were shaking *bad*."

"You have any idea where he might have gone?"

A look flashed through her eyes, some emotion she concealed by dropping her gaze. "He only had one friend and that was Billy Polo up in Santa Teresa. If he needed help, that's where he'd go. I think he used to have family up there too, but I don't know what happened to them. He never talked much about that."

"So Polo's out of prison?"

"I heard he got out just recently."

"Well, maybe I'll track him down since that's the only lead I have. In the meantime, would you find a phone and call me if you hear from either one?" I took out a business card and jotted my home address and phone on the back. "Call collect."

She looked at both sides of the card. "What do you think is goin' on?"

"I don't know and I don't much care. As soon as I run him down, I'll clean up this business and *bail out*."

3

As long as I was in the area, I went by the bank. The woman in charge of customer service couldn't have been less helpful. She was dark haired, in her early twenties, and new at the job I gathered because she greeted my every request with the haunted look of someone who isn't quite sure of the rules and therefore says no to everything. She would not verify "Alvin Limardo's" account number or the fact that the account had been closed. She would not tell me if there was, perhaps, another account in John Daggett's name. I knew there had to be a registered copy of the cashier's check itself, but she refused to verify the information he'd given at the time. I kept thinking there was some other tack I might take, especially with that much money at stake. Surely, the bank must care what happened to twenty-five thousand dollars. I stood at the counter and stared at the woman, and she stared back. Maybe she hadn't understood.

I took out the photostat of my license and pointed. "Look," I said, "You see this? I'm a private investigator. I've got a real problem here. I was hired to deliver a cashier's check, but now I can't find the man who gave it to me and I don't know the whereabouts of the person who's supposed to receive it and I'm just trying to get a lead so I can do what I was hired to do."

"I understand that," she said.

"But you won't give me any information, right?"

"It's against bank regulations."

"Isn't it against bank regulations for Alvin Limardo to write me a bad check?"

"Yes."

"Then what am I supposed to do with it?" I said. I really knew the answer . . . eat it, dum-dum . . . but I was feeling stubborn and perverse.

"Take him to small claims court," she said.

"But I can't find him. He can't be hauled into court if nobody knows where he is."

She stared at me blankly, offering no comment.

"What about the twenty-five thousand?" I said. "What am I supposed to do with that?"

"I have no idea."

I stared down at the desk. When I was in kindergarten, I was a biter and I still struggle with the urge. It just feels good, you know? "I want to speak to your supervisor."

"Mr. Stallings? He's gone for the day."

"Well, is there anybody else here who might give me some help on this?"

She shook her head. "I'm in charge of customer service."

"But you're not doing a thing. How can you call it customer service when you don't do shit?"

Her mouth turned prim. "Please don't use language like that around me. It's very offensive."

"What do I have to do to get help around here?"

"Do you have an account with us?"

"If I did, would you help?"

"Not with this. We're not supposed to divulge information about bank customers."

This was silly. I walked away from her desk. I wanted to make a withering remark, but I couldn't think of one. I knew I was just mad at myself for taking the job to begin with, but I was hoping to lay a little ire off on her . . . a pointless enterprise. I got back in my car and headed toward the freeway. When I reached Santa Teresa, it was 4:35. I bypassed the office altogether and went home. My disposition improved the minute I walked in. My apartment was once a single-car garage and consists now of one room, fifteen feet on a side, with a narrow extension on the right that serves as a kitchenette, separated from the living area by a counter. The space is arranged with cunning: a stackable washer-dryer tucked in beside the kitchenette, bookshelves, drawers and storage compartments built into the wall. It's tidy and self-contained and all of it suits me absolutely. I have a six-foot convertible sofa that I usually sleep on as is, a desk, a chair, an endtable, and plump pillows that serve as additional seating if anyone comes over to sit. My bathroom is one of those pre-formed fiberglass units with everything molded into it, including a towel bar, a soap holder, and a cutout for a window that looks out at the street. Sometimes I stand in the bathtub, elbows resting on the sill, and stare at passing cars, just thinking how lucky I am. I love being single. It's almost like being rich.

I dropped my handbag on the desk and hung my jacket on a peg. I sat on the couch and pulled off my boots, then padded over to the refrigerator and took out a bottle of white zinfandel and a corkscrew. At intervals, I try to behave like a person with class, which is to say I drink wine from a bottle instead of a cardboard box. I pulled the cork and poured myself a glass. I crossed to the desk, taking the telephone book from the top drawer, trailing telephone cord, directory, and wine glass over to the sofa. I set the wine glass on the endtable and thumbed through the book to see if Billy Polo was listed. Of course, he wasn't. I looked up the name Gahan. No dice. I drank some wine and tried to think what to do next.

On an impulse, I checked for the name Daggett. Lovella had mentioned that he once lived up here. Maybe he still had relatives in town.

There were four Daggetts listed. I started dialing them in order, saying the same thing each time. "Oh, hi. I'm trying to reach a John Daggett, who used to live in this area. Can you tell me if this is the correct number?"

On the first two calls, I drew a blank, but with the third, the man who answered responded to my query with one of those odd silences that indicate that information is being processed.

"What did you want with him?" he asked. He sounded like he was in his sixties, his phrasing tentative, alert to my response, but undecided how much he was willing to reveal.

He was certainly skipping right down to the tricky part. From everything I'd heard about Daggett, he was a bum, so I didn't dare claim to be a friend of his. If I admitted he owed me money, I was going to have the phone slammed down in my ear. Ordinarily, in a situation like this, I'd insinuate that I had money for *him*, but somehow I didn't think that would fly. People are getting wise to that shit.

I laid out the first lie that occurred to me. "Well, to tell you the truth," I said, "I've only met John once, but I'm trying to get in touch with a mutual acquaintance and I think John has his address and telephone number."

"Who were you looking to get in touch with?"

That caught me off-guard, as I hadn't made that part up yet. "Who? Um . . . Alvin Limardo. Has John ever mentioned Alvin?"

"No, I don't believe so. But, now, you may have the wrong party. The John Daggett that used to live here is currently in prison and he's been there, oh I'd say nearly two years." His manner suggested a man whose retirement has invested even a wrong number with some interesting possibilities. Still, it was clear I'd hit pay dirt.

"That's the one I'm talking about," I said. "He was up in San Luis Obispo."

"He still is."

"Oh, no. He's out. He was released six weeks ago."

"John? *No*, ma'am. He's still in prison and I hope he stays there. I don't mean to speak ill of the man, but you'll find he's what I call a problematic person."

"Problematic?"

"Well, yes. That's how I'd have to put it. John is the type of person that creates problems and usually of a quite serious nature."

"Oh, really," I said. "I didn't realize that." I loved it that this man was willing to chat. As long as I could keep him going, I might figure out how to get a bead on Daggett. I took a flyer. "Are you his brother?"

"I'm his brother-in-law, Eugene Nickerson."

"You must be married to his sister then," I said.

He laughed. "No, he's married to *my* sister. She was a Nickerson before she became a Daggett."

"You're Lovella's brother?" I was trying to picture siblings with a forty-year age span.

"No, Essie's."

I held the receiver away from my ear and stared at it. What was he talking about? "Wait a minute. I'm confused. Maybe we're *not* talking about the same man." I gave a quick verbal sketch of the John Daggett I'd met. I didn't see how there could be two, but there was something going on here.

"That's him all right. How did you say you knew him?"

"I met him last Saturday, right here in Santa Teresa."

The silence on the other end of the line was profound.

I finally broke into it. "Is there some way I might stop by so we can talk about this?"

"I think you'd best," he said. "What would your name be?"

"Kinsey Millhone."

He told me how to get to the place.

The house was white frame with a small wooden porch, tucked into the shadow of Capillo Hill on the west side of town. The street was abbreviated, only three houses on each side before the blacktop petered out into the gravel patch that formed a parking pad beside the Daggett residence. Beyond the house, the hill angled upward into sparse trees and underbrush. No sunlight whatever penetrated the yard. A sagging chicken wire fence cut along the lot lines. Bushes had been planted at intervals, but had failed to thrive, so that now there were only globes of dried twigs. The house had a hangdog look, like a stray being penned up until the dogcatcher comes.

I climbed the steep wooden steps and knocked. Eugene Nickerson opened the door. He was much as I had pictured him: in his sixties, of medium height, with wiry gray hair and eyebrows drawn together in a knot. His eyes were small and pale, his lashes nearly white. Narrow shoulders, thick waist, suspenders, flannel shirt. He carried a Bible in his left hand, his index finger closed between the covers, keeping his place.

Uh-oh, I thought.

"I'll have to ask your name again," he said as he admitted me. "My memory's not what it was."

I shook his hand. "Kinsey Millhone," I said. "Nice to meet you, Mr. Nickerson. I hope I didn't interrupt anything."

"Not at all. We're preparing for our Bible class. We usually get together on Wednesday nights, but our pastor has been down with the flu this week, so the meeting was postponed. This is my sister, Essie Daggett. John's wife," he said, indicating the woman seated on the couch. "You can call me Eugene if you like," he added. I smiled briefly in assent and then concentrated on her.

"Hello. How are you? I appreciate your letting me stop by like this." I moved over and offered my hand. She allowed a few fingers to rest in mine briefly. It was like shaking hands with a Playtex rubber glove.

She was broad-faced and colorless, with graying hair in an unbecoming cut and glasses with thick lenses and heavy plastic frames. She had a wen on the right side of her nose about the size of a kernel of popcorn. Her lower jaw jutted forward aggressively, with protrusive cuspids on either side. She smelled virulently of lilies of the valley.

Eugene indicated that I should have a seat, my choice being the couch where Essie sat, or a Windsor chair with one of the wooden spokes popped out. I opted for the chair, sitting forward slightly so as not to pop anything else. Eugene seated himself in a wicker rocker that creaked under his weight. He took up the narrow purple ribbon hanging out of the Bible and marked his place, then set the book on the table in front of him. Essie had said nothing, her gaze fixed on her lap.

"May I get you a glass of water?" he asked. "We don't hold with caffeinated beverages, but I'd be happy to pour you some 7-Up, if you like."

"I'm fine, thanks," I said. I was seriously alarmed. Being with devout Christians is like being with the very rich. One senses that there are rules at work, some strange etiquette that one might inadvertently breech. I tried to hold bland and harmless thoughts, hoping I wouldn't blurt out any four-letter words. How *could* John Daggett be related to these two?

Eugene cleared his throat. "I was explaining to Essie this confusion we're having over John Daggett's whereabouts. Our understanding is that John is still incarcerated, but now you seem to have a different point of view."

"I'm as baffled as you are," I said. I was thinking fast, wondering how much information I might elicit without giving anything away. As bugged as I was with Daggett, I still didn't feel I should be indiscreet. Not only was there the issue of his being out on parole— there was Lovella. I didn't want to be the one to spill the beans about this new bride of his to a woman he was apparently still married to. "Do you happen to have a picture of him?" I asked. "I suppose it's possible the man I talked to was simply claiming to be your brother-in-law."

"I don't know," Eugene said, dubiously. "It surely sounded like him from what you described."

Essie reached over and picked up a color studio photograph in an ornate silver frame. "This was taken on our thirty-fifth wedding anniversary," she said. Her voice had a nasal cast and a grudging undertone. She passed the photograph to her brother as though he'd never seen it before and might like to have a peek.

"Shortly before John left for San Luis," Eugene amended, passing the photo to me. His tone suggested John was off on a business trip.

I studied the picture. It was Daggett all right, looking as self-conscious as someone in one of those booths where you dress up as a Confederate soldier or a Victorian gent. His collar looked too tight, his hair too slicked down with pomade. His face looked tight too, as if any minute he might cut and run. Essie was seated beside him, as placid as a blancmange. She was wearing what looked like a crepe de chine dress in lilac, with shoulder pads and glass buttons, a big orchid corsage pinned to her left shoulder.

"Lovely," I murmured, feeling guilty and false. It was a terrible picture. She looked like a bulldog and John looked like he was suppressing a fart.

I handed the picture to Essie again. "What sort of crime did he commit?"

Essie inhaled audibly.

"We prefer not to speak of that," Eugene interjected smoothly. "Perhaps you should tell us of your own acquaintance with him."

"Well, of course, I don't know him well. I think I mentioned that on the phone. We have a mutual friend and he's the one I was hoping to get in touch with. John mentioned that he had family in this area and I just took a chance. I'm assuming you haven't spoken to him recently."

Essie shifted on the couch. "We stuck by him as long as we could. The pastor said in his opinion we'd done enough. We don't know what John might be wrestling with in the dark of his soul, but there's a limit to what others can *take*." The edge was there in her voice and I wondered what it was made of: rage, humiliation perhaps, the martyrdom of the meek at the hands of the wretched.

I said, "I gather John's been a bit of a trial."

Essie pressed her lips together, clutching her hands in her lap. "Well, it's just like the Bible says. '*Love* your enemies, *bless* them that curse you, do *good* to them that hate you, and pray for them which despitefully use you and persecute you'!" Her tone was accusatory. She began to rock with agitation.

Whoa, I thought, this lady's heat gauge has shot right up into the red.

Eugene creaked in his chair, snagging my attention with a gentle clearing of his throat. "You said you saw him on Saturday. May I ask what the occasion was?"

I realized then that I should have devoted a lot more time to the fib I'd told because I couldn't think how to respond, I was so unnerved by Essie Daggett's outburst that my mind went blank.

She leaned forward then. "Have you been saved?"

"Excuse me, what?" I said, squinting.

"Have you taken Jesus into your heart? Have you set aside *sin*? Have you *repented*? Have you been washed in the Blood of the *Lamb*?"

A spark of spit landed on my face, but I didn't dare react. "Not lately," I said. What is it about me that attracts women like this?

"Now Essie, I'm sure she didn't come by to ponder the state of her soul," Eugene said. He glanced at his watch. "My goodness, I believe it's time for your medication."

I took the opportunity to rise. "I don't want to take up any more of your time," I said, conversationally. "I really appreciate your help on this and if I need any more information, I'll give you a call." I fumbled in my handbag for a business card and left it on the table.

Essie had kicked into high gear by now. "'And they shall stone thee with stones, and *thrust* thee through with their swords. And they shall burn thine houses with fire, and execute judgments upon thee in the sight of many women; and I will cause thee to *cease* from playing harlot, and thou also shalt give no hire anymore . . .'"

"Well, okay now, thanks a lot," I called, easing toward the door. Eugene was patting Essie's hands, too distracted to worry about my departure.

I closed the door and trotted back to my car at a quick clip. It was getting dark and I didn't like the neighborhood.

4

Friday morning I got up at 6:00 and headed over to the beach for my run. For much of the summer, I'd been unable to jog because of an injury, but I'd been back at it for two months and I was feeling good. I've never rhapsodized about exercise and I'd avoid it if I could, but I notice the older I get, the more my body seems to soften, like butter left out at room temp. I don't like to watch my ass drop and my thighs spread outward like jodhpurs made of flesh. In the interest of tight-fitting jeans, my standard garb, I jog three miles a day on the bicycle path that winds along the beach front.

The dawn was laid out on the eastern skyline like water-colors on a matte board: cobalt blue, violet, and rose bleeding together in horizontal stripes. Clouds were visible out on the ocean, plump and dark, pushing the scent of distant seas toward the tumbling surf. It was cold and I ran as much to keep warm as I did to keep in shape.

I got back to my apartment at 6:25, showered, pulled on a pair of jeans, a sweater, and my boots, and then ate a bowl of cereal. I read the paper from front to back, noting with interest the weather map, which showed the radiating spiral of a storm sweeping toward us from Alaska. An 80 percent chance of showers was forecast for the afternoon, with scattered showers through the weekend, clearing by Monday night. In Santa Teresa, rain is not a common event, and it takes on a festive air when it comes. My impulse, always, is to shut myself inside and curl up with a good book. I'd just picked up a new Len Deighton novel and I was looking forward to reading it.

At 9:00, reluctantly, I dug out a windbreaker and picked up my handbag, locked the apartment, and headed over to the office. The sun was shining with a brief show of warmth while the bank of charcoal clouds crept in from the islands twenty-six miles out. I parked in the lot and went up the back stairs, passing the glass double doors of California Fidelity, where business was already under way.

I unlocked my office and dropped my bag on the chair. I really didn't have much to do. Maybe I'd put in a little bit of work and then head home again.

My answering machine showed no messages. I sorted through the mail from the day before and then typed up the notes from my visit with Lovella Daggett, Eugene Nickerson, and his sister, Essie. Since no one seemed to know where John Daggett was, I decided I'd try to get a line on Billy Polo instead. I was going to need data for an effective paper search. I put a call through to the Santa Teresa Police Department and asked to be connected to Sergeant Robb.

I'd met Jonah back in June when I was working on a missing persons case. His erratic marital status made a relationship between us inadvisable from my point of view, but I still eyed him with interest. He was what they called Black Irish: dark-haired, blue-eyed, with (perhaps) a streak of masochism. I didn't know him well enough to determine how much of his suffering was of his own devising and I wasn't sure I wanted to find out. Sometimes I think an unconsummated affair is the wisest course, in any event. No hassles, no demands, no disappointments, and both partners keep all their neuroses under wraps. Whatever the surface appearances, most human beings come equipped with convoluted emotional machinery. With intimacy, the wreckage starts to show, damage rendered in the course of passions colliding like freight trains on the same track. I'd had enough of that over the years. I wasn't in any better shape than he was, so why complicate life?

Two rings and the call was picked up.

"Missing Persons, Sergeant Robb."

"Hello, Jonah. It's Kinsey."

"Hey, babe," he said, "What can I do for you that's legal in this state?"

I smiled. "How about a field check on a couple of ex-cons?"

"Sure, no sweat," he said.

I gave him both names and what little information I had. He took it down and said he'd get back to me. He'd fill out a form and have the inquiry run through the National Crime Information Computer, a federal offense since I'm really not entitled to access. Generally, a private investigator has no more rights than the average citizen and relies on ingenuity, patience, and resourcefulness for facts that law enforcement agencies have available as a matter of course. It's a frustrating, but not impossible, state of affairs. I simply cultivate relationships with people plugged into the system at various points. I have contacts at the telephone company, the credit bureau, Southern California Gas, Southern Cal Edison, and the DMV. Occasionally I can make a raid on certain government offices, but only if I have something worthwhile to trade. As for information of a more personal sort, I can usually depend on people's tendencies to rat on one another at the drop of a hat.

I made up a check sheet for Billy Polo and went to work.

Knowing Jonah, he'd call Probation and pick up Polo's current address. In the meantime, I wanted to tag some bases of my own. A personal search always pays unexpected dividends. I didn't want to bypass the possibility of surprise, as that's half the fun. I knew Polo wasn't listed in the current phone book, but I tried information, thinking he might have had a phone put in. There was no new listing for him.

I put a call through to my pal at the utility company, inquiring about a possible service connection. Their records showed nothing. Apparently he hadn't applied for water, gas, or electricity in the area in his own name, but he could be renting a room somewhere, paying a flat rate, with utilities thrown in.

I put calls through to five or six fleabag hotels on lower State Street. Polo wasn't registered and nobody seemed to spark to the name. While I was at it, I tried John Daggett's name and got nowhere.

I knew I wouldn't get so much as a by-your-leave from the local Social Security office and I doubted I'd find Billy Polo's name among the voter registration files.

Which left what?

I checked my watch. Only thirty minutes had passed since I talked to Jonah. I wasn't sure how long it would take him to call back and I didn't want to waste time sitting around until I heard from him. I grabbed my windbreaker, locked the office, and went down the front stairs to State Street, walking two blocks over and two blocks up to the public library.

I found an empty table in the reference department and hauled out Santa Teresa telephone directories for the past five years, checking back year by year. Four books back, I found Polo. Great. I made a note of the Merced Street address, wondering if his prison sentence accounted for the absence of a listing since then.

I went over to the section on Santa Teresa history and pulled out the city directory for that year. In addition to an alphabetical listing by name, the city directory lists *addresses* alphabetically so that if you have

an address and want to know the resident, you can
thumb to the street and number and pick up the name
of the occupant and a telephone number. In the back
half, telephone numbers are listed sequentially. If all
you have is a telephone number, the city directory will
provide you with a name and address. By cross referenc-
ing the address, you can come up with the name again,
an occupation, and the names of neighbors all up and
down the same street. In ten minutes, I had a list of
seven people who had lived in range of Billy Polo on
Merced. By checking for those seven in the current
directory, I determined that two were still living there. I
jotted down both current telephone numbers, returned
the books to their proper places, and headed back
toward my office.

The sunlight, intermittent for the last hour, was
now largely blocked by incoming clouds which had
crowded out blue sky, leaving only an occasional patch,
like a hole in a blanket. The air was beginning to cool
rapidly, a damp breeze worrying at women's hems. I
looked toward the ocean and spotted that silent veil of
gray that betokens rain already falling some miles out. I
quickened my pace.

Once in my office again, I entered the new information in the file I'd opened. I was just on the verge of
closing up for the day when I heard a tap at the door. I
hesitated, then crossed to the door and peered out.

There was a woman standing in the corridor, late
thirties, expressionless and pale.

"Can I help you?" I said.

"I'm Barbara Daggett."

Quickly, I prayed this wasn't wife number three. I
tried the optimistic approach. "John Daggett's
daughter?"

"Yes."

She was one of those icy blondes, with skin as finely
textured as a percale bedsheet, tall, substantially built,

with short coarse hair fanning straight back from her
face. She had high cheekbones, a delicate brow, and her
father's piercing gaze. Her right eye was green, her left
eye blue. I'd seen a white cat like that once and it had
had the same disconcerting effect. She was wearing a
gray wool business suit and a prim, high-necked white
blouse with a froth of lace at the throat. Her heels were a
burgundy leather and matched her shoulder bag. She
looked like an attorney or a stockbroker, someone
accustomed to power.

"Come on in," I said, "I was trying to figure out how
to get in touch with him. I take it your mother told you I
stopped by."

I was making small talk. She wasn't having any of it.
She sat down, turning those riveting eyes on me as I
moved around to my side of the desk and took a seat. I
thought of offering her coffee, but I really didn't want
her to stay that long. Even the air around her seemed
chilly and I didn't like the way she looked at me. I
rocked back in my swivel chair. "What can I do for you?"

"I want to know why you're looking for my father."

I shrugged, underplaying it, sticking to the story I'd
started with. "I'm not really. I'm looking for a friend of
his."

"Why weren't we told Daddy was out of prison? My
mother's in a state of collapse. We had to call the doctor
and have her sedated."

"I'm sorry to hear that," I said.

Barbara Daggett crossed her legs and smoothed her
skirt, her movements agitated. "Sorry? You don't know
what this has done to her. She was just beginning to feel
safe. Now we find out he's in town somewhere and she's
very upset. I don't understand what's going on."

"Miss Daggett, I'm not a parole officer," I said. "I
don't know when he got out or why nobody notified you.
Your mother's problems didn't start yesterday."

A bit of color came to her cheeks. "That's true. Her

problems started the day she married him. He's ruined her life. He's ruined life for all of us."

"Are you referring to his drinking?"

She brushed right over that. "I want to know where he's staying. I have to talk to him."

"At the moment, I have no idea where he is. If I find him, I'll tell him you're interested. That's the best I can do."

"My uncle tells me you saw him on Saturday."

"Only briefly."

"What was he doing in town?"

"We didn't discuss that," I said.

"But what did you talk about? What possible business could he have had with a private detective?"

I had no intention of giving her information, so I tried her technique and ignored the question.

I pulled a legal pad over and picked up a pen. "Is there a number where you can be reached?"

She opened her handbag and took out a business card which she passed across the desk to me. Her office address was three blocks away on State and her title indicated that she was chairman and chief executive officer of a company called FMS.

As if in response to a question, she said, "I develop financial management software systems for manufacturing firms. That's my office number. I'm not listed in the book. If you need to reach me at home, this is the number."

"Sounds interesting," I remarked. "What's your background?"

"I have a math and chemistry degree from Stanford and a double masters in computer sciences and engineering from USC."

I felt my brows lift appreciatively. I couldn't see any evidence that Daggett had ruined *her* life, but I kept the observation to myself. There was clearly more to Barbara Daggett than her professional status indicated. Maybe she was one of those women who succeeds in business and fails in relationships with men. As I'd been accused of that myself, I decided not to make a judgment. Where is it written that being part of a couple is a measure of anything?

She glanced at her watch and stood up. "I have an appointment. Please let me know if you hear from him."

"May I ask what you want with him?"

"I've been urging Mother to file for divorce, but so far she's refused. Maybe I can persuade him instead."

"I'm surprised she didn't divorce him years ago."

Her smile was cold. "She says she married him 'for better or for worse.' To date, there hasn't been any 'better.' Maybe she's hoping for a taste of that before she gives up."

"What about his imprisonment? What was that for?"

Something flickered in her face and I thought at first she wouldn't answer me. "Vehicular manslaughter," she said, finally. "He was drunk and there was an accident. Five people were killed, two of them kids."

I couldn't think of a response and she didn't seem to expect one. She stood up, closed the conversation with a perfunctory handshake, and then she was gone. I could hear her high heels tapping away down the corridor.

5

By the time I closed up the office and got down to my car, the clouds overhead looked like dark gray vacuum cleaner fluff and the rain had begun to splatter the sidewalk with polka dots. I stuck Daggett's file on the passenger seat and backed out of my space, turning right from the parking lot onto Cannon, and right again onto Chapel. Three blocks up, I made a stop, ducking into the supermarket to pick up milk, Diet Pepsi, bread, eggs, and toilet paper. I was into my siege mentality, looking forward to pulling up the drawbridge and waiting out the rain. With luck, I wouldn't have to go out for days.

The phone was ringing as I let myself in. I put the grocery bag on the counter and snatched up the receiver.

"God, I was just about to give up," Jonah said. "I tried the office, but all I got was your answering machine."

"I closed up for the day. I can work at home if I'm in the mood, which I'm not. Have you seen the rain?"

"Rain? Oh yeah, so there is. I haven't even looked out the window since I got in. God, that's great," he said. "Listen, I have some of the information you're looking for and the rest will have to wait. Woody's got a priority

37

request and I had to back off. I'm working tomorrow so I can pick it up then."

"You're working Saturday?"

"I'm filling in for Sobel. My good deed for the week," he said. "Got a pencil? Polo's the one I got a line on."

He rattled out Billy Polo's age, date of birth, height, weight, hair and eye color, his a.k.a., and a hasty rundown of his record, all of which I noted automatically. He'd picked up the name of Billy's parole officer, but the guy was out of the office and wouldn't be available until Monday afternoon.

"Thanks. In the meantime, I'm nosing around on my own," I said. "I bet I'll get a line on him before you do." He laughed and hung up.

I put groceries away and then sat down at my desk, hauling out the little portable Smith-Corona I keep in the knee hole. I consigned the data Jonah'd given me to index cards and then sat and stared at it. Billy Polo, born William Polokowski, was thirty years old, five-foot-eight, a hundred and sixty pounds, brown hair, brown eyes, no scars, tattoos, or "observable physical oddities." His rap sheet sounded like a pop quiz on the California Penal Code, with arrests that ranged from misdemeanors to felonies. Assault, forgery, receiving stolen property, grand theft, narcotics violations. Once he was even convicted of "injuring a public jail," a misdemeanor in this state. Had this occurred in the course of an escape attempt, the charge would have been bumped up to a felony. As it was, he'd probably been caught scratching naughty words on the jail house walls. A real champ, this one.

Apparently, Billy Polo was pretty shiftless when it came to breaking the law and had never even settled on an area of expertise. He'd been arrested sixteen times, with nine convictions, two acquittals, five dismissals. Twice, he'd been put on probation, but nothing seemed o have affected the nature of his behavior, which appeared nearly pathological in its thrust. The man was determined to screw up. Since the age of eighteen, he'd spent an accumulated nine years in jail. No telling what his juvenile record looked like. I assumed his acquaintance with John Daggett dated from his latest offense, an armed robbery conviction, for which he'd served two years and ten months at the California Men's Colony at San Luis Obispo, a medium security facility about ninety miles north of Santa Teresa.

I pulled out the telephone book again and checked for a listing under the name Polokowski. Nothing. God, why can't anything be simple in this business? Oh well. I wasn't going to worry about it for the moment.

By now, I could hear the rain tapping on the glass-enclosed breezeway that connects my place to Henry Pitt's house. He's my landlord and has been for nearly two years. In dry weather, he places an old Shaker cradle out there, filled with rising bread. When the sun is out, the space is like a solar oven, warm and sheltered, dough puffing up above the rim of the cradle like a feather pillow. He can proof twenty loaves at a time, then bake them in the big industrial-sized oven he had installed when he retired from commercial baking. Now he trades fresh bread and pastries for services in the neighborhood and stretches his Social Security payments by clipping coupons avidly. He picks up additional income constructing crossword puzzles which he sells to a couple of those pint-sized "magazines" you can purchase in a supermarket checkout line. Henry Pitts is eighty-one years old and everyone knows I'm half in love with him.

I considered popping over to see him, but even the fifty-foot walk seemed like too much to deal with in the wet. I put some tea water on and picked up my book, stretching out on the sofa with a quilt pulled over me. And that's how I spent the rest of the day.

During the night, the rain escalated and I woke up twice to hear it lashing at the windows. It sounded like somebody spraying the side of the place with a hose. At intervals, thunder rumbled in the distance and my windows flickered with blue light, tree branches illuminated briefly before the room went black again. It was clear I'd have to cancel my 6:00 A.M. run, an obligatory day off, so I burrowed into the depths of my quilt like a little animal, delighted at the idea of sleeping late.

I woke at 8:00, showered, dressed, and fixed myself a soft-boiled egg on toast with lots of Lawry's Seasoned Salt. I'm not going to give up salt. I don't care what they say.

Jonah called as I was washing my plate. He said, "Hey, guess what? Your friend Daggett showed."

I tucked the receiver into the crook of my neck, turning off the water and drying my hands. "What happened? Did he get picked up?"

"More or less. A scruffy drifter spotted him face down in the surf this morning, tangled up in a fishing net. A skiff washed ashore about two hundred yards away. We're pretty sure it connects."

"He died last night?"

"Looks like it. The coroner estimates he went into the water sometime between midnight and five A.M. We don't have a determination yet on the cause and manner of death. We'll know more after the autopsy's done, of course."

"How'd you find out it was him?"

"Fingerprints. He was over at the morgue listed as a John Doe until we ran the computer check. You want to take a look?"

"I'll be right there. What about next of kin? Have they been notified?"

"Yeah, the beat officer went over as soon as we made the I.D. You know the family?"

"Not well, but we've met. I wouldn't want to be quoted on this, but I think you'll find out he's a bigamist. There's a woman down in L.A. who also claims she's married to him."

"Cute. You better come talk to us when you leave St. Terry's," he said and hung up.

The Santa Teresa Police Department doesn't really have a morgue of its own. There's a coroner-sheriff, an elected officer in this county, but the actual forensic work is contracted out among various pathologists in the tri-county area. The morgue space itself is divided between Santa Teresa Hospital (commonly referred to as St. Terry's) and the former County General Hospital facility on the frontage road off 101. Daggett was apparently at St. Terry's, which was where I headed as soon as I'd rounded up my slicker, an umbrella, and my handbag.

The visitors' lot at the hospital was half empty. It was Saturday and doctors would probably be making rounds later in the day. The sky was thick with clouds and, high up, I could see the wind whipping through like a fan, blowing white mist across the gray. The pavement was littered with small branches, leaves plastered flat against the ground. Puddles had formed everywhere, pockmarked by the steady rainfall. I parked as close to the rear entrance as I could and then locked my car and made a dash for it.

"Kinsey!"

I turned as I reached the shelter of the building. Barbara Daggett hurried toward me from the far side of the lot, her umbrella tilted against the slant of the rain. She was wearing a raincoat and spike-heeled boots, her white-blonde hair forming a halo around her face. I held the door open for her and we ducked into the foyer.

"You heard about my father?"

"That's why I'm here. Do you know how it happened?"

"Not really. Uncle Eugene called me at eight-fifteen
I guess they tried to notify Mother and he intercede
The doctor has her so doped up it doesn't make an
sense to tell her yet. He's worried about how she'll tak
it, as unstable as she is."

"Is your uncle coming down?"

She shook her head. "I said I'd do it. There's n
doubt it's Daddy, but somebody has to sign for the bod
so the mortuary can come pick it up. Of course, they'
autopsy first. How did you find out?"

"Through a cop I know. I'd told him I was trying t
get a line on your father, so he called me when they got
match on the fingerprints. Did you manage to locat
him yesterday?"

"No, but it's clear someone did." She closed he
umbrella and gave it a shake, then glanced at m
"Frankly, I'm assuming somebody killed him."

"Let's not be too quick off the mark," I said, thoug
privately, I agreed.

The two of us moved through the inner door an
into the corridor. The air was warmer here and smelle
of latex paint.

"I want you to look into it for me, in any event," sh
said.

"Hey, listen. That's what the police are for. I don
have the scope for that. Why don't you wait and see wha
they have to say first?"

She studied me briefly and then moved on. "The
don't give a damn what happened to him. Why woul
they care? He was a drunken bum."

"Oh come on. Cops don't have to *care*," I said. "If it
homicide, they have a job to do and they'll do it well.'

When we reached the autopsy room, I knocked an
a young black morgue attendant came out, dressed i
surgical greens. His name tag indicated that his nam
was Hall Ingraham. He was lean, his skin the color o
pecan wood with a high-gloss finish. His hair wa

cropped close and gave him the look of a piece of sculpture, his elongated face nearly stylized in its perfection.

"This is Barbara Daggett," I said.

He looked in her direction without meeting her eyes. "You can wait right down here," he said. He moved two doors down and we followed, pausing politely while he unlocked a viewing room and ushered us in.

"It'll be just a minute," he said.

He disappeared and we took a seat. The room was small, maybe nine by nine, with four blue molded-plastic chairs hooked together at the base, a low wooden table covered with old magazines, and a television screen affixed, at an angle, up in one corner of the room. I saw her gaze flick to it.

"Closed circuit," I said. "They'll show him up there."

She picked up a magazine and began to flip through it distractedly. "You never really told me why he hired you," she said. An ad for pantyhose had apparently caught her eye and she studied it as if my reply were of no particular concern.

I couldn't think of a reason not to tell her at this point, but I noticed that I censored myself to some extent, a habit of long standing. I like to hold something back. Once information is out, it can't be recalled so it's better to exercise caution before you flap your mouth. "He wanted me to find a kid named Tony Gahan," I said.

That remarkable two-toned gaze came up to meet mine and I found myself trying to decide which eye color I preferred. The green was more unusual, but the blue was clear and stark. The two together presented a contradiction, like the signal at a street corner, flashing Walk and Don't Walk simultaneously.

"You know him?" I asked.

"His parents and a younger sister were the ones

killed in the accident, along with two other people in the car with them. What did Daddy want with him?"

"He said Tony Gahan helped him once when he was on the run from the cops. He wanted to thank him."

Her look was incredulous. "But that's bullshit!"

"So I gather," I said.

She might have pressed for more information, but the television screen flashed with snow at that moment and then flipped over to a closeup of John Daggett. He was lying on a gurney, a sheet neatly pulled up to his neck. He had the blank, plastic look that death sometimes brings, as if the human face were no more than an empty page on which the lines of emotion and experience are transcribed and then erased. He looked closer to twenty years old than fifty-five, with a stubble of beard and hair carelessly arranged. His face was unmarked.

Barbara stared at him, her lips parting, her face diffused with pink. Tears rose in her eyes and hung there, captured in the well of her lower lids. I looked away from her, unwilling to intrude any more than I had to. The morgue attendant's voice reached us through the intercom.

"Let me know when you're done."

Barbara turned away abruptly.

"Thank you. That's fine," I called. The television screen went dark.

Moments later, there was a tap at the door and he reappeared with a sealed manila envelope and a clipboard in hand.

"We'll need to know what arrangements you want made," he said. He was using that tone of studied neutrality I've heard before from those who deal with the bereaved. Its effect is impersonal and soothing, liberating one to transact business without intrusive emotionalism. He needn't have bothered. Barbara Daggett was a businesswoman, bred to that awesome poise

that so unsettles men accustomed to female subservience. Her manner now was smooth and detached, her
tone as impassive as his.

"I've talked to Wynington-Blake," she said, indicating one of the funeral homes in town. "If you'll notify
them once the autopsy's done, they'll take care of
everything. Is that form for me?"

He nodded and held the clipboard out to her with a
pen attached. "A release for his personal effects," he
said.

She dashed off a signature as if she were signing an
autograph for a pesky fan. "When will you have the
autopsy results?"

He handed her the envelope, which apparently
contained Daggett's odds and ends. "Probably by late
afternoon."

"Who's doing the post?" I asked.

"Dr. Yee. He's scheduled it for two-thirty."

Barbara Daggett glanced at me. "She's a private
investigator. I want all information released to her. Will
I need to sign a separate authorization for that?"

"I don't know. There's probably some procedure,
but it's a new one on me. I can check into it and contact
you later, if you like."

She slipped her business card under the clamp as
she handed the clipboard back to him. "Do that."

His eyes met hers for the first time and I could see
him register the oddity of the mismatched irises. She
brushed past him, moving out of the room. He stared
after her. The door closed.

I held my hand out. "I'm Kinsey Millhone, Mr.
Ingraham."

He smiled for the first time. "Oh yeah. I heard
about you from Kelly Borden. Nice to meet you."

Kelly Borden was a morgue attendant I'd met
during a homicide investigation I'd worked on in
August.

"Nice to meet you too," I said. "What's the story on this one?"

"I can't tell you much. They brought him in about seven, just as I was coming to work."

"Do you have any idea how long he'd been dead?"

"I don't know for sure, but it couldn't have been long. The body wasn't bloated and there wasn't any putrefaction. From what I've seen of drowning victims, I'd guess he went in the water late last night. Don't quote me on that. The watch he had on was stopped at two thirty-seven, but it could have been broken. It's a crummy watch and looks all beat up. It's in with his effects. Hell, what do I know? I'm just a flunkie, lowest of the low. Dr. Yee hates it if we talk to people like this."

"Believe me, I'm not going to say anything. I'm just asking for my own purposes. What about his clothing? How was he dressed?"

"Jacket, pants, shirt."

"Shoes and socks?"

"Well, shoes. He didn't have socks on and he didn't have a wallet or anything like that."

"Any signs of injury?"

"None that I've seen."

I couldn't think of anything else I wanted to ask for the moment so I thanked him and said I'd be in touch.

Then I went out to look for Barbara Daggett. If I was going to work for her, we needed to get business squared away.

6

I found her standing in the foyer, looking out at the parking lot. The rain was falling monotonously, occasional gusts of wind tossing the treetops. Cozy-looking lights were on in all the buildings that rimmed the parking lot, which only emphasized the dampness and the chill outside. A nurse, her white uniform flashing from the flaps of a dark blue raincoat, approached the doorway, leaping over puddles like a kid playing hopscotch. Her white hose were speckled with flesh-colored blotches where the rain had soaked through and the tops of her white shoes were spattered with mud. She reached the entrance and I held the door for her.

She flashed me a smile. "Whoo! Thanks. It's like an obstacle course out there." She shook the water from her raincoat and padded down the hallway, crepe soles leaving a pattern of damp footprints in her wake.

Barbara Daggett seemed rooted to the spot. "I have to go to Mother's," she said. "Somebody has to tell her." She turned and looked at me. "How much do you charge for your services?"

"Thirty an hour, plus expenses, which is standard for the area. If you're serious, I can drop a contract off at your office this afternoon."

"What about a retainer?"

I made a quick assessment. I usually ask for an

47

advance, especially in a situation like this, when I know
I'll be talking to the cops. There's no concept of privilege
between a P.I. and a client, but at least the front money
makes it clear where my loyalties lie.

"Four hundred should cover it," I said. I wondered
if the figure came to mind because of Daggett's bounced
check. Oddly enough, I felt protective of him. He'd
conned me—there was no doubt of that—but I *had*
agreed to work for him, and in my mind, I still had a
duty to discharge. Of course, I might not have felt as
charitable if he were still alive, but the dead are
defenseless, and somebody in this world has to look out
for them.

"I'll have my secretary cut you a check first thing
Monday morning," she said. She turned back, looking
out the double doors into the gloom. She leaned her
head against the glass.

"Are you okay?"

"You don't know how many times I've wished him
dead," she said. "Have you ever dealt with an alcoholic?"

I shook my head.

"They're so maddening. I used to look at him and I
was convinced he could quit drinking if he wanted to. I
don't know how many times I talked to him, begging
him to stop. I thought he didn't understand. I thought
he just wasn't aware of what we were going through, my
mother and me. I can remember the look he'd get in his
eyes when he was drunk. Little pink piggy eyes. His
whole body radiated this odor. Bourbon. God, I hate
that stuff. He smelled like somebody'd dropped a bottle
of Early Times down a heater vent . . . waves of smell.
He reeked of it."

She looked over at me, her eyes dry and pitiless.
"I'm thirty-four and I've hated him with every cell in my
body for as long as I can remember. And now I'm stuck
with it. He won, didn't he? He never changed, never
straightened up, never gave us an inch. He was such a

shitheel. It makes me want to smash this glass door out. I don't even know why I care how he died. I should be relieved, but I'm pissed. The irony is that he's probably still going to dominate my life."

"How so?"

"Look what he's done to me already. I think of him every time I have a drink. I think of him if I decide *not* to have a drink. If I even *meet* a man who drinks or if I see a bum on the street or smell bourbon, his face is the first thing that comes to mind. Oh God, and if I'm around someone who's had too much, I can't stand it. I disconnect. My life is filled with reminders of him. His apologies and his phony, wheedling charm, his boo-hooing when the booze got to him. The times he fell, the times he got put in jail, the times he spent every dime we had. When I was twelve, Mother got religion and I don't know which was worse. At least Daddy woke up most days in okay shape. She had Jesus for breakfast, lunch, and dinner. It was grotesque. And then there were the joys of being an only child."

She broke off abruptly and seemed to shake herself. "Oh hell. What difference does it make? I know I sound sorry for myself, but it's been such a bitch and there's no end in sight."

"Actually, you look like you've done pretty well," I said.

She turned her gaze back to the parking lot and I could see her faint, bitter smile reflected in the glass. "You know what they say about living well as the best revenge. I did well because it was the one defense I had. Escape has been the motivating force in my life. Getting away from him, getting away from her, putting that household behind me. The funny thing is, I haven't moved an inch, and the harder I run, the faster I keep slipping back to them. There are spiders that work like that. They bury themselves and create a little pocket of loose dirt. Then when their prey comes along, the soil gives way and the victim slides right down into the trap. There are laws for everything except the harm families do."

She turned, shoving her hands down in her rain coat pockets. She pushed the door open with her backside and a draft of cold air rushed in. "What about you? Are you leaving or will you stick around?"

"I guess I'll hit the office as long as I'm out," I said.

She pressed a button on the handle of her umbrella and it lifted into the open position with a muffled *thunk*. She held it for me and we walked toward my car together. The raindrops tapping on the umbrella fabric made a muted sound, like popcorn in a covered sauce pan.

I unlocked my car and got in, while she moved off toward hers, calling back over her shoulder. "Try me at the office as soon as you hear anything. I should be there by two."

My office building was deserted. California Fidelity is closed on weekends so their offices were dark. I let myself in, picking up the batch of morning mail that had been shoved through the slot. There were no messages on my answering machine. I pulled a contract out of my top drawer and spent a few minutes filling in the blanks. I checked Barbara Daggett's business card to verify the address, then I locked up again and went down the front stairs.

I walked the three blocks and dropped the contract off at her office, then headed over to the police station on Floresta. The combination of the weekend and the bad weather lent the station much the same deserted air as my office building. Crime doesn't adhere to a forty-hour week, but there are days when even the criminals don't seem to feel like doing much. The linoleum showed a gridwork of wet footprints, like a pattern of dance steps too complex to learn. The air smelled of cigarette smoke and damp uniforms. I could see where someone had fashioned a folded newspaper into a rain hat and then abandoned it on the wooden bench just inside the door.

One of the clerks in the identification and records section buzzed Jonah and he came out to the locked foyer door and admitted me.

He wasn't looking good. During the summer, he'd shed an excess twenty pounds and he'd told me he was still working out at the gym, so it wasn't that. His dark hair seemed poorly trimmed and the lines around his eyes were pronounced. He also had that weary aura that unhappiness seems to breed.

"What happened to you?" I asked as we walked back to his office. He'd been reconciled with his wife since June, after a year's separation, and from what I'd gathered, it was not going well.

"She wants an open relationship," he remarked.

"Oh come *on*," I said, with disbelief.

That netted me a tired smile. "That's what the lady says." He held the door open for me and we passed into an L-shaped room, furnished with big wooden desks.

Missing Persons is included in Crimes Against Persons, which in turn is considered part of the Investigations Division, along with Crimes Against Property, Narcotics, and Special Investigations. The room was deserted at the moment, but people came and went at intervals. From the interview room off the inside corridor, I could hear the rise and fall of a shrill female voice and I guessed that an interrogation was under way. Jonah closed the hall door, automatically protective of department business.

He filled two Styrofoam cups with coffee and brought them over, handing me packets of Cremora and Equal. Just what I needed, a cup of hot chemicals. We went through the motions of doctoring the coffee, which smelled like it'd been on the burner too long.

I took a few minutes to lay out the Daggett

situation. At this point, we didn't have the results of the autopsy, so the idea of murder was purely theoretical. Still, I told Jonah what had gone on to date, detailing the principal characters. I was talking to him as a friend instead of a cop and he listened as an interested, but unofficial, party.

"So how long was he up here before he died?" Jonah asked.

"Since Monday presumably," I said. "It's possible he went somewhere else first, but Lovella seemed to think he'd head straight for Billy Polo if he needed help."

"Did that information on Polo do you any good?"

"Not yet, but it will. I'm just waiting to see what we've got on our hands before I proceed. Even if the death was accidental, I suspect Barbara Daggett will want me to look into it. I mean, for starters, what was he doing on a boat in a rainstorm? And where has he been all this time?"

"Where have *you* been?" Jonah asked.

I focused on him and realized he'd shifted the subject. "Who, me? I've been around."

He picked up a pencil and began to tap out a beat, like a man auditioning for a tiny blues band. He was giving me a look I'd seen before, full of heat and speculation. "Are you dating anyone?"

I shook my head, smiling slightly. "The only good men I know are married." I was being flirtatious and he seemed to like that.

His blue eyes locked into mine and the color rose in his face. "What do you do for sex?"

"Jog on the beach. How about you?"

He smiled, breaking off eye contact. "In other words, it's none of my business."

I laughed. "I'm not avoiding the question. I'm telling the truth."

"Really? That's funny. I always pictured you out raising hell."

"I did some of that years ago, but I can't stand it these days. Sex is a bonding process. I'm careful who I connect up with. Besides, you don't know what the marketplace is like. A one-night stand is more like a wrestling match with a couple of quick take-downs. Talk about demoralizing. I'd rather be alone."

"I know what you mean. I was out there hustling some the year she was gone, but I never got the hang of it. I'd go in a bar and some babe would sidle up to me, but I never made the right moves. Couple of times, women told me I was rude when I just thought I was making small talk."

"It's worse if you're successful at it," I said. "Be grateful you never learned the gamesmanship. I know a couple of guys on the circuit and they're hard as nails, you know? Unhappy. Hostile toward women. They get laid, but that's about all they get."

Behind him, Lieutenant Becker came in and took a seat at a desk across the room. Jonah's pencil tapping started again and then stopped. He tossed it aside and rocked back in his chair.

"I wish life were simple," he said.

I kept my tone of voice mild. "Life *is* simple. You're the one making things complex. You were doing great without Camilla, as far as I could see. She crooks her finger, though, and you go running back. And now you can't figure out what went wrong. Quit acting like a victim when you did it to yourself."

This time he laughed. "God, Kinsey. Why don't you just say what's on your mind."

"Well, I don't understand voluntary suffering. If you're unhappy, change something. If you can't make it work, then bail out. What's the big deal?"

"Is that what you did?"

"Not quite. I dumped the first and the second one dumped me. With both, I did my share of suffering, but when I look back on it, I can't understand why I endured so long. It was dumb. It was a big waste of time and cost me a lot."

"I've never even heard you mention those guys."

"Yeah, well I'll tell you about them sometime."

"You want to have a drink when I get off work?"

I looked at him briefly and then shook my head. "We'd end up in bed, Jonah."

"That's the point, isn't it?" He smiled and did a Groucho Marx wiggle with his eyebrows.

I laughed and turned the subject back to Daggett as I got up. "Call me when Dr. Yee has results on the post."

"I'll call for more than that."

"Get your life squared away first."

When I left, he was still staring after me, and it was all I could do to get out of there. I had this troubling urge to gallop over and leap onto his lap, laughing while I covered his face with licks, but I didn't think the department would ever be the same. As I glanced back, I could see Becker giving us a speculative look while he pretended to check his "in" box.

7

Daggett's death was ruled accidental. Jonah called me at home at 4:00 to give me the news. I'd spent the afternoon again wrapped up in a quilt, hoping to finish the book. I'd just put on a fresh pot of coffee and I was scurrying back under the covers as the phone rang. When he told me, I was puzzled, but I wasn't convinced. I kept waiting for the punchline, but there wasn't one.

"I don't get it," I said. "Does Yee know the background on this?"

"Babe, Daggett's blood alcohol was point three-five. You're talking acute ethanol intoxication, almost coma stage."

"And that was the cause of death?"

"Well no, he drowned, but Yee says there's no evidence of foul play. None. Daggett went out in a boat, got tangled up in a fishing net, and fell overboard, too drunk to save himself."

"Bullshit!"

"Kinsey, some people die accidentally. It's a fact."

"I don't believe it. Not this one."

"The crime scene investigation unit didn't find a thing. Not even a *hint*. What can I say? You know these guys. They're as good as they come. If you think it's murder, come up with some evidence. In the meantime, we're calling it an accident. As far as we're concerned, the case is closed."

"What was he doing dead drunk in a boat?" I asked. "The man was broke and it was raining cats and dogs. Who'd he rent the boat from?"

I could hear Jonah sigh. "He didn't. Apparently, he took a little ten-foot skiff from its mooring off the dock at Marina One. The harbor master identified the boat and you can see where the line was cut."

"Where'd they find it?"

"On the beach near the pier. There weren't any usable prints."

"I don't like it."

"Look, I know what you're saying and you've got a point. I tend to agree, if that makes you feel any better, but who's asking us? Look at it as a gift. If the death is ruled a homicide, you can't get near it. This way, you've got carte blanche . . . within limits, of course."

"Does Dolan know I'm interested?" Lieutenant Dolan was an assistant division commander and an old antagonist of mine. He hated private investigators getting involved in police business.

"The case is Feldman's. He won't give a shit. You want me to talk to him?"

"Yeah, do that," I said. "And clear it with Dolan, while you're at it. I'm tired of getting my hand smacked."

"Okay. I'll get back to you first thing Monday then," Jonah said. "In the meantime, let me know if anything turns up."

"Right. Thanks."

I put a call through to Barbara Daggett, repeating the information I'd just received. When I finished, she was silent.

"What do you think?" she asked, finally.

"Let's put it this way. *I'm* not satisfied, but it's your money. If you like, I can nose around for a couple of

days and if nothing turns up, we'll dump the whole
business and you'll just have to live with it."

"What are the odds?"

"I have no idea. All I know to do is pick up a thread
and see where it leads. We may come up with six dead
ends, but at least you'll know we gave it a shot."

"Let's do it."

"Great. I'll be in touch."

I pushed the quilt aside and got up. I hoped Billy
Polo was still around. I didn't know where else to start.

I unplugged the coffeepot, poured the balance of
the coffee into a thermos, and then made myself a
peanut butter and dill pickle sandwich, which I put in a
brown paper bag like a school kid. I had just about that
same feeling in my gut too . . . the dull dread I'd
experienced when I was eight, trudging off to Woodrow
Wilson Elementary. I didn't want to go out in the rain. I
didn't want to connect up with Billy Polo, who was
probably a creep. He sounded like one of the sixth-
grade boys I'd been so fearful of . . . lawless, out of
control, and mean.

I searched through my closet until I found my
slicker and an umbrella. I left my warm apartment
behind and drove over to Billy Polo's old address on
Merced. It was 4:15 and getting prematurely dark. The
neighborhood had probably been charming once, but it
was gradually being overtaken by apartment buildings
and was now no more than a hapless mix of the down-at-
the-heel and the bland. The little gingerbread structures
were wedged between three-story stucco boxes with
tenant parking underneath and everywhere there was
evidence of the same tasteless disregard for history.

I parked under a pepper tree, using the overhang-
ing branches as brief shelter while I put up my umbrella.
I checked the names and house numbers of the two
former neighbors, hoping one of them could give me a
lead on Polo's current whereabouts.

The first door I knocked on was answered by an
elderly woman in a wheelchair, her legs wrapped in Ace
bandages and stuffed into lace-up shoes with slices cut
out of the sides to accommodate her bunions. I stood on
her leaky front porch, talking to her through the screen
door, which she kept latched. She had a vague recollec-
tion of Billy, but had no idea what had happened to him
or where he'd gone. She did direct me to a little rental
unit at the rear of the property next door. This was not
one of the addresses I'd picked up from the city
directory. She said Billy's family had lived in the front
house, while the rear was still occupied by an old gent
named Talbot, who had been there for the last thirty
years. I thanked her and picked my way down the rain-
slicked stairs and back along the driveway.

The front unit must have been one of the early
houses in the area—a story and a half of white frame,
with a peaked roof, two dormers, and a front porch that
was screened in now and furnished with junk. I could
see the coils on the backside of an old refrigerator and
beside it, what looked like a pillar of milk cartons, filled
with paperback books. Hydrangeas and bougainvillea
grew together in a tangle along the side of the house and
the runoff from the rain gutter threw a gush of water
out on the drive, forcing me to cut wide to the right.

The rear unit looked like it was originally a tool
shed, with a lean-to attached to the left side and a tiny
carport on the right. There was no car visible and most
of the sheltered space was taken up by a cord of fire-
wood, stacked against the wall. There was room left for
a bicycle maybe, but not much else.

The structure was white frame, propped up on
cinderblocks, with a window on either side of a central
door, and a tiny chimney poking up through the roof. It
looked like the drawing we all did in grade school, even
to the smoke curling up from the chimney pipe.

I knocked and the door was opened by a wizened

old man with no teeth. His mouth was a wide line barely separating the tip of his nose from the upward thrust of his chin. When he caught sight of me and realized that I was no one he knew, he left the doorway briefly and returned with his dentures, smiling slightly as he shifted them into place. His false teeth made a crunching sound like a horse chewing on a bit. He looked to be in his seventies, frail, his pale skin speckled with red and blue. His white hair was brushed into a pompadour in front, shaggy over his ears and touching his collar in the back. He wore a shirt that looked soft from years of washing and a cardigan sweater that probably belonged to a woman at some point. The buttons were rhinestone and the buttonholes were on the wrong side. He smoothed his hair back with a trembling hand and waited to see what I could possibly want.

"Are you Mr. Talbot?"

"Depends on who's asking," he said.

"I'm Kinsey Millhone. The woman next door suggested that I talk to you. I'm looking for Billy Polo. His family lived in that front house about five years ago."

"I know Billy quite well. Why are you looking for him?"

"I need some information about a friend of his," I said and then gave him a brief explanation. I couldn't see any reason to prevaricate so I simply stated my purpose and left it at that.

He blinked at me. "Billy Polo's a very bad fella. I wonder if you're aware of that." His voice was powdery and I noticed that he had a tremor, his head oscillating as he spoke. I guessed that he suffered from some form of parkinsonism.

"Yeah, I am. I heard he was up at the California Men's Colony until recently. I think that's where he met the man I'm referring to. Do you have any idea how I might reach him?"

"Well, you know, his mother is the one who owned

that place," he said, nodding toward the front house. "She sold it about two years ago when she remarried."

"Is she still here in town?"

"Yes, and I believe she's living on Tranvia. Her married name is Christopher. Just a minute and I'll give you the address." He shuffled away and a few moments later was back with a small address book in hand. "She's a lovely woman. Sends me a card every year at Christmastime. Yes, here it is. Bertha Christopher. Goes by the nickname of Betty. If you chance to see her, I wish you'd give her my best."

"I'll do that, Mr. Talbot. Thanks so much."

Tranvia turned out to be a wide, treeless street off Milagro on the east side of town, a neighborhood of one-story frame houses on small lots, with chicken wire fences, unruly head-high poinsettia bushes pelted by the rain, and soggy children's toys abandoned in driveways paved with parallel strips of concrete. The level of maintenance here seemed erratic, but the address I now had for Bertha Christopher showed one of the better-kept houses on the block, mustard-colored with dark brown trim. I parked my VW on the opposite side of the street, about fifty yards away, so I could sit and watch the place inconspicuously. Most of the parked cars were crummy so mine fit right in.

It was now after 5:00 and the light was fading fast, the chill in the air more pronounced. The rain had eased somewhat so I left my umbrella where it was. I grabbed my yellow slicker and slipped into it, pulling up the hood. I locked the car and crossed the street, splashing through puddles that darkened the leather of my boots. The rain drummed against the fabric of the slicker with a pocking sound that made me feel like I was in a pup tent.

The Christopher property was surrounded by a low rock wall, constructed with sandstone boulders the size of cantaloupes, held together with concrete. A row of hanging planters screened the front windows from the street and a set of glass windchimes, suspended in one corner of the porch, tinkled with the wind. There were two lightweight aluminum lawn chairs arranged on either side of a metal table. Everything was soggy and smelled of wet grass.

There was no doorbell, but I tapped on the pane of glass in the front door, cupping a hand so I could peer in. The interior was in shadow, no lights showing from the rear of the house. I moved to the porch rail and checked the adjacent houses, both of which were dark. My guess was that many of these people were off at work. After a few minutes, I went back to my car.

I started the engine and ran the heater for a while, fogging up the windows until I could barely see. I rubbed a clear spot in the middle of the windshield and then sat and stared. Streetlights came on. At 5:45, I ate my sandwich just for something to do. At 6:15, I drank some coffee and flipped on my car radio, listening to a talk-show host interview a psychic. Fifteen minutes later, right after the 6:30 news, a car approached and slowed, turning into the Christophers' driveway.

A woman got out, dimly illuminated by the street light. She paused as if to raise her umbrella and then apparently decided to make a dash for it. I watched her scuttle up the driveway and around toward the back of the house. Moments later, the lights went on in sequence . . . first the rear left room, probably a kitchen, then the living room, and finally the front porch light. I gave her a few minutes to get her coat hung up and then I returned to her front door.

I knocked again. I could see her peer into the hallway from the rear of the house and then approach the front door. She stared at me blankly, then leaned her head close to the glass for a better look.

She appeared to be in her fifties, with a sallow complexion and a deeply creased face. Her hair was too

uniform a shade to be a natural brown. She wore it
parted on the side with big puffy bangs across her lined
forehead. Her eyes were the size and color of old
pennies and her makeup looked like it needed renewing
at this hour of the day. She wore a uniform I'd seen
before, brown pants and a brown-and-yellow-checked
tunic. I couldn't place the outfit offhand.

"Yes?" she called through the glass.

I raised my voice against the sound of the rain. "I'm
looking for Billy. Is he back yet?"

"He don't live here, hon, but he said he'd be by at
eight o'clock. Who are you?"

I picked a name at random. "Charlene. Are you his
mother?"

"Charlene who?"

"A friend of his said I should look him up if I was
ever in Santa Teresa. Is he at work?"

She gave me an odd look, as if the notion of Billy
working had never crossed her mind. "He's out checking
the used car lots for an automobile."

She had one of those faces that seemed tantalizingly
familiar and it dawned on me, belatedly, that she was a
checker at the supermarket where I shop now and then.
We'd even chatted idly about the fact that I was a P.I. I
eased back out of the porch light, hoping she hadn't
recognized me at the same time I recognized her. I held
the corner of the slicker up as though to shield my face
from the wind.

She seemed to pick up on the fact that something
odd was going on. "What'd you want him for?"

I ignored that, pretending I couldn't hear. "Why
don't I come back when he gets home?" I hollered. "Just
tell him Charlene stopped by and I'll catch up with him
when I can."

"Well, all right," she said reluctantly. I gave her a
casual wave as I turned. I went down the porch steps
and into the dark, aware that she was peering after me

uspiciously. I must have disappeared from her field of ision then because she turned the porch light off.

I got back in my car with one of those quick, nvoluntary shudders that racks you from head to toe. When I caught up with Billy, I might well admit who I vas and what I wanted with him, but for the moment, I lidn't want to tip my hand. I checked my watch and ettled in, prepared to wait. Already, it was feeling like a ong night.

8

Four hours passed. The rain stopped. It becam[e]
apparent that Billy was not only late, but possibly n[o]
coming at all. Maybe he'd bought a car and hightailed
out of town, or maybe at some point he'd phoned h[is]
mother and decided to skip the visit when he hear[d]
about "Charlene." I finished all the coffee in th[e]
thermos, my brain fairly crackling from caffeine. If [I]
smoked cigarettes, I could have gone through a pac[k]
Instead, I listened to eight more installments of th[e]
news, the farm report, and an hour of Hispanic music. [I]
pondered the possibility of learning the Spanish la[n]
guage by simply listening to these gut-wrenching tune[s]
I thought about Jonah and the husbands I'd know[n]
Surely, if my heart broke again, it would sound just lik[e]
this, though for all I knew, the lyrics were about c[ut]
worms and inguinal hernias, matters only made soulf[ul]
through soaring harmonies. Altogether, I came per[il]
ously close to boring myself insensible with my ow[n]
mental processes, so it was with real relief that I saw th[e]
car approach and pull into the curb in front of the hous[e]
across the street. It looked like a 1967 Chevrolet, whit[e]
with a temporary registration sticker on the windshie[ld]
I couldn't tell much about the guy who got out, but [I]
watched with interest as he took the porch steps in tw[o]
bounds and rang the bell.

Betty Christopher came to the door to let him in. The two of them disappeared. A moment later, shadows wavered against the kitchen light. I figured they'd sit down for a couple of beers and a heart-to-heart talk. The next thing I knew, however, the front door opened again and he came out. I slipped down on the car seat until my eyes were level with the bottom of the window. The cloud cover was still heavy, obscuring the moon, and the cars along the curb created deeper shadows still. He stared out at the street, taking in the line of parked cars one by one. I felt my heart start to thump as I watched him come down the steps and head in my direction.

He paused in the middle of the street. He moved over to a van parked two cars away from mine. He flicked on a flashlight and opened the door on the driver's side, apparently to check the registration. I lost sight of him. Moments went by. I watched the shadows, wondering if he'd crept around the other side and was coming up on my right. I heard a muffled sound as he closed the door to the van. The beam from his flashlight swept over the car in front of me and flashed across my windshield, the light too diffused by the time it reached me to illuminate much. He flicked it off. He waited, scanning the street on both sides. Apparently, he decided there was nothing to worry about. He crossed back to the house. As he reached the porch, she came out, clutching a robe around her. They talked for a few minutes and then he got in his car and took off. The minute she went inside, I started the VW and did a big U-turn, following. I hoped this wasn't all some elaborate ruse to flush me into the open.

He had already made a left turn and then a right by the time I caught sight of him two blocks ahead of me. We were driving along the back streets with no traffic lights at all and only an occasional stop sign to slow our progress. I had to close the gap or risk losing him. A

"one-man" tail is nearly pointless unless you know wh
you're following and where he's going to begin with. A
this hour, there were very few cars on the road, and if h
drove far, he'd realize the presence of my VW was n
accident.

I thought he was headed toward the freeway, bu
before he reached the northbound on-ramp, he slowe
and made a right-hand turn. By then, I was only half
block back so I whipped over to the curb and parked
killing the engine. I locked the car and took off on foo
heading diagonally across the corner lot at a dead run.
caught sight of his taillights half a block ahead. The ca
was making a left-hand turn into a shabby trailer park

Puente is a narrow street that parallels Highway 10
on the east side of town, with the trailer park itsel
squeezed into the space between the two roadways
screened off from the highway by a ten-foot board fenc
and masses of oleander. I was covering ground at
quick clip. The houses I passed were dark, driveway
crowded with old cars, most of them sporting dents. Th
street lighting here was poor, but ahead of me I caugh
traces of light from the trailer park, which was strun
with small multicolored bulbs.

By the time I got to the entrance, there was no sig
of the Chevrolet, but the place was small and I didn
think the car would be hard to spot. The road twistin
through the trailer park was two lanes wide. Th
blacktop still glistened from the rain and water wa
dripping from the eucalyptus trees that towered a
intervals. There were signs posted everywhere: SLOW
SPEED BUMPS. TENANT PARKING ONLY. DO NOT BLOC
DRIVEWAY.

Most of the trailers were "single-wides," fifteen t
twenty feet long, the kind that once upon a time yo
could actually hitch to your car and travel in. Nomad
Airstream, and Concord seemed to predominate. Eac
had a numbered cardboard sign in the window, indicat

ing the number of the lot on which it sat. Some were moored in narrow patches of grass, temporary camper spaces for RVs passing through, but many were permanent and, by the look of them, had been there for years. The lots were stingy squares of poured concrete, surrounded by sections of white picket fence two feet high, or separated from one another by sagging lengths of bamboo matting. The yards, when they existed, harbored an assortment of plastic deer and flamingos.

It was almost eleven and many of the trailers were dark. Occasionally, I could see the blue-gray flicker of a TV set. I found the Chevrolet, hood warm, the engine still ticking, parked beside a dark green battered trailer with a torn awning and half the aluminum skirting ripped away. From inside, I could hear the dull thump of rock and roll music being played too loudly in too small a space.

The trailer windows were ovals of hot yellow light, positioned about a foot higher than eye level. I edged around to the right-hand side, easing in as close as I could, checking the area to see if any of the neighbors had spotted me. The trailer next door had a FOR RENT sign taped to the siding, and the one across the lane had the curtains pulled. I turned back to the window and got up on tiptoe, peering in. The window was opened slightly and the air seeping out was hot and smelled of fried onions. The curtains consisted of old cotton dish towels, with a brass rod threaded through one end, hanging crookedly enough to provide a clear view of Billy Polo and the woman he was talking to. They were both seated at a flop-down table in the galley, drinking beer, mouths working, words inaudible in the thumping din of music. The interior of the trailer was a depressing collage of cheap paneled walls, dirty dishes, junk, torn upholstery, newspapers, and canned goods stacked on counter tops. A bumper sticker pasted above the front door said, I'VE BEEN TO ALL 48 STATES!

There was a small black-and-white television set perched on a cardboard box, tuned to what looked like the tag end of a prime-time private-eye show. The action was speeding up. A car careened out of control, flipping end over end before it went off a cliff, exploding in midair. The picture cut to two men in an office, one talking on the phone. Neither Billy nor his companion seemed to be watching and the music must have made it impossible for them to hear the dialogue anyway.

I could feel a cramp forming in my right calf. I cast about for something to stand on to ease the strain. The yard next door was a jungle of overgrown shrubs, the parking space choked with discards. There was a set of detached wooden steps tucked up under the trailer door. I blundered through the bushes, my jeans and boots getting drenched in the process. I was counting on the thunder of music to cover the sound of my labors as I hefted the box steps, tramped back through the shrubs, and set the steps under the window.

Cautiously, I mounted, peering in again. Billy Polo had a surprisingly boyish face for a man who'd lived his thirty years as a thug. His hair was dark, a curly mass standing out around his face. His nose was small, his mouth generous, and he had a dimple in his chin that looked like a puncture wound. He wasn't a big man, but he had a wiry musculature that suggested strength. There was something manic about him, a hint of tension in his gestures. His eyes were restless and he tended to stare off to one side when he spoke, as if direct eye contact made him anxious.

The woman was in her early twenties, with a wide mouth, strong chin, and a pug nose that looked as if it was made of putty. She wore no makeup and her fair hair was dense, a series of tight ripples that she wore shoulder length, brittle and illcut. Her skin was very pale, mottled with freckles. She was wearing a man's oversized silk bathrobe and apparently nursing a cold.

She kept a wad of Kleenex in her pocket which she honked into from time to time. She was so close to me I could see the chapping where the frequent blowing had reddened her nose and upper lip. I wondered if she was an old girlfriend of Billy's. There was no overt sexuality in the way they related to one another, but there was a curious intimacy. An old love affair gone flat perhaps.

The continuous rock and roll music was driving me nuts. I was never going to hear what they were saying with that stuff booming out all over the place. I got down off the steps and went around the other side of the trailer to the front door. The window to the right was wide open, though the curtains were pinned shut.

I waited until there was a brief pause between cuts. I took a deep breath and pounded on the door. "Hey! Could you cut the goddamn noise," I yelled. "We're tryin' to get some sleep over here!"

From inside the trailer, the woman hollered, "Sorry!" The music ceased abruptly and I went back around to the other side to see how much of their conversation I could pick up.

The quiet was divine. The volume on the television set must have been turned all the way down, because the string of commercials that now appeared was antic with silence and I could actually catch snatches of what they were saying, though they mumbled unmercifully.

". . . course, she's going to say that. What did you expect?" she said.

"I don't like the pressure. I don't like havin' her on my back . . ." He said something else I couldn't make out.

"What difference does it make? Nobody forced her. Shit, she's free, white, and twenty-one . . . the point is . . . getting into . . . just so she doesn't think . . . the whole thing, right?"

Her voice had dropped and when Billy answered,

he had one hand across his mouth so I couldn't
understand him at all. He was only half attentive
anyway, talking to her with his gaze straying to the
television picture. It must have been 11:00 because the
local news came on. There was the usual lead-in, a long
shot of the news desk with two male newscasters, one
black, one white, like a matched set, sitting there in suits.
Both looked properly solemn. The camera cut to a head
shot of the black man. A photograph of John Daggett
appeared briefly behind him. There was a quick shot of
the beach. It took me a moment to realize that it must
have been the spot where Daggett's body had been
found. In the background, I could see the mouth of the
harbor and the dredge.

Billy jerked upright, grabbing the woman's arm.
She swiveled around to see what he was pointing to. The
announcer talked on, smoothly moving the top sheet of
paper aside. The camera cut to the co-anchor and the
picture shifted to a still shot of a local waste disposal site.

Billy and the woman traded a long, anxious look.
Billy started cracking his knuckles. "Christ!"

The woman snatched up the paper and tossed it at
him. "I told you it was him the minute I read some bum
washed up on the beach. Goddamn it, Billy! Everything
with you comes down to the same old bullshit. You think
you're so smart. You got all the angles covered. Oh sure.
Turns out you don't even know what you're talking
about!"

"They don't even know we knew him. How would
they know that?"

She gave him a scornful look, exasperated that he'd
try to defend himself. "Give the cops some credit! They
probably identified him by his fingerprints, right? So
they know he was up in San Luis. It's not going to take a
genius to figure out you were up there with him. Next
thing we know somebody's coming around knocking at
the door. 'When'd you last see this guy?' Shit like that."

He got up abruptly. He crossed to a kitchen cabinet and opened it. "You got any Black Jack?"

"No, I don't have any Black Jack. You drank it all last night."

"Get some clothes on. Let's go over to the Hub."

"Billy, I've got a cold! I'm not going out at this hour. You go. Why do you need a drink anyway?"

He reached for his jacket, hunching into it. "You have any cash? All I got on me is a buck."

"Get a job. Pay your own way. I'm tired of givin' you money."

"I said you'd get it back. What are you worried about? Come on, come on," he said, snapping his fingers impatiently.

She took her time about it, but she did root through her purse, coming up with a crumpled five-dollar bill, which he took without comment.

"Are you crashing here?" she asked.

"I don't know yet. Probably. Don't lock up."

"Well, just keep it down, okay? I feel like hell and I don't want to be woke up."

He put his hands on her arms. "Hey," he said. "Cool it. You worry too much."

"You know what your problem is? You think all you have to do is say shit like that and it's all okay. The world doesn't work that way. It never did."

"Yeah, well there's always a first time. Your problem is you're a pessimist. . . ."

At that point, I figured I'd better cut out and head back to my car. I eased down off my perch, debating briefly about whether I should move the steps or leave them there. Better to move them. I hefted them, swiftly pushing through the undergrowth to a cleared space where the junk was stacked up. I set the box down and then took off through the darkened trailer park and out to the street.

I jogged to my car, started it, and did another

U-turn, anticipating that Billy would head back the same way he came. Sure enough, in my rearview mirror I saw the Chevrolet make a left turn onto the main thoroughfare, coming up behind me. He followed me for a block and a half, tailgating, a real A-type. With an impatient toot of the horn, he passed me, squealed into another left-hand turn, and zoomed off toward Milagro. I knew where he was headed so I took my time. There's a bar called the Hub about three blocks up. I walked into the place maybe ten minutes after he did. He'd already bought his Jack Daniel's, which he was nursing while he played pool.

9

The Hub is a bar with all the ambience of a converted warehouse. The space is too vast for camaraderie, the air too chill for relaxation. The ceiling is high, painted black, and covered with a gridwork of pipes and electrical conduits. The tables in the main room are sparse, the walls lined with old black-and-white photographs of the bar and its various clientele over the years. Through a wide archway is a smaller room with four pool tables. The juke box is massive, outlined in bands of yellow, green, and cherry red, with bubbles blipping through the seams. The place was curiously empty for a Saturday night. A Willie Nelson single was playing, but it wasn't one I knew.

I was the only woman in the bar and I could sense the male attention shift to me with a bristling caution. I paused, feeling sniffed at, as if I were a dog in an alien neighborhood. Cigarette smoke hung in the air, and the men with their pool cues were caught in the hazy light, bent above the tables in silhouette. I identified Billy Polo by the great puff of hair around his head. Upright, he was taller than I'd pictured him, with wide, hard shoulders and slim hips. He was playing pool with a Mexican kid, maybe twenty-two, with a gaunt face, tattooed arms, and a strip of pinched-looking chest

which was visible in the gap of the Hawaiian shirt h[
wore unbuttoned to the waist. He sported maybe si[
chest hairs in a shallow depression in the middle of hi[
sternum.

I crossed to the table and stood there, waiting fo[
Billy to finish his game. He glanced at me with disinter[
est and lined up the cue ball with the six ball, which h[
smacked smartly into a side pocket. He moved around[
the table without pause, lining up the two ball which h[
fired like a shot into the corner pocket. He chalked hi[
cue, eyeing the three ball. He tested an angle and[
rejected it, leaning into the table then with a shot tha[
sent the three ball rocketing into the side pocket, whil[
the five ball glanced off the side, rolled into range of th[
corner pocket, hung there, and finally dropped in. [
trace of a smile crossed Billy's face, but he didn't look up[

Meanwhile, the Mexican kid stood there and[
grinned at me, leaning on his cue stick. He mouthed, "[
love you." One of his front teeth was rimmed in gold[
like a picture frame, and there was a smudge of blu[
chalk near his chin. Behind him, Billy cleaned up th[
table and put his cue stick back in the rack on the wall[
As he passed, he plucked a twenty from the kid's shir[
pocket and tucked it into his own. Then, with his fac[
averted, he said, "You the chick came looking for me a[
my mom's house earlier?"

"That's right. I'm a friend of John Daggett's."

He cocked his head, squinting, his right hand[
cupped behind his ear. "Who?"

I smiled lazily. We were apparently playing cha[
rades. I raised my voice, enunciating. "Daggett. John.'[

"Oh, yeah, him. How's he doing these days?" H[
started snapping his fingers lightly to the music, which[
had switched from Willie Nelson to a George Benson[
tune.

"He's dead."

I have to credit him. He did a nice imitation of casual surprise, not overdoing it. "You're shittin' me. Daggett's dead? Too bad. What happened to the dude, heart attack?"

"Drowned. It just happened last night, down at the marina." I wagged a thumb over my shoulder in the direction of the beach so he'd know which marina I meant.

"Here in town? Hey, that's tough. I didn't know that. He was in L.A. last I heard."

"I'm surprised you didn't see it on the news."

"Yeah, well I never pay attention to that shit, you know? Bums me out. I got better things to do with my time."

His eyes were all over the place and his body was half turned away. I had to guess that he was busy trying to figure out who I was and what I was up to. He flicked a look at me. "I'm sorry. I didn't catch your name."

"Kinsey Millhone."

He studied me fleetingly. "I thought my mom said the name was Charlene."

I shook my head. "I don't know where she got that."

"And you do what?"

"Basic research. I free-lance. What's that got to do with it?"

"You don't look like a friend of Daggett's. He was kind of a lowlife. You got too much class for a scumbag like him."

"I didn't say we were close. I met him recently through a friend of a friend."

"Why tell me about it? I don't give a damn."

"I'm sorry to hear that. Daggett said if anything happened to him, I should talk to you."

"Me? Naww," he said with disbelief. "That's fuckin' weird. You must have got me mixed up with somebody else. I mean, I knew Daggett, but I didn't *know* him, you dig?"

"That's funny. He told me you were the best of friends."

He smiled and shook his head. "Old Daggett gave you a bum steer, baby doll. I don't know nothin' about it. I don't even remember when I saw him last. Long time."

"What was the occasion?"

He glanced at the Mexican kid who was eavesdropping shamelessly. "Catch you later, man," he said to him. Then under his breath, with contempt, he said, "Paco." Apparently, this was a generic insult that applied to all Hispanics.

He touched my elbow, steering me into the other room. "These beaners are all the same," he confided. "Think they know how to play pool, but they can't do shit. I don't like talking personal in front of spics. Can I buy you a beer?"

"Sure."

He indicated an empty table and held a chair out for me. I hung my slicker over the back and sat down. He caught the bartender's eye and held up two fingers. The bartender pulled out two bottles of beer which he opened and set on the bar.

Billy said, "You want anything else? Potato chips? They make real nice french fries. Kinda greasy, but good."

I shook my head, watching him with interest. At close range, he had a curious charisma . . . a crude sexuality that he probably wasn't even aware of. I meet men like that occasionally and I'm always startled by the phenomenon.

He ambled over and picked up the beers, dropping a couple of crumpled bills on the bar. He said something to the bartender and then waited while the guy placed a glass upside down on each bottle, shooting a smirk in my direction.

He came back to the table and sat down. "Jesus, ask for a glass in this place and they act like you're puttin' on airs. Bunch of bohunks. I only hang out here because I got a sister works here three nights a week."

Ah, I thought, the woman in the trailer.

He poured one of the beers and pushed it over to me, taking his time then as he poured his own. His eyes were deepset, and he had dimples that formed a crease on either side of his mouth. "Look," he said, "I can see you got your mind made up I know something I don't. The truth is, I didn't like Daggett much and I don't think he liked me. Where you got this yarn about me bein' some pal of his, I don't know, but it wasn't from him."

"You called him Monday morning, didn't you?"

"Nuh-uh. Not me. Why would I call him?"

I went on as though he hadn't said anything. "I don't know what you told him, but he was scared."

"Sorry I can't help you out. Must have been somebody else. What was he doin' up here anyway?"

"I don't know. His body washed up in the surf this morning. I thought maybe you could fill me in on the rest. Do you have any idea where he was last night?"

"Nope. Not a clue." He'd gotten interested in a speck of dust in the foam on his beer and he had to pick that out.

"When did you see him last? I don't think you said."

His tone became facetious. "Geez, I don't have my Day-Timer with me. Otherwise, I could pin it down. We might've had lunch at some little out of the way place, just him and me."

"San Luis perhaps?"

There was a slight pause and his smile dimmed a couple of watts. "I was at San Luis with him," he said, cautiously. "Me and thirty-seven hundred other guys. So what?"

"I thought maybe you'd kept in touch."

"I can tell you didn't know Daggett too good. Being with him is like walking around with dog-do on your shoe, you know? It's not something you'd seek out."

"Who else did he know here in town?"

"Can't help you there. It's not my week to keep track."

"What about your sister? Did he know her?"

"Coral? No way. She don't hang out with bums like that. I'd break her neck. I don't get why you're goin' on and on about this. I told you I don't know nothin'. I didn't see him, didn't hear from him. Why can't you just take my word for it?"

"Because I don't think you're telling the truth."

"Says who? I mean, you came lookin' for me, remember? I don't have to talk to you. I'm doin' you a favor. I don't know who you are. I don't even know what the fuck you're up to."

I shook my head, smiling slightly. "God, Billy. Such foul talk. I didn't think you dealt with women that way. I'm shocked."

"Now you're makin' fun of me, right?" He scrutinized my face. "You some kind of cop?"

I ran my thumbnail down the bottle, snagging an accordion strip of label, which I picked off. "Actually I am."

He snorted. Now he'd heard everything. "Come on. Like what," he said.

"I'm a private investigator."

"Bullshit."

"It's a fact."

He tipped back in his chair, amused that I'd try to lay such a line on him. "Jesus, you're too much. Who do you think you're talkin' to? I might have been born at ight, but it wasn't *last* night. I know the private eyes round town and you ain't one, so try somethin' else."

I laughed. "All right, I'm not. Maybe I'm just a nosy hick looking into the death of a man I once met."

"Now, that I'd buy, but it still don't explain why ou're crankin' on my case."

"You introduced him to Lovella, didn't you?"

That stopped him momentarily. "You know Lo-ella?"

"Sure. I met her down in L.A. She has an apartment n Sawtelle."

"When was this?"

"Day before yesterday."

"No foolin'. And she told you to look me up?"

"How else would I know where you were?"

He stared at me, going through some sort of mental debate.

I thought a little coaxing might loosen his tongue. "Are you aware that Daggett's been beating the shit out of her?"

That made him restless and his eyes dropped away from mine. "Yeah, well Lovella's a big girl. She has to learn how to take care of herself."

"Why don't you help her out?"

He smiled bitterly. "I know people who'd laugh at the notion of me helping anyone," he said. "Besides, she's tough. You don't want to underestimate that one, 'm tellin' you."

"You've known her a long time, haven't you?"

His knee had started to jump. "Seven years, eight. I met her when she was seventeen. We lived together for a while, but it didn't work out. We used to knock heads too much. She's a bullheaded bitch, but I loved her a lot. Then I got busted on a burglary rap and me and her, hell, I don't know what it was. We wrote to each other or a while, but you can't go back to something once it's

dead, you know? Anyway, now we're friends, I guess. A
least I dig her. I don't know how she feels about me.

"Have you seen her recently?"

The knee stopped. "No, I haven't seen her recent
ly," he said. "What about you? Why'd you go dow
there?"

"I was looking for Daggett. The phone was dis
connected."

"What exactly did she say?"

I shrugged. "Nothing much. I wasn't there long an
she wasn't feeling that good. She was nursing a big blac
eye."

"Jesus," he said. He rocked back in his chair. "Te
me something. How come women do that? Let guy
punch 'em out?"

"I have no idea."

He drained his beer glass and set it down. "I bet yo
don't take crap from anyone, am I right?"

"We all take crap from someone," I said.

Billy got up. "Sorry to cut this off, but I gotta split.
He turned, tucking his shirt down into his pants mor
securely. His body language said he'd already taken o
and hoped his clothing would catch up with him by th
time he hit the street.

I got up, reaching for my slicker. "You're no
leaving town, are you?"

"What business is it of yours?"

"It doesn't seem like a good idea with Daggett
death hanging fire. Suppose the cops want to talk t
you."

"About what?"

"Where you were last night, for starters."

His tone rose. "Where *I* was? What are you talkin
about?"

"They might want to know about the connectio
between Daggett and you."

"What connection? That's a crock. I don't know where you come up with that."

"It's not me you have to worry about. It's the cops who count."

"What cops?"

I shook my head. "You know who your friendly local cops are," I said. "If somebody puts a bug in the wrong ear, you'll be sitting in the hot seat."

He was all outrage. "Why would you do that to me?"

"Because you're not leveling with me, William."

"I *am* leveling with you! I've told you everything I know."

"I don't think so. I think you knew about Daggett's death. I think you saw him this week."

He put his hands on his hips and looked off across the room, shaking his head. "Man, this is all I need. This is no lie. I've been straight. I'm minding my own business, doing like I been told. I didn't even know the dude was up here."

"You can stick to your story if you like," I said, "but I'll give you a word of advice. I've got the license number of that car you bought. You bolt and I'm calling Lieutenant Dolan down at Homicide."

He seemed as much puzzled as dismayed. "What is this? A shakedown? Is that what this is about?"

"What's to shake? You don't have a cent. I want information, that's all."

"I don't *have* any information. How many times I gotta tell you that?"

"Look," I said patiently. "Why don't I let you think about the situation and then we can talk again."

"Why don't you go fuck yourself!"

I put my slicker on, tucking the strap of my handbag over my shoulder. "Thanks for the beer. I'll buy yours next time."

He made an exaggerated gesture of dismissal, too

pissed off to reply. He headed toward the door and
watched him go. I glanced at my watch. It was well after
midnight and I was exhausted. My head was starting to
ache and I knew everything about me smelled like stale
cigarette smoke. I wanted to go home, strip down,
shower, and then crawl into the folds of my quilt.
Instead, I took a deep breath and went after him.

10

I gave him a good head start, then followed him back to the trailer. The temperature felt like it had dropped into the fifties. The eucalyptus trees were still tossing occasional showers at me when the wind cut through, but for the most part, the night was clear. Above me, I could see pale puffs of rain clouds receding, wide patches of starry sky breaking through. I parked half a block away and padded into the park on foot as I had before. Billy's car was parked beside the trailer. I was getting bored, but I had to be certain he wasn't heading off to consult with some confederate I didn't know about.

The same lights were on in the galley, but a dim light now glowed at the rear of the trailer, where I imagined the bedroom to be. I picked my way through the bushes to that end. Curtains were pulled across the windows, but the venting system was piping a mur- mured conversation right out through a mesh-covered opening. I hunkered down by the torn skirting, leaning my head against the aluminum. I could smell cigarette smoke, which I guessed was Coral's.

". . . want to know why she showed up now," she was saying. "That's what we have to worry about. For all we know, they're in it together."

"Yeah, but doin' what? That's what I can't figure out."

"When'd she say she'd get in touch?"

"She didn't. Said I should think about the situation. Jesus. How'd she get a bead on the Chevy so fast? That's what bugs me. I had that car two hours."

"Maybe she followed you, dimwit."

The silence was profound. "Goddamn it," he said.

I heard footsteps thump toward the front of the trailer. By the time the door banged open I was easing my way around the end. I peered out into the carport. The nose of the Chevy was about six feet away, the space on either side of it crowded with junk.

The door to the trailer had been flung open. Light poured out, washing as far as the point where the asphalt began. With a quick look over my shoulder, I waded into the refuse, picking my way around to the far side of the car, where I crouched, listening intently. Sometimes I feel like I spend half my life this way. I heard Billy fumble his way around the bedroom end of the trailer just as I had.

"Jesus!" he hissed.

Coral peered out the side window, whispering hoarsely. "What's wrong?"

"Shut up! Nothing. I banged my goddamn shin on the trailer hitch. Why don't you clean up this crap?"

My sentiments exactly.

Coral laughed and the curtain dropped back into place.

Billy appeared again at the far end of the carport, rubbing his left shin. He did a quick visual survey, apparently convinced by then there wasn't anybody lurking about the premises. He shook his head and thumped up the steps, banging the door shut behind him. The carport went dark. I let out my breath.

I could hear them murmuring together, but by then I didn't really care what else they discussed. As soon as I was convinced it was safe, I crept out of the driveway and headed for my car.

Sunday morning was overcast. The very air looked gray, and dampness seemed to rise up out of the earth like a mist. I went through my usual morning routine, getting a three-mile run in before the skies opened up again. At 9:00, I put a call through to Barbara Daggett at home. I brought her up to date, filling her in on my night's activities.

"What now?" she asked.

"I'm going to let Billy Polo stew for a day or two and then get back to him."

"What makes you think he won't skip?"

"Well, he *is* on parole and I'm hoping he won't want to mess that up. Besides, it feels like a waste of money to pay me to sit there all day."

"I thought you said he was the only lead you had."

"Maybe not," I said cautiously. "I've been thinking about Tony Gahan and the other people killed in the accident."

"Tony Gahan?" she said with surprise. "How could he be involved in this?"

"I don't know. Your father hired me originally to track him down. Maybe he found the kid himself and that's where he was early in the week."

"But Kinsey, why would Daddy want to track him down? That boy must hate his guts. His whole family was wiped out."

"That's my point."

"Oh."

"Do you have any idea how to locate him? Your father had an address on Stanley Place, but the house was apparently empty. I can't find a Gahan listed in the telephone book."

"He lives with his aunt now, I think, somewhere in Colgate. Let me see if I've got an address."

Colgate is the bedroom community, attached to Santa Teresa like a double star. The two are just about the same size, but Santa Teresa has all the character and Colgate has the affordable housing, along with hardware stores, paint companies, bowling alleys, and drive-in theaters. Colgate is the Frostee-Freeze capital of the world.

There was a pause and I could hear pages rattle. She came back on the line. "My mistake. They live near the Museum. Her last name is Westfall. Ramona."

"I wonder why your father didn't know about her."

"I don't know. She was there for the trial. I do remember that, because someone pointed her out to me. I wrote her a note afterwards, saying that of course we'd do anything we could to help, but I never heard back."

"You know anything else about her? Is she married, for instance?"

"I think so, yes. Her husband manufactures industrial supplies or something like that. Actually, now that I think about it, she *was* working at that kitchenware place on Capilla because I spotted her when I was in there shopping a couple of months ago. Maybe you could catch her this afternoon if she still works there."

"On Sunday?"

"Sure, they're open from twelve to five."

"I'll try her first and see how far I get," I said. "What about your mother? How's she holding up?"

"Surprisingly well. Turns out she handles death like a champ. If it's covered in the Bible, she trots out all the appropriate attitudes and goes through the sequence automatically. I thought she'd flip out, but it seems to have put her back on her feet. She's got church women sitting with her, and the pastor's there. The kitchen table's stacked with tuna casseroles and chocolate cakes. I don't know how long it will last, but for now, she's in her element."

"When's the funeral?"

"Tuesday afternoon. The body's been transported to the mortuary. I think they said he'd be ready for viewing early this afternoon. Are you coming by?"

"Yes, I think I will. I can tell you then if I've talked to this Westfall woman or the kid."

Jorden's is a gourmet cook's fantasy, with every imaginable food preparation device. Rack after rack of cookware, utensils, cookbooks, linens, spices, coffees, and condiments; chafing dishes, wicker baskets, exotic vinegars and oils, knives, baking pans, glassware. I stood in the entrance for a moment, amazed by the number and variety of food-related implements. Pasta machines, cappuccino makers, food warmers, coffee grinders, ice cream freezers, food processors. The air smelled of chocolate and made me wish I had a mother. I spotted three saleswomen, all wearing wraparound aprons made of mattress ticking, with the store's name embroidered in maroon across the bib.

I asked for Ramona Westfall and was directed toward the rear aisle. She was apparently doing a shelf count. I found her perched on a small wooden stool, clipboard in hand, checking off items on a list that included most of the non-electrical gadgets. She was sorting through a bin of what looked like small stainless steel sliding boards with a blade across the center that would slice your tiny ass off.

"What are those?" I asked.

She glanced up at me with a pleasant smile. She appeared to be in her late forties, with short, pale sandy hair streaked with gray, hazel eyes peering at me over a pair of half-glasses which she wore low on her nose. She used little if any makeup, and even seated, I could tell she was small and slim. Under the apron, she wore a white, long-sleeved blouse with a Peter Pan collar, a gray tweed skirt, hose, and penny loafers.

"That's a mandoline. It's made in West Germany."

"I thought a mandolin was a musical instrument."

"The spelling's different. This is for slicing raw vegetables. You can waffle-cut or julienne."

"Really?" I said. I had sudden visions of homemade French fries and cole slaw, neither of which I've ever prepared. "How much is that?"

"A hundred and ten dollars. With the slicing guard, it's one thirty-eight. Would you like a demonstration?"

I shook my head, unwilling to spend that much money on behalf of a potato. She got to her feet, smoothing the front of her apron. She was half a head shorter than I and smelled like a perfume sample I'd gotten in the mail the week before. Lavender and crushed jasmine. I was impressed with the price of the stuff, if not the scent. I stuck it in a drawer and I'm assailed with the fragrance now every time I pull out fresh underwear.

"You're Ramona Westfall, aren't you?"

Her smile was modified to a look of expectancy. "That's right. Have we met?"

I shook my head. "I'm Kinsey Millhone. I'm a private investigator here in town."

"Is there something I can help you with?"

"I'm looking for Tony Gahan. I understand you're his aunt."

"Tony? Good heavens, what for?"

"I was asked to locate him on a personal matter. I didn't know how else to get in touch with him."

"What personal matter? I don't understand."

"I was asked to deliver something to him. A check from a man who's recently deceased."

She looked at me blankly for a moment and then I saw recognition leap into her eyes. "You're referring to John Daggett, aren't you? Someone told me it was on the news last night. I assumed he was still in prison."

"He's been out for six weeks."

Her face flooded with color. "Well, isn't that typi-

l," she snapped. "Five people dead and he's back on
ie streets."

"Not quite," I said. "Could we go someplace and
ilk?"

"About what? About my sister? She was thirty-eight,
beautiful person. She was decapitated when he ran a
oplight and plowed into them. Her husband was
illed. Tony's sister was crushed. She was six, just a
aby. . . ." She bit off her sentence abruptly, suddenly
ware that her voice had risen. Nearby, several people
aused, looking over at us.

"Who were the others? Did you know them?" I
.ked.

"You're the detective. You figure it out."

In the next aisle, a dark-haired woman in a striped
pron caught her eye. She didn't open her mouth, but
er expression said, "Is everything all right?"

"I'm taking a break," Ramona said to her. "I'll be in
ie back room if Tricia's looking for me."

The dark-haired woman glanced at me briefly and
ien dropped her gaze. Ramona was moving toward a
oorway on the far side of the room. I followed. The
ther customers had lost interest, but I had a feeling
iat I'd be facing an unpleasant scene.

By the time I entered the back room, Ramona was
imbling in her handbag with shaking hands. She
pened a zippered compartment and took out a vial of
ills. She extracted a tablet and broke it in half, downing
with a slug of cold coffee from a white mug with her
ame on the side. On second thought, she took the
:cond half of the tablet as well.

I said, "Look, I'm sorry to have to bring this
p . . ."

"Don't apologize," she spat. "It doesn't do any
ood." She searched through the bag and came up with
hard pack of Winston's. She pulled out a cigarette and
imped it repeatedly on her thumbnail, then lit it with a

Bic disposable lighter she'd tucked in her apron pock
She hugged her waist with her left arm, propping t
right elbow on it so she could hold the cigarette near h
face. Her eyes seemed to have darkened and she fixe
me with a blank, rude stare. "What is it you want?"

I could feel my face warm. Somehow the money w
suddenly beside the point and seemed like too paltry
sum in any event. "I have a cashier's check for Tor
John Daggett asked me to deliver it."

Her smile was supercilious. "Oh, a *check*. Well, ho
much is it for? Is it per *head* or some sort of lump su
payment by the carload?"

"Mrs. Westfall," I said patiently.

"You can call me Ramona, dear, since the subje
matter's so intimate. We're talking about the people
loved best in this world." She took a deep drag of h
cigarette and blew smoke toward the ceiling.

I clamped down on my temper, controlling n
response. "I understand that the subject is painful,"
said. "I know there's no way to compensate for wh
happened, but John Daggett was making a gesture, an
regardless of your opinion of him, it's possible that Tor
might have a use for the money."

"We provide for him very nicely, thanks. We don
need anything from John Daggett *or* his daughter c
from *you*." -

I plowed on, heading into the face of her wrath lil
a swimmer through churning surf. "Let me just s;
something first. Daggett came to me last week with
cashier's check made out to Tony."

She started to speak, but I held up one han
"Please," I said.

She subsided, allowing me to continue.

"I put the check in a safe deposit box until I coul
figure out how to deliver it, as agreed. You can toss it i
the trash for all I care, but I'd like to do what I said I'
do, which is to see that Tony Gahan gets it. In theory, it

Tony's to do with as he sees fit, so I'd appreciate it if you'd talk to him before you do anything else."

She thought about that one, her eyes locked on mine. "How much?"

"Twenty-five thousand. That's a good chunk of education for Tony, or a trip abroad. . . ."

"I get the point," she cut in. "Now maybe you'll allow me to have my say. That boy has been with us for almost three years now. He's fifteen years old and I don't think he's slept a full eight hours since the accident. He has migraines, he bites his nails. His grades are poor, school attendance is *shit*. We're talking about a kid with an I.Q. right off the charts. He's a wreck and John Daggett did that to him. There's no way . . . no *way* anyone can ever make up to Tony for what that man did."

"I understand that."

"No, you don't." Her eyes filled suddenly with tears. She was silent, hands shaking again so badly now that she could scarcely get the Winston to her lips. She managed to take another drag, fighting for control. The silence lengthened. She seemed to shudder and I could almost see the tranquilizer kick in. She turned away abruptly, dropped the cigarette, and stepped on it. "Give me a number where I can reach you. I'll talk to my husband and see what he says."

I handed her my card, taking a moment to jot down my home address and telephone number on the back, in case she needed to reach me there.

11

After I left Ramona Westfall, I stopped by my apartment and changed into pantyhose, low heels, and my all-purpose dress. This garment, which I've owned for five years, is made of some magic fabric that doesn't wilt, wrinkle, or show dirt. It can be squashed down to the size of a rain hat and shoved in the bottom of my handbag without harm. It can also be rinsed out in any bathroom sink and hung to dry overnight. It's black, lightweight, has long sleeves, zips up the back, and should probably be "accessorized," a women's clothing concept I've never understood. I wear the dress "as is" and it always looks okay to me. Once in a while I see this look of recognition in someone's eye, but maybe it's just a moment of surprise at seeing me in something other than jeans and boots.

The Wynington-Blake Mortuary—Burials, Cremation, and Shipping, Serving All Faiths—is located on the east side of town on a shady side street with ample parking. It was originally built as a residence and retains the feeling of a substantial single-family dwelling. Now of course, the entire first floor has been converted into the equivalent of six spacious living rooms, each furnished with metal folding chairs and labeled with some serene-sounding word.

The gentleman who greeted me, a Mr. Sharonson, wore a subdued navy blue suit, a neutral expression, and used a public library voice. John Daggett was laid out in 'Meditation," which was just down the corridor and to my left. The family, he murmured, was in the Sunrise Chapel if I cared to wait. I signed in. Mr. Sharonson removed himself discreetly and I was left to do as I pleased. The room was rimmed with chairs, the casket at the apex. There were two sprays of white gladioli that looked somehow like pristine fakes provided by the mortuary, instead of wreaths sent by those who mourned Daggett's passing. Organ music was being piped in, a nearly subliminal auditory cue meant to trigger thoughts about the brevity of life.

I tiptoed across the room to have a peek at him. The color and texture of Daggett's skin looked about like a Betsy-Wetsy doll I'd had as a kid. His features had a flattened appearance, which I suspected was a side effect of the autopsy process. Peel somebody's face back and it's hard to line it all up again. Daggett's nose looked crooked, like a pillowcase put on with the seam slightly skewed.

I was aware of a rustling behind me and Barbara Daggett appeared on my right. We stood together for a moment without a word. I don't know why people stand and study the dead that way. It makes about as much sense as paying homage to the cardboard box your favorite shoes once came in. Finally, she murmured something and turned away, moving toward the entrance where Eugene Nickerson and Essie Daggett were just coming in through the archway.

Essie was wearing a dark navy dress of rayon jersey, her massive arms dimpled with pale flesh. Her hair looked freshly "done," puffed and thick, sprayed into a turban of undulating gray. Eugene, in a dark suit, steered her by the elbow, working her arm as if it were

the rudder on a ship. She took one look at the casket and
her wide knees buckled. Barbara and Eugene caught
her before she actually hit the floor. They guided her to
an upholstered chair and lowered her into the seat. She
fumbled for a handkerchief, which she pressed to her
mouth as if she meant to chloroform herself.

"Sweet Jesus Lord," she mewed, her eyes turned up
piteously. "Lamb of God . . ." Eugene began to pat at
her hand and Barbara sat down beside her, putting one
arm around her protectively.

"You want me to bring her some water?" I asked.
Barbara nodded and I moved toward the doorway.
Mr. Sharonson had sensed the disturbance and had
appeared, his face forming a question. I passed the
request along and he nodded. He left the room and
returned to Mrs. Daggett's side. She was having a pretty
good time by now, rolling her head back and forth
reciting scriptures in a high-pitched voice. Barbara and
Eugene were working to restrain her and I gathered
that Essie had expressed a strong desire to fling herself
into the coffin with her beloved. I might have given her
a boost myself.

Mr. Sharonson returned with a paper envelope full
of water, which Barbara took, holding it to Essie's lips.
She jerked her head back, unwilling to accept even this
small measure of solace. "By night on my bed, I sought
him whom my soul loveth," she warbled. "I sought him
but I found him not. I will rise now, and go about the
city in the streets, and in the broad ways I will seek him
whom my soul loveth. The watchmen that go about the
city found me . . . Lord in Heaven . . . O God. . . ."

With surprise, I realized she was quoting fragments
from the Song of Solomon, which I recognized from my
old Methodist Sunday School days. Little kids were
never allowed to read that part of the Bible as it was
considered too smutty, but I was real interested in the

idea of a man with legs like pillars of marble set upon sockets of fine gold. There was some talk of swords and thighs that caught my attention too. I believe I lasted three Sundays before my aunt was asked to take me down the street to the Presbyterians.

Essie was rapidly losing control, whipping herself into such an agitated state that Eugene and Mr. Sharonson had to assist her to her feet and help her out of the room. I could hear her cries becoming feebler as she was moved down the hall. Barbara rubbed her face wearily. "Oh God. Count on Mother," she said. "How has your day been?"

I sat down beside her. "This doesn't seem like the best time to talk," I said.

"Oh, don't worry about it. She'll calm down. This is the first she's seen of him. There's some kind of lounge upstairs. She can rest for a while and she'll be fine. What about Ramona Westfall? Did you talk to her?"

I filled her in on my brief interview, bringing the subject around to my real question at this point, which had to do with the two other victims in the accident. Barbara closed her eyes, the matter clearly causing her pain.

"One was a little friend of Hilary Gahan's. Her name was Megan Smith. I'm sure her parents are still in the area. I'll check the address and telephone number when I get home. Her father's name is Wayne. I forget the name of the street, but it's probably listed."

I took my notebook out and jotted the name down. "And the fifth?"

"Some kid who'd bummed a ride with them. They picked him up at the on-ramp to the freeway to give him a lift into town."

"What was his name?"

"Doug Polokowski."

I stared at her. "You're kidding."

"Why? Do you know him?"

"Polokowski is Billy Polo's real last name. It's on his rap sheet."

"You think they're related?"

"They'd almost have to be. There's only one Polokowski family in town. It's got to be a cousin or a brother, *something*."

"But I thought Billy Polo was supposed to be Daddy's best friend. That doesn't make sense."

Mr. Sharonson returned to the room and caught her eye. "Your mother is asking for you, Miss Daggett."

"You go ahead," I said. "I've got plenty to work on at this point. I'll call you later at home."

Barbara followed Mr. Sharonson while I headed out to the foyer and hustled up a telephone book. Wayne and Marilyn Smith were listed on Tupelo Drive out in Colgate, right around the corner from Stanley Place, if my memory served me correctly. I considered calling first, but I was curious what the reaction would be to the fact of Daggett's death, if the news hadn't already reached them. I stopped to get gas in the VW and then headed out to the freeway.

The Smiths' house was the single odd one in a twelve-block radius of identical tract homes and I guessed that theirs was the original farmhouse at the heart of what had once been a citrus grove. I could still spot orange trees in irregular rows, broken up now by winding roads, fenced lots, and an elementary school. The Smiths' mailbox was a small replica of the house and the street number was gouged out of a thick plank of pine, stained dark and hung above the porch steps. The house itself was a two-story white frame with tall, narrow windows and a slate roof. A sprawling vegetable garden stretched out behind the house, with the garage beyond that. A tire swing hung by a rope from a sycamore that grew in the yard. Orange trees extended on all sides, looking twisted and barren, their producing years long past. It was probably cheaper to leave them there than to tear them out. An assortment of boys' bicycles in a rack on the porch suggested the presence of male offspring or an in-progress meeting of a cycling club.

The bell consisted of a metal twist in the middle of the door. I cranked it once and it trilled harshly. As with the Christopher house, the upper portion of the door was glass, allowing me a glimpse of the interior—high ceilings, waxed pine floors, a scattering of rag rugs, and Early American antiques that looked authentic to my untrained eye. The walls were covered with patchwork quilts, the colors washed out to pale shades of mauve and blue. Numerous children's jackets hung from a row of pegs to the left, rainboots lined up underneath.

A woman in jeans and an oversized white shirt trotted down the stairs, trailing one hand along the banister. She gave me a quick smile and opened the front door.

"Oh hi. Are you Larry's mom?" She read instantly from my expression that I hadn't the faintest idea what she was talking about. She gave a quick laugh. "I guess not. The boys got back from the movie half an hour ago and we've been waiting for Larry's mother to pick him up. Sorry."

"That's all right. I'm Kinsey Millhone," I said. "I'm a private investigator here in town." I handed her my card.

"Can I help you with something?" She was in her mid-thirties, her blonde hair pulled straight back from her face in a clumsy knot. She was dark-eyed, with the tanned good looks of someone who works outdoors. I imagined her to be the kind of mother who forbade her children to eat refined sugar and supervised the television shows they watched. Whether such vigilance pays off or not, I'm never sure. I tend to place kids in a class with dogs, preferring the quiet, the smart, and the well trained.

"John Daggett was killed here in town Friday night," I said.

Something flickered across her face, but maybe it was just the realization that a painful subject was coming up again. "I hadn't heard about that. What happened?"

"He fell out of a boat and drowned."

She thought about that briefly. "Well, that's not too bad. Drowning's supposed to be fairly easy, isn't it?" Her tone of voice was light, her expression pleasant. It took me a minute to realize the savagery of the sentiment. I wondered what kind of torture she'd wished on him.

"Most of us don't get to choose our death," I said.

"My daughter certainly didn't," she said tartly. "Was it an accident or did someone give him a nice push?"

"That's what I'm trying to find out," I said. "I heard he came up from L.A. on Monday, but nobody seems to know where he spent the week."

"Not here, I can assure you. If Wayne so much as set eyes on him, he'd have. . . ." The words tapered off to a faint smile and her tone became almost bantering. "I was going to say, he'd have killed him, but I didn't mean that literally. Or maybe I did. I guess I shouldn't speak for Wayne."

"What about you? When did you see him last?"

"I have no idea. Two years ago at least."

"At the trial?"

She shook her head. "I wasn't there. Wayne sat in for a day, but he couldn't take it after that. He talked to Barbara Daggett once, I think, but I'm sure there's been nothing since. I'm assuming somehow that the man was murdered. Is that what you're getting at?"

"It's possible. The police don't seem to think so, but

I'm hoping they'll revise their opinion if I can come up with some evidence. I get the impression a lot of people wanted Daggett dead."

"Well, I sure did. I'm thrilled to hear the news. Somebody should have killed him at birth," she said. "Would you like to come in? I don't know what I can tell you, but we might as well be comfortable." She glanced at my business card again, double-checking the name and then tucking it in her shirt pocket.

She held the door and I passed over the threshold, pausing to see where she meant for us to go. She led me into the living room.

"You and your husband were home Friday night?"

"Why? Are we suspects?"

"There isn't even a formal investigation yet," I said.

"I was here. Wayne was working late. He's a C.P.A."

She indicated a chair and I sat down. She took a seat on the couch, her manner relaxed. She was wearing a thin gold bracelet on her right wrist and she began to turn that, straightening a kink in the chain. "Did you ever meet John Daggett yourself?" she asked.

"Once. He came to my office a week ago Saturday."

"Ah. Out on parole, no doubt. He must have served his ten minutes."

I made no comment, so she went on.

"What was he doing in Santa Teresa? Returning to the scene of the slaughter?"

"He was trying to locate Tony Gahan."

This seemed to amuse her. "To what end? It's probably none of my business, but I'm curious."

I was discomfited by her attitude, which seemed an odd mix of the wrathful and the jocular. "I'm not really sure what his intentions were," I said carefully. "The story he told me wasn't true anyway, so it's probably not worth repeating. I gathered he wanted to make restitution."

Her smile faded, dark eyes boring into mine with a look that chilled me. "There's no such thing as 'restitution' for what that man did. Megan died horribly. Five-and-a-half years old. Has anyone given you the details?"

"I have the newspaper clippings in the car. I talked to Ramona Westfall too, and she filled me in," I said, lying through my teeth. I didn't want to hear about Megan's death. I didn't think I could bear it, whatever it was. "Have you kept in touch with the other families?"

For a moment, I didn't think I could distract her. She was going to sit there and tell me some blood-curdling tale that I was never going to forget. Cruel images seemed to play across her face. She faltered and her expression underwent that transformation that precedes tears—her nose reddening, mouth changing shape, lines drawing down on either side. Then her self-control descended and she looked at me with clouded eyes. "I'm sorry. What?"

"I was wondering if you'd talked to the others recently. Mrs. Westfall or the Polokowskis."

"I've hardly even talked to Wayne. Megan's death has just about done us in."

"What about your other children? How are they handling it?"

"Better than we are, certainly. People always say, 'Well, you still have the boys.' But it doesn't work that way. It's not like you can substitute one child for another." Belatedly, she took out a Kleenex and blew her nose.

"I'm sorry I had to bring it all up again," I said. "I've never had children, but I can't imagine anything more painful than losing one."

Her smile returned, fleeting and bitter. "I'll tell you what's worse. Knowing there's a man out there doing a few months in jail for 'vehicular manslaughter' when he murdered five people. Do you know how many times he got picked up for drunk driving before that accident? Fifteen. He paid a few fines. He got his hand smacked. Once he did thirty days, but most of the time. . . ." She broke off, then changed her tone. "Oh hell. What difference does it make? Nothing changes anyway and it never ends. I'll tell Wayne you stopped by. Maybe he knows where Daggett was."

12

I sat in the car and shuddered. I couldn't think when an interview had made me feel so tense. Daggett *had* to have been murdered. I just didn't see how it could come down any other way. What I couldn't figure out was how to get my thinking straight. Usually the morality of homicide seems clear to me. Whatever the shortcomings of the victim, murder is wrong and the penalties levied against the perpetrator had better be substantial to balance out the gravity of the crime. In this case, that seemed like a simplistic point of view. It was *Daggett* who had caused the world to tilt on its axis. Because of him, five people had died, so that his death, whatever the instrument, was swinging the planet upright again, restoring a moral order of sorts. At the moment, I still didn't know whether his desire to make restitution was sincere or part of some elaborate con. All I knew was that I'd been caught up in the loop and I had a part to play, though I had no idea yet what it was.

I started the car and headed back to my place. The sky was clouding over again. It was after 5:00 and a premature twilight already seemed to be spilling down the mountainside. I pulled up in front of my apartment and switched off the ignition. I glanced over at my windows, which were dark. I was feeling edgy and I wasn't ready to go home yet. On impulse, I started the

ar again and headed for the beach, drawn by the scent
f salt in the air. Maybe a walk would ease my restless-
ess.

I pulled into one of the municipal lots and parked,
lipping out of my shoes and pantyhose, which I tossed
n the back seat along with my handbag. I zipped up my
vindbreaker and locked the car, tucking my keys in my
acket pocket as I crossed the bike path to the beach.
The ocean was silver, but the breaking waves were a
nuddy brown and the sand along the surf line was
eppered with rocks. This was the winter beach, dark
oulders having surfaced with the shifting coastal sands.
Gulls hovered overhead, eyeing the thundering waves
or signs of edible sea life.

I walked along the wet sand with a buffeting wind at
ny back. A windsurfer clung to the crossbar on a bright
green sail, arching himself against the force of the wind,
iis board streaking toward the beach. Two big fishing
oats were chugging into the marina. Everywhere there
vas the sense of urgency and threat—the torn white of
torm surf, the darkening gray of the sky. Across the
aarbor, the ocean drove at the shore without pity,
ounding at the breakwater with a grudging monotony.
A rocketing spray shot straight up on impact, fanning
along the seawall. I could almost hear the splats as
uccessive waves hit the concrete walkway on the land-
vard side.

I passed the entrance to the wharf. Ahead the beach
videned, curving left toward the marina where the bare
nasts of sailboats tilted in the wind like metronomes.
The sand was softer here, deeper too, so that walking
ecame a labor. I turned and walked backwards for a
ew steps, trying to get my bearings. Somewhere along
his part of the beach was the spot where Daggett's body
aad been found. A brief glimpse of the site had
ppeared on the newscast and I was hoping now to get a
ix on the place. I thought it was probably this side of the

boat launch. Ahead and to my right was the kiddie park
with its playground equipment and a fenced-in area
with a wading pool.

The newscast had shown a portion of the dredge in
the background, intersected by the breakwater and a
line of rocks. I trudged on until I had the three lined up
in the same configuration. The dry sand was trampled
and there were signs that vehicles had crossed the beach.
Where waves slapped against the shore, all traces of
activity had been erased. The crime scene investigators
had, no doubt, done at least a cursory search. I scanned
the area without any expectation of finding "evidence."
If you murder a man by tossing him, dead drunk, out of
a rowboat, there aren't any telltale clues to dispose of
afterward. The boat itself had been left to drift and
from what Jonah said, must have washed ashore closer
to the pier.

I drank in the heady perfume of the sea, watching
the restless surge of the waves, turning myself slowly
until the ocean was at my back and I was staring at the
line of motels across the boulevard. Daggett had apparently died sometime between midnight and 5:00 A.M. I
wondered if it would be productive to canvas the
neighborhood for witnesses. It was possible, of course,
that Daggett had actually cut the line on the skiff
himself, rowing out of the harbor alone. With a 0.35
blood alcohol level, it seemed unlikely. By the time blood
alcohol concentrations reach 0.40 percent, a drunk is
essentially in a state of deep anesthesia, incapable of
anything so athletic as working an oar. He might have
maneuvered his way out of the harbor first and *then* sat
in the bobbing boat, drinking himself insensible, but I
couldn't picture that. I kept visualizing somebody with
him . . . waiting, watching . . . finally hefting his feet
and toppling him backwards. "A lesson in the back flip,
Daggett. Oh shit, you blew it. Too bad, sucker. You die."

Getting him in the boat in the first place might have

en a trick, as drunk as he was, but the rest of it must
ve been a snap.

I glanced to my right. An old bum with a shopping
't was picking through a trash container. I crossed the
id, heading toward him. As I approached, I could see
at his skin was nearly gray with accumulated filth,
ined by the wind, with an overlay of rosiness from
:ent sunburn or Mogen David wine . . . Mad Dog
–20, as it's better known among the scruffy drifters.
: looked in his seventies and was bulked up by layers
clothing. He wore a watch cap, his gray hair hanging
t of it like mop strings. He smelled as musky as an old
ffalo. The odor radiated from his body in nearly
ible wavy lines, like a cartoon rendition of a skunk.

"Hello," I said.

He went about his business, ignoring me. He pulled
t a pair of spike heels, inspecting them briefly before
tucked them into one of his plastic trash bags. A two-
y-old newspaper didn't interest him. Beer cans? Yes,
seemed to like those. A Kentucky Fried Chicken
rrel was a reject. A skirt? He held it up with a critical
e and then shoved it into the trash bag with the shoes.
meone had discarded a plastic beach ball with a hole
nched in it. The old man set that aside.

"Did you hear about the guy they found in the surf
sterday?" I asked. No response. I felt like an appari-
n, calling to him from the netherworld. I raised my
ice. "I heard somebody down here spotted him and
led the cops. Do you happen to know who?"

I guess he didn't care to discuss it. He resolutely
)ided eye contact. I didn't have my handbag with me
I didn't have a business card or even a dollar bill as a
ter of reference. I had no choice but to let it drop. I
)ved away. By then, he had worked his way down in
: bin, his head almost out of sight. So much for my
erviewing techniques.

By the time I got back to the parking lot, the light

had faded, so I registered the fact that something w
wrong long before I realized what it was. The door
the passenger side of my car was ajar. I stopped in
tracks.

"Oh no," I said.

I approached with caution, as if the vehicle mig
be booby-trapped. It looked like someone had run
coathanger in through the wind-wing in an attempt
jimmy the lock. Failing that, the shitheel had simp
smashed the window out on the passenger side and h
opened the door. The glove compartment hung op
the contents spilling out across the front seat.
handbag was missing. *That* generated a flash of irri
tion, swiftly followed by dread. I jerked the seat forwa
and hauled out my briefcase. The strap that secured t
opening had been cut and my gun was gone.

"Oh nooo," I wailed. I gave vent to a string
expletives. In high school, I had hung out with so
bad-ass boys who taught me to cuss to perfection. I tri
some combinations I hadn't thought of in years. I v
mad at myself for leaving the stuff in plain sight on t
seat and mad at the jerk who ripped me off. Mine v
one of the last cars left in the lot and had probably sto
out like a beacon. I slammed the car door shut a
headed off across the street, still barefoot, gesturing a
muttering to myself like a mental case. I didn't ev
have the spare change to call the cops.

There was a hamburger stand close by and
conned the fry cook into making the call for me. The
went back and waited until the black-and-white arriv
The beat officers, Pettigrew and Gutierrez (Gerald a
Maria, respectively), I'd encountered some months b
fore when they made an arrest in my neighborhoo

She took the report now, while he made symp
thetic noises. Somehow the two of them managed
console me insofar as that was possible, calling for
crime scene investigator who obligingly came out a

lusted for prints. We all knew it was pointless, but it made me feel better. Pettigrew said he'd check the computer for the serial number on my gun, which was registered, thank God. Maybe it would turn up later in a pawn shop and I'd get it back.

I love my little semiautomatic, which I've had for years . . . a gift from the aunt who raised me after my parents' death. That gun was my legacy, representing the odd bond between us. She'd taught me to shoot when I was eight. She had never married, never had children of her own. With me, she'd exercised her many odd notions about the formation of female character. Firing a handgun, she felt, would teach me to appreciate both safety and accuracy. It would also help me develop good hand-eye coordination, which she thought was useful. She'd taught me to knit and crochet so that I'd learn patience and an eye for detail. She'd refused to teach me to cook as she felt it was boring and would only make me fat. Cussing was okay around the house, though we were expected to monitor our language in the company of those who might take offense. Exercise was important. Fashion was not. Reading was essential. Two out of three illnesses would cure themselves, said she, so doctors could generally be ignored except in case of accident. On the other hand, there was no excuse for having bad teeth, though she viewed dentists as the persons who came up with ludicrous schemes for the human mouth. Drilling out all of your old fillings and replacing them with gold, was one. She had dozens of these precepts and most are still with me.

Rule Number One, first and foremost, above and beyond all else, was financial independence. A woman should never, never, never be financially dependent on anyone, especially a man, because the minute you were dependent, you could be abused. Financially dependent persons (the young, the old, the indigent) were inevi-

tably treated badly and had no recourse. A woman
should *always* have recourse. My aunt believed that
every woman should develop marketable skills, and the
more money she was paid for them the better. An
feminine pursuit that did not have as its ultimate goal
increased self-sufficiency could be disregarded. "How to
Get Your Man" didn't even appear on the list.

When I was in high school, she'd called Home E
"Home Ick" and applauded when I got a D. She thought
it would make a lot more sense if the boys took Home E
and the girls took Auto Mechanics and Wood Shop
Make no mistake about it, she liked (some) men a lot, but
she wasn't interested in tending to one like a charwoman
or a nurse. She was nobody's mother, said she, not even
mine, and she didn't intend to behave like one. All of
which constitutes a long-winded account of why
wanted my gun back, but there it is. I didn't have to
explain any of this to G. Pettigrew or M. Gutierrez. The
both knew I'd been a cop for two years and they both
understood the value of a gun.

By the time everyone left the parking lot, it was
fully dark and starting to rain again. Oh perfect.

I drove home and started making out a list of items
I'd have to replace, including my driver's license, gaso
line charge card, checkbook, and God knows what else
While I was at it, I looked up three "800" numbers
phoning in the loss of my credit cards from the Xerox
copy I keep in my file drawer at home. I'd only been
carrying about twenty bucks in cash, but I resented the
loss. It was all too irritating to contemplate for long. I
showered, pulled on jeans, boots, and a sweater, and
headed up to Rosie's for a bite to eat.

Rosie's is the tavern in my neighborhood, run by
herself, a Hungarian woman in her sixties, short and
top-heavy, with dyed red hair that recently had looked
like a cross between terra cotta floor tile and canned
pumpkin pie filling. Rosie is an autocrat—outspoken

verbearing, suspicious of strangers. She cooks like a
ream when it suits her, but she usually wants to dictate
hat you should eat at any given meal. She's protective,
ometimes generous, often irritating. Like your best
riend's cranky grandmother, she's someone you endure
or the sake of peace. I hang out at her establishment
ecause it's unpretentious and it's only half a block away
rom my place. Rosie apparently feels that my pa-
ronage entitles her to boss me around . . . which is
enerally true.

That night when I walked in, she took one look at
ny face and poured me a glass of white wine from her
ersonal supply. I moved to my favorite booth at the
ear. The backs are high, cut from construction grade
lywood and stained dark, with side pieces shaped like
ne curve of a wingback chair. Within moments, Rosie
naterialized at the table and set the glass of wine in
ront of me.

"Somebody just busted out the window of my car
nd stole everything I hold dear, including my gun," I
aid.

"I've got some *sóska leves* for you," she announced.
And after that, you gonna have a salad made with
elery root, some chicken paprikas, some of Henry's
ood rolls, cabbage strudel, and deep-fried cherries if
ou're good and clean up your plate. It's on the house,
n account of your troubles, only think about this one
hing while you eat. If you had a good man in your life,
his would never happen to you and that's all I'm gonna
ay."

I laughed for the first time in days.

13

The next morning, Monday, I began the laboriou process of replacing the contents of my handbag. I h the DMV first, since the offices opened at 8:00 A.M. I s in motion the paperwork for a new driver's licens paying three dollars for a duplicate. The minute th bank opened, I closed out my checking account an opened a new one. I stopped by the apartment then an put a call through to Sacramento to the Bureau Collection and Investigative Services, Department Consumer Affairs, requesting application for a certifie replacement for my private investigator's registratio card. I armed myself with a batch of business cards fro my ready supply and hunted up an old handbag to u until I could buy a new one. I drove over to th drugstore and made purchases to replace at least a fe of the odds and ends I carry with me as a matter course, birth control pills being one. At some point, I' have to have my car window replaced, too. Irksome, a of it.

I didn't reach the office until almost noon and th message light on my answering machine was blinkin insistently. I tossed the morning mail aside and punche the playback button as I passed the desk, listening to th caller as I opened the French doors to let in some fres air.

"Miss Millhone, this is Ferrin Westfall at 555-6790. My wife and I have discussed your request to speak with our nephew, Tony, and if you'll get in touch, we'll see what we can work out. Please understand, we don't want the boy upset. We trust you'll conduct whatever business you have with him discreetly." There was a click, breaking the connection. His tone had been cold, perfectly suited to his formal, well-organized speaking voice. No "uh"s, no hesitations, no hiccups in the presentation. I lifted my brows appreciatively. Tony Gahan was in capable hands. Poor kid.

I made myself a pot of coffee and waited until I'd downed half a cup before I returned the call. The phone rang twice.

"Good morning. PFC," the woman said.

PFC turned out to be Perforated Formanek Corporation, a supplier of industrial abrasives, grinders, clamps, epoxy, cutters, end mills, and precision tools. I know this because I asked and she recited the entire inventory in a sing-song tone, thinking perhaps that I was in the market for one of the above. I asked to speak to Ferrin Westfall and was thanked for my request.

There was a click. "Westfall," said he.

I identified myself. There was a silence, meant (perhaps) to intimidate. I resisted the urge to rush in with a lot of unnecessary chatter, allowing the pause to go on for as long as it suited him.

Finally, he said, "We'll see that Tony's available this evening between seven and eight if that's acceptable." He gave me the address.

"Fine," I said. "Thank you." Ass, I added mentally. Then I hung up.

I tipped back in my swivel chair and propped my feet up. So far, it was a crummy day. I wanted my handbag back. I wanted my gun. I wanted to get on with life and quit wasting time with all this clerical nonsense. I glanced out at the balcony. At least it wasn't raining at the moment. I pulled the mail over and started going through it. Most of it was junk.

I was feeling restless again, thinking about John Daggett and his boat trip across the harbor. Yesterday, at the beach, the notion of canvassing the neighborhood for witnesses had seemed pointless. Now I wasn't so sure. Somebody might have seen him. Public drunkenness is usually conspicuous, especially at an hour when not many people are about. Weekend guests at the beach motels had probably checked out by now, but it might still be worth a shot. I grabbed my jacket and my car keys, locked the office, and headed down the back stairs.

My VW was looking worse every time I turned around. It's fourteen years old, an oxidized beige model with dents. Now the window was smashed out on the passenger side. Not a class act by any stretch of the imagination, but it was paid for. Every time I think about a new car, it makes my stomach do a flip-flop. I don't want to be saddled with car payments, a jump in insurance premiums, and hefty registration fees. My current registration costs me twenty-five dollars a year, which suits me just fine. I turned the ignition key and the engine fired right up. I patted the dashboard and backed out of the space, taking State Street south toward the beach.

I parked on Cabana, just across from the entrance to the wharf. There are eight motels strung out along the boulevard, none with rooms for under sixty dollars a night. This was the "off" season and there were still no vacancies. I started with the first, the Sea Voyager, where I identified myself to the manager, found out who'd been working the night desk the previous Friday, jotted down the name, and left my card with a handwritten note on the back. As with many other aspects of the job I do, this door-to-door inquiry requires dogged patience and a fondness for repetition that doesn't really come naturally. The effort has to be made, however, on the off chance that someone, somewhere can fill in a detail that might help. Having worked my way to the last motel, I returned to my car and headed on down the boulevard toward the marina, half a mile away.

I parked this time near the Naval Reserve Building, in the lot adjacent to the harbor. There didn't seem to be much foot traffic in the area. The sky was overcast, the air heavy with the staunch smells of fresh fish and diesel fuel. I ambled along the walk that skirts the waterfront, with its eighty-four acres of slips for eleven hundred boats. A wooden pier, two lanes wide, juts out into the water topped with a crane and pulleys for hoisting boats. I could see the fuel dock and the city guest dock, where two men were securing the lines on a big power boat that they'd apparently just brought in.

On my right, there was a row of waterfront businesses—a fish market with a seafood restaurant above, a shop selling marine and fishing supplies, a commercial diving center, two yacht brokers. The building fronts are all weathered gray wood, with bright royal blue awnings that echo the blue canvas sail covers on boats all through the harbor. For a moment, I paused before a plate glass window, scanning the snapshots of boats for sale—catamarans, luxury cabin cruisers, sailboats designed to sleep six. There's a small population of "live-aboards" in the harbor—people who actually use their boats as a primary residence. The idea is mildly appealing to me, though I wonder about the reality of chemical toilets in the dead of night and showering in marina restrooms. I crossed the walk and leaned on the iron railing, looking out across the airy forest of bare boat masts.

The water itself was dark hunter green. Big rocks were submerged in the gloomy depths, looking like sunken ruins. Few fish were visible. I spotted two little crabs scuttling along the boulders at the water's edge, but for the most part, the shallows seemed cold and sterile, empty of sea life. A beer bottle rested on a shelf of sand and mud. Two harbor patrol boats were moored not far away.

I spotted a line of skiffs tied up at one of the docks below and my interest perked up. Four of the marinas are kept locked and can only be entered with a card key issued by the Harbor Master's Office, but this one was accessible to the public. I moved down the ramp for a closer look. There were maybe twenty-five small skiffs, wood and fiberglass, most of them eight to ten feet long. I had no way of knowing if one of these was the boat Daggett had taken, but this much seemed clear: if you cut the line on one of these boats, you'd have to row it out around the end of the dock and through the harbor. There was no current here and a boat left to drift would simply bump aimlessly against the pilings without going anyplace.

I went up the ramp again and turned left along the walkway until I reached Marina One. At the bottom of the ramp, I could see the chain-link fence and locked gate. I loitered on the walk, keeping an eye on passersby. Finally, a middle-aged man approached, his card key in one hand, a bag of groceries in the other. He was trim and muscular, tanned to the color of rawhide. He wore Bermuda shorts, Topsiders, and a loose cotton sweater, a mat of graying chest hairs visible in the V.

"Excuse me," I said. "Do you live down there?"

He paused, looking at me with curiosity. "Yes." His face was as lined as a crumpled brown grocery bag pressed into service again.

"Do you mind if I follow you out onto Marina One? I'm trying to get a line on the man who washed up on the beach Saturday."

"Sure, come on. I heard about that. The skiff he stole belongs to a friend of mine. By the way, I'm Aaron. You are?"

"Kinsey Millhone," I said, trotting down the ramp after him. "How long have you lived down here?"

"Six months. My wife and I split up and she kept the house. Nice change, boat life. Lot of nice people. You a cop?"

"Private investigator," I said. "What sort of work do you do?"

"Real estate," he said. "How'd you get into it?" He inserted his card and pushed the gate open. He held it while I passed through. I paused on the other side so he could lead the way.

"I was hired by the dead man's daughter," I said.

"I meant how'd you get into investigative work."

"Oh. I used to be a cop, but I didn't like it much. The law enforcement part of it was fine, but not the bureaucracy. Now I'm self-employed. I'm happier that way."

We passed a cloud of sea gulls converging rapidly on an object bobbing in the water. The screeches from the birds were attracting gulls from a quarter of a mile away, streaking through the air like missiles.

"Avocado," Aaron said idly. "The gulls love them. This is me." He had paused near a thirty-seven-foot twin-diesel trawler, a Chris-Craft, with a flying bridge.

"God, it's a beautiful boat."

"You like it? I can sleep eight," he said, pleased. He hopped down into the cockpit and turned, holding a hand out to me. "Pop your boots off and you can come on board and take a look around. Want a drink?"

"I better not, thanks. I've got a lot of ground to cover yet. Is there any way you can introduce me to the guy whose skiff was stolen?"

Aaron shrugged. "Can't help you there. He's out on a fishing boat all day, but I can give him your name and telephone number if you like. I think the police impounded the skiff, so if you want to see that, you better talk to them."

I didn't expect anything to come of it, but I thought I'd leave the door open just in case. I took out a business card, jotting down my home number on the back before I passed it on to him. "Have him give me a call if he knows anything," I said.

"I'll tell you who you might want to talk to. Go down here six slips and see if that guy's in. *The Seascape* is the name of the boat. His is Phillip Rosen. He knows all the gossip down here. Maybe he can help."

"Thanks."

The Seascape was a twenty-four-foot Flicka, a gaff-rigged sloop with a twenty-foot mast, teak deck, and a fiberglass hull that mimicked wood.

I tapped on the cabin roof, calling a hello toward the open doorway. Phillip Rosen appeared, ducking his head as he came up from down below. His emerging was like a visual joke: he was one of the tallest men I'd seen except on a basketball court. He was probably six-foot-ten and built on a grand scale—big hands and feet, big head with a full head of red hair, a big face with red beard and moustache, bare-chested and barefoot. Except for the ragged blue jean cut-offs, he looked like a Viking reincarnated cruelly into a vessel unworthy of him. I introduced myself, mentioning that Aaron had suggested that I talk to him. I told him briefly what I wanted.

"Well, I didn't see them, but a friend of mine did. She was coming down here to meet me and passed 'em in the parking lot. Man and a woman. She said the old guy was drunk as a skunk, staggering all over the place. The little gal with him had a hell of a time trying to keep him upright."

"Do you have any idea what she looked like?"

"Nope. Dinah never said. I can give you her number though, if you want to ask her about it yourself."

"I'd like that," I said. "What time was this?"

"I'd say two-fifteen. Dinah's a waitress over at the Wharf and she gets off at two. I know she didn't close up that night and it only takes five minutes to get here. Shoot, if she walked on water, she could skip across the harbor in the time it takes her to get to the parking lot."

"Is she at work now by any chance?"

"Monday afternoon? Could be. I never heard what her schedule was this week, but you can always try. She'd be up in the cocktail lounge. A redhead. You can't miss her if she's there."

Which turned out to be true. I drove the half mile from the marina to the wharf, leaving my car with the valet who handles restaurant parking. Then I went up the outside staircase to the wooden deck above. Dinah was crossing from the bar to a table in the corner, balancing a tray of margaritas. Her hair was more orange than red, too carroty a shade to be anything but natural. She was probably six feet tall in heels, wearing dark mesh hose, and a navy blue "sailor" suit with a skirt that skimmed her crotch. She had a little sailor cap pinned to her head and an air about her that suggested she'd known starboard from port since the day she reached puberty.

I waited until she'd served the drinks and was on her way back to the bar. "Dinah?"

She looked at me quizzically. Up close, I could see the overlay of pale red freckles on her face and a long, narrow nose. She wore false eyelashes, like a series of commas encircling her pale hazel eyes, lending her a look of startlement. I gave her a brief rundown, patiently repeating myself. "I know who the old guy is," I said. "What I'm trying to get a fix on is the woman he was with."

Dinah shrugged. "Well, I can't tell you much. I just saw them as I went past. I mean, the marina's got *some* lights, but not that great. Plus, it was raining like a son of a bitch."

"How old would you say she was?"

"On the young side. Twenties, maybe. Blonde. Not real big, at least compared to him."

"Long hair? Short? Buxom? Flat-chested?"

"The build, I don't know. She was wearing a raincoat. Some kind of coat, anyway. Hair was maybe shoulder length, not a lot of curl. Kind of bushy."

"Pretty?"

She thought briefly. "God, all I remember thinking was there was something off, you know? For starters, he was such a mess. I could smell him ten feet away. Bourbon fumes. Phew! Actually, I kind of thought she might be a hooker on the verge of rolling him. I nearly said something to her, but then I decided it was none of my business. He was having a great old time, but you know how it is. Drunk as he was, she really could have ripped him off."

"Yeah, well, she did. *Dead* is about as ripped off as you can get."

14

By the time I pulled out of the restaurant parking lot, it was 2:00 and the air felt dank. Or maybe it was only the shadowy image of Daggett's companion that chilled me. I'd been half convinced there was someone with him that night and now I had confirmation—not proof of murder, surely, but some sense of the events leading up to his death, a tantalizing glimpse of his consort, that "other" whose ghostly passage I tracked.

From Dinah's description, Lovella Daggett was the first name that popped into my head. Her trashy blonde looks had made me think she was hooking when I met her in L.A. On the other hand, most of the women I'd run across to date were on the young side and fair-haired—Barbara Daggett, Billy Polo's sister Coral, Ramona Westfall, even Marilyn Smith, the mother of the other dead child. I'd have to start pinning people down as to their whereabouts the night of the murder, a tricky matter as I had no way to coerce a reply. Cops have some leverage. A P.I. has none.

In the meantime, I went by the bank and removed the cashier's check from my safe deposit box. I ducked into a coffee shop and grabbed a quick lunch, then spent the afternoon in the office catching up on paperwork. At 5:00, I locked up and went home, puttering around until 6:30 when I left for Ferrin and Ramona Westfall's house to meet Tony Gahan.

The Westfalls lived in an area called the Close, a deadend street lined with live oaks over near the Natural History Museum. I drove through stone gates into the dim hush of privacy. There are only eight homes on the cul-de-sac, all Victorian, completely restored, immaculately kept. The neighborhood looks, even now, like a small, rural community inexplicably lifted out of the past. The properties are surrounded by low walls of fieldstone, the lots overgrown with bamboo, pampas grass, and fern. It was fully dark by then and the Close was wreathed in mist. The vegetation was dense, intensely scented, and lush from the recent rain. There was only one street light, its pale globe obscured by the branches of a tree.

I found the number I was looking for and parked on the street, picking my way up the path to the front. The house was a putty-colored, one-story wood frame with a wide porch, white shutters and trim. The porch furniture was white wicker with cushions covered in a white-and-putty print. Two Victorian wicker plant stands held massive Boston ferns. All too perfect for my taste.

I rang the bell, refusing to peer in through the etched glass oval in the door. I suspected the interior was going to look like something out of *House and Garden* magazine, an elegant blend of the old, the new, and the offbeat. Of course, my perception was probably colored by Ferrin Westfall's curt treatment of me and Ramona's outright hostility. I'm not above holding grudges.

Ramona Westfall came to the door and admitted me. I kept my tone pleasant, but I didn't fall all over myself admiring the place, which, at a glance, did appear to be flawlessly done. She showed me into the front parlor and removed herself, closing the oak paneled sliding doors behind her. I waited, staring resolutely at the floor. I could hear murmuring in the hall. After a moment, the doors slid open and a man entered, introducing himself as Ferrin Westfall . . . as if I hadn't guessed. We shook hands.

He was tall and slim, with a cold, handsome face and silver hair. His eyes were a dark green, as empty of warmth as the harbor. There were hints of something submerged in the depths, but no signs of life. He wore charcoal gray pants and a soft gray cashmere sweater that fairly begged to be stroked. He indicated that I should have a seat, which I did.

He surveyed me for a moment, taking in the boots, the faded jeans, the wool sweater beginning to pill at the elbows. I was determined not to let his disapproval get through to me, but it required an effort on my part. I stared at him impassively and warded off his withering assessment by picturing him on the toilet with his knickers down around his ankles.

Finally, he said, "Tony will be out in a moment. Ramona's told me about the check. I wonder if I might examine it."

I removed the check from my jeans pocket and smoothed it out, passing it to him for his inspection. I wondered if he thought it was forged, stolen, or in some way counterfeit. He scrutinized it, fore and aft, and returned it, apparently satisfied that it was legitimate.

"Why did Mr. Daggett come to you with this?" he asked.

"I'm not really sure," I said. "He told me he'd tried to find Tony at an old address. When he had no luck, he asked me to track him down and deliver it."

"Do you know how he acquired the money?"

Again, I found myself feeling protective. It was really none of this man's business. He probably wanted to assure himself that Daggett hadn't come by the money through some tacky enterprise—drugs, prostitutes, selling dogs and kitty cats to labs for medical experiments.

"He won it at the track," I said. Personally, I hadn't quite believed this part of Daggett's tale, but I didn't mind if Ferrin Westfall got sucked in. He didn't seem any more convinced than I. He shifted the subject.

"Would you prefer to be alone with Tony?"

I was surprised at the offer. "Yes, I would. I'd really like to go off somewhere with him and have a Coke."

"I suppose that would be all right, as long as you don't keep him too long. This is a school night."

"Sure. That's very nice of you."

There was a tap at the door. Mr. Westfall rose and crossed the room. "This will be Tony," he said.

The doors slid back and Tony Gahan came in. He looked like an immature fifteen. He was maybe five-foot-six, a hundred and twenty-five pounds. His uncle introduced me. I proferred my hand and we fumbled through a handshake. Tony's eyes were dark, his hair a medium brown, attractively cut, which struck me as odd. Most of the high school kids I've seen lately look like they're being treated for the same scalp disease. I suspected Tony's hairstyle was a concession to Ferrin Westfall's notions of good taste and I wondered how that sat with him.

His manner was anxious. He seemed like a kid trying desperately to please. He shot a cautious look at his uncle, searching for visual cues as to what was expected of him and how he was meant to behave. It was painful to watch.

"Miss Millhone would like to take you out for a Coke, so she can talk to you," Mr. Westfall said.

"How come?" he croaked. Tony looked like he was going to drop dead on the spot and I remembered in a flash how much I'd hated eating and drinking in the presence of strange adults when I was his age. Meals represent a series of traps when you haven't yet mastered the appropriate social skills. I hated adding to his distress, but I was convinced I'd never have a decent conversation with him in this house.

"She'll explain all that," Mr. Westfall said. "Obviously, you're not required to go. If you'd prefer to stay here, simply say so."

Tony seemed unable to get a reading from his uncle's statement, which was neutral on the surface, but contained some tricky side notes. It was the word "simply" that tripped him, I thought, and the "obviously" didn't help.

Tony glanced at me with a half shrug. "It's okay, I guess. Like, right now?"

Mr. Westfall nodded. "It won't be for long. You'll need a jacket, of course."

Tony moved out into the hall and I followed, waiting until he found his jacket in the hall closet.

At fifteen, I thought he could probably figure out if he needed a jacket or not, but neither of them consulted me on the subject. I opened the front door and held it while he went out. Mr. Westfall watched us for a moment and then closed the door behind us. God, it was just like a date. I nearly swore I'd have him home by 10:00. Absurd.

We made our way down the path in the dark. "You go to Santa Teresa High School?"

"Right."

"What year?"

"Sophomore."

We got in the car. Tony tried to roll down the smashed window on his side without much success. A shard of glass tinkled down into the door frame. He finally gave up.

"What happened to this?"

"I was careless," I said, and let it go at that.

I did a U-turn in the lane and I headed for the Clockworks on State Street, a teen hangout generally regarded as seedy, unclean, and corrupt, which it is . . . a training ground for junior thugs. Kids come here (stoned, no doubt) to drink Cokes, smoke clove cigarettes, and behave like bad-asses. I'd been introduced to the place by a seventeen-year-old pink-haired dope dealer named Mike, who made more money than I did. I hadn't seen him since June, but I tend to look for him around town.

We parked in a small lot out back and went in through the rear entrance. The place is long and narrow, painted charcoal gray, the high ceiling rimmed with pink and purple neon. A series of mobiles, looking like big black clock gears, revolve in the smoky air. The noise level, on weekends, is deafening, the music so loud it makes the floor vibrate. On week nights, it's quiet and oddly intimate. We found a table and I went over to the counter to pick up a couple of Cokes. There was a tap on my shoulder and I turned to find Mike standing there. I felt a rush of warmth. "I was just thinking about you!" I said. "How are you?"

A pink tint crept across his cheeks and he gave me a slow seductive smile. "I'm okay. What are you doin' these days?"

"Nothing much," I said. "Great hair." Formerly he'd sported a Mohawk, a great cockscomb of pink down the center of his head, with the sides shaved close. Now it was arranged in a series of purple spurts, each clump held together with a rubber band, the feathery tips bleached white. Aside from the hair, he was a good-looking kid, clear skin, green eyes, good teeth.

I said, "Actually, I'm about to have a talk with that guy over there . . . a schoolmate of yours."

"Yeah?" He turned and gave Tony a cursory inspection.

"You know him?"

"I've seen him. He doesn't hang out with the kind of people I do." His gaze returned to Tony and I thought he was going to say more, but he let it pass.

"What are you up to?" I asked. "Still dealing?"

"Who me? Hey, no. I told you I'd quit," he said, sounding faintly righteous. The look in his eyes, of course, suggested just the opposite. If he was doing something illegal, I didn't want to know about it anyway, so I bypassed the subject.

"What about school? You graduate this year?"

"June. I got college applications out and everything."

"Really?" I couldn't tell if he was putting me on or not.

He caught the look. "I get good grades," he protested. "I'm not just your average high school dunce, you know. The bucks I got, I could go anyplace I want. That's what private enterprise is about."

I had to laugh. "For sure," I said. The "bar maid" set two Cokes on the counter and I paid her. "I have to get back to my date."

"Nice seeing you," he said. "You ought to come in sometime and talk to me."

"Maybe I'll do that," I said. I smiled at him, mentally shaking my head. Flirtatious little shit. I moved over to the table where Tony was sitting. I handed him a Coke and sat down.

"You know that guy?" Tony asked cautiously.

"Who, Mike? Yes, I know him."

Tony's eyes strayed to Mike and back again, resting on my face with something close to respect. Maybe I wasn't such a geek after all.

"Did your uncle tell you what this is about?" I asked.

"Some. He said the accident and that old drunk."

"You feel okay discussing it?"

He shrugged by way of reply, avoiding eye contact.

"I take it you weren't in the car," I said.

He smoothed the front of his hair to the side. "Uh-uh. Me and my mom got into this argument. They were going to my granny's for this Easter egg hunt and I didn't want to go."

"Your grandmother's still in town someplace?"

He shifted in his chair. "In a rest home. She had a stroke."

"She's your mother's mother?" I didn't care particularly about any of this. I was just hoping the kid would relax and open up.

"Yeah."

"What's it like living with your aunt and uncle?"

"Fine. No big deal. He comes down on my case all the time, but she's nice."

"She said you were having some problems at school."

"So?"

"Just curious. She says you're very smart and your grades are in the toilet. I wondered what that was about."

"It's about school sucks," he said. "It's about I don't like people butting into my fuckin' business."

"Really," I said. I took a sip of Coke. His hostility was like a sewer backing up and I thought I'd give the efflux a chance to subside. I didn't care if he cussed. I could outcuss him any day of the week.

When I didn't react, he filled the silence. "I'm trying to get my grades pulled up," he said somewhat grudgingly. "I had to take all this bullshit math and chemistry. That's why I didn't do good."

"What's your preference? English? Art?"

He hesitated. "You some kind of shrink?"

"No. I'm a private investigator. I assumed you knew that."

He stared at me. "I don't get it. What's this got to do with the accident?"

I took out the check and laid it on the table. "The man responsible wanted me to look you up and give you this."

He picked the check up and glanced at it.

"It's a cashier's check for twenty-five thousand ollars," I said.

"What for?"

"I'm not really sure. I think John Daggett was oping to make restitution for what he did."

Tony's confusion was clear and so was the anger that ccompanied it. "I don't want this," he said. "Why give it) me? Megan Smith died too, you know, and so did that ther guy, Doug. Are they gettin' money too, or just ie?"

"Just you, as far as I know."

"Take it back then. I don't want it. I hate that old astard." He tossed the check on the table and gave it a ush.

"Look. Now just wait and let me say something first. t's your choice. Honestly. It's up to you. Your aunt was ffended by the offer and I understand that. No one can orce you to accept the money if you don't want it. But ist hear me out, okay?"

Tony was staring off across the room, his face set.

I lowered my voice. "Tony, it's true John Daggett as a drunk, and maybe he was a totally worthless uman being, but he did something he felt bad about nd I think he was trying to make up for it. Give him redit for that much and don't say no without giving it onsideration first."

"I don't *want* money for what he did."

"I'm not done yet. Just let me finish this."

His mouth trembled. He made a dash at his eyes ith the sleeve of his jacket, but he didn't get up and alk away.

"People make mistakes," I said. "People do things iey never meant to do. He didn't kill anyone deliber- tely . . ."

"He's a fuckin' drunk! He was out on the fuckin' reet at fuckin' nine in the morning. Dad and Mom and

Hilary . . ." His voice broke and he fought for contro
"I don't want anything from him. I hate his guts and
don't want his crummy check."

"Why don't you cash it and give it all away?"

"No! You take it. Give it back to him. Tell him I sai
he could get fucked."

"I can't. He's dead. He was killed Friday night."

"Good. I'm glad. I hope somebody cut his heart ou
He deserved it."

"Maybe so. But it's still possible that he felt some
thing for you and wanted to give you back some of wha
he took away."

"Like what? It's done. They're all dead."

"But you're not, Tony. You have to find a way to ge
on with life . . ."

"Hey! I'm doing that, okay? But I don't have t
listen to this bullshit! You said what you had to say an
now I want to go home."

He got up, radiating rage, his whole body stiff. H
moved swiftly toward the rear entrance, knocking chair
aside. I snatched up the check and followed.

When I reached the parking lot, he was kick-boxin
the remaining glass out of the smashed window of m
car. I started to protest and then I stopped myself.

Oh why not, I thought. I had to replace the dam
thing anyway. I stood and watched him without a word
When he was done, he leaned against the car and wept

15

By the time I got Tony home again, he was calm,
shut down, as if nothing out of the ordinary had
occurred. I pulled up in front of the house. He got out,
slammed the door, and headed up the path without a
word. I was reasonably certain he wouldn't mention his
outburst to his aunt and uncle, which was fortunate as
I'd sworn I could talk to him without his getting upset. I
was, of course, still in possession of Daggett's check,
wondering if I'd be toting it around for life, trying in
vain to get someone to take it off my hands.

When I got back to my place, I spent twenty
minutes unloading my VW. While I tend to maintain an
admirable level of tidiness in the apartment, my organi-
zational skills have never extended to my car. The back
seat is usually crowded with files, law books, my briefcase, piles of miscellaneous clothing—shoes, pantyhose,
jackets, hats, some of which I use as "disguises" in the
various aspects of my trade.

I packed everything in a cardboard box and then
proceeded around to the backyard where the entrance
to my apartment is located. I opened the padlock on the
storage bin attached to the service porch and stowed the
box, snapping the padlock into place again.

As I reached my door, a dark shape loomed out of
the shadows. "Kinsey?"

I jumped, realizing belatedly that it was Billy Polo.
couldn't distinguish his features in the dark, but hi
voice was distinctly his own.

"Oh Jesus, what are you doing here?" I said.

"Hey, I'm sorry. I didn't mean to scare you. I wante
to talk to you."

I was still trying to recover from the jolt he'd give
me, my temper rising belatedly. "How'd you know
where to find me?"

"I looked you up in the telephone book."

"My home address isn't in the book."

"Yeah, I know. I tried your office first. You weren
in, so I asked next door at that insurance place."

"California Fidelity gave you my home address?"
said. "Who'd you talk to?" I didn't believe for a minut
that CF would release that kind of information to him

"I didn't get her name. I told her I was a client an
it was urgent."

"Bullshit."

"No, it's the truth. She only gave it to me because
leaned on her."

I could tell he wasn't going to budge on the point, s
I let it pass. "All right, what is it?" I said. I kncw
sounded cranky, but I didn't like his coming to my plac
and I didn't believe his tale about how he found ou
where it was.

"We're just gonna stand around out here?"

"That's right, Billy. Now get on with it."

"Well, you don't have to get so huffy."

"Huffy! What the hell are you talking about? Yo
loom up out of the dark and scare me half to death!
don't know you from Jack the Ripper so why should
invite you in?"

"Okay, okay."

"Just say what you have to say. I'm beat."

He did some fidgeting around . . . for effect,

ught. Finally, he said, "I talked to my sister, Coral,
d she told me I should be straight with you."

"Oh goody, what a treat. Straight about what?"

"Daggett," he mumbled. "He did get in touch."

"When was this?"

"Last Monday when he got to town."

"He called you?"

"Yeah, that's right."

"How'd he know where you were?"

"He tried my mom's house and talked to her. I
sn't home at the time, so she got his number and I
led him back."

"Where'd he call from?"

"I don't know for sure. Some dive. There was all
s noise in the background. He was drunk and I
ured he must have parked himself in the first bar he
nd."

"What time of day was this?"

"Maybe eight at night. Around in there."

"Go on."

"He said he was scared and needed help. Somebody
ed him down in Los Angeles and told him he was
d meat on account of a scam he pulled up in prison
t before he got out."

"What scam?"

"I don't know all the details. What I heard was his
mate got snuffed and Daggett helped himself to a big
d of cash the guy had hidden in his bunk."

"How much?"

"Nearly thirty grand. It was some kind of drug deal
nt sour, which is why the guy got killed in the first
ce. Daggett walked off with the whole stash and
nebody wanted it back. They were comin' after him.
least that's what they told him."

"Who?"

"I don't want to mention names. I got a fair idea
d I could find out for sure if I wanted to, but I don't

like puttin' my neck in a noose unless I have to. T
point is I shined him on. I wasn't going to help that
coot. No way. He got himself in a hole, let him
himself out. I didn't want to be involved. Not with th
guys after him. I'm too fond of my health."

"So what happened? You talked on the phone a
that was it?"

"Well, no. I met him for a drink. Coral said I sho
level with you about that."

"Really," I said. "What for?"

"In case something came up later. She didn't wan
to look like I was holding out."

"So you think they caught up with him?"

"He's dead, ain't he?"

"Proving what?"

"Don't ask me. I mean, all I know is what Dagg
said. He was on the run and he thought I'd help."

"How?"

"A place to hide."

"When did you meet with him?"

"Not till Thursday. I was tied up."

"Pressing social engagements, no doubt."

"Hey, I was looking for work. I'm on parole an
got requirements to meet."

"You didn't see him Friday?"

"Uh-uh. I just saw him once and that was Thursc
night."

"What'd he do in the meantime?"

"I don't know. He never said."

"Where'd you meet him?"

"At the bar where Coral works."

"Ah, now I see. She got worried I'd ask around a
somebody'd say they saw you with him."

"Well, yeah. Coral don't like me to mess with
law, especially with me on parole anyway."

"How come it took the bad guys so long to catch
with him? He's been out of prison for six weeks."

"Maybe they didn't figure it was him at first. Daggett wasn't the brightest guy, you know. He never did nothin' right in his life. They prob'bly figured he was too dumb to stick his hand in a mattress and walk off with the cash."

"Did Daggett have the money with him when you talked to him?"

"Are you kidding? He tried to borrow ten bucks from me," Billy said, aggrieved.

"What was the deal?" I asked. "If he gave the money back, they'd let him off the hook?"

"Probably not. I doubt that."

"So do I," I said. "How do you think Lovella figures into this?"

"She doesn't. It's got nothing to do with her."

"I wouldn't be too sure about that. Somebody saw Daggett down at the marina last Friday night, dead drunk, in the company of a trashy-looking blonde."

Even in the dark, I could tell Billy Polo was staring at me.

"A blonde?"

"That's right. She was on the young side from what I was told. He was staggering, and she had to work to keep him on his feet."

"I don't know nothin' about that."

"Neither do I, but it sure sounded like Lovella to me."

"Ask her about it then."

"I intend to," I said. "So what happens next?"

"About what?"

"The thirty thousand, for starters. With Daggett dead, does the money go back to the guys who were after him?"

"If they found it, I guess it does," he said, uncomfortably.

"What if they didn't find it?"

Billy hesitated. "Well, I guess if it's stashed somewhere, it'd belong to his widow, wouldn't it? Part of his estate?"

I was beginning to get the drift here, but I wondered if he did. "You mean Essie?"

"Who?"

"Daggett's widow, Essie."

"He's divorced from her," Billy said.

"I don't think so. At least not as far as the law is concerned."

"He's married to Lovella," he said.

"Not legally."

"You're shittin' me."

"Come to the funeral tomorrow and see for yourself."

"This Essie has the money?"

"No, but I know where it is. Twenty-five thousand of it, at any rate."

"Where?" he said, with disbelief.

"In my pocket, sweetheart, in the form of a cashier's check made out to Tony Gahan. You remember, Tony, don't you?"

Dead silence.

I lowered my voice. "You want to tell me who Doug Polokowski is?"

Billy Polo turned and walked away.

I stood there for a moment and then followed reluctantly, still pondering the fact that he had my home address. Last time I'd talked to him, he didn't even buy the fact that I was a private investigator. Now suddenly he was seeking me out, having confidential chats about Daggett on my front step. It didn't add up.

I heard his car door slam as I reached the street. hung back in the shadows, watching as he swung the Chevrolet out of a parking place four doors down. He gunned it, speeding off toward the beach. I debated about whether to pursue him, but I couldn't bear the thought of lurking about outside Coral's trailer again.

nough of that stuff. I turned back and let myself into
ny apartment. I kept thinking about the fact that my car
vas broken into, my handbag stolen, along with all of
ny personal identification. Had Billy Polo done that? Is
hat how he came up with my home address? I couldn't
figure out how he'd tracked me to the beach in the first
place, but it would explain how he knew where to find
ne now.

I was sure he was maneuvering, but I couldn't
figure out what he'd hoped to get. Why the yarn about
Daggett and the bad guys in jail? It did fit with some of
he facts, but it didn't have that nice, untidy ring of
ruth.

I hauled out a stack of index cards and wrote it all
own anyway. Maybe it would make sense later, when
ther information came to light. It was 10:00 by the time
finished. I pulled the white wine out of the re-
rigerator, wiggled the cork loose, and poured myself a
lass. I stripped my clothes off, turned the lights out,
nd toted the wine into the bathroom where I set it on
he window sill in the bathtub and stared out at the
arkened street. There's a streetlight out there, buried
n the branches of a jacaranda tree, largely denuded
ow by the rain. The window was half opened and a
amp slat of night wind wafted in, chilly and secretive. I
ould hear rain begin to rattle on my composition roof. I
vas restless. When I was a young girl, maybe twelve or
o, I wandered the streets on nights like this, barefoot, in
raincoat, feeling anxious and strange. I don't think my
unt knew about my nocturnal excursions, but maybe
he did. She had a reckless streak of her own and she
nay have honored mine. I was thinking a lot about her,
f late, perhaps because of Tony. His family had been
iped out in a car accident, just as mine had, and he was
eing raised now by an aunt. Sometimes, I had to admit
o myself . . . especially on nights like this . . . that
he death of my parents may not have been as tragic as it

seemed. My aunt, for all her failings, was a perfec
guardian for me . . . brazen, remote, eccentric, inde
pendent. Had my parents lived, my life would hav
taken an altogether different route. There was no doub
of that in my mind. I like my history just as it is, bu
there was something else going on as well.

Looking back on the evening, I realized how muc
I'd identified with Tony's kicking my car window ou
The rage and defiance were hypnotic and touched o
deep feelings of my own. Daggett's funeral was comin
up the next afternoon and that touched off somethin
else . . . old sorrows, good friends gone down into th
earth. Sometimes I picture death as a wide ston
staircase, filled with a silent procession of those being le
away. I see death too often to worry about it much, but
miss the departed and I wonder if I'll be docile when m
turn comes.

I finished my wine and went to bed, sliding nake
into the warm folds of my quilt.

16

The dawn was accompanied by drizzle, dark gray sky gradually shading to a cold white light. Ordinarily, I don't run in the rain, but I hadn't slept well and I needed to clear away the dregs of nagging anxiety. I wasn't even sure what I was worried about. Sometimes I awaken uncomfortably aware of a low-level dread humming in my gut. Running is the only relief I can find short of drink and drugs, which at 6:00 A.M. don't appeal.

I pulled on a sweat suit and hit the bike path, jogging a mile and a half to the recreation center. The palm trees along the boulevard had shed dried fronds in the wind and they lay on the grass like soggy feathers. The ocean was silver, the surf rustling mildly like a taffeta skirt with a ruffle of white. The beach was a drab brown, populated by sea gulls snatching at sand fleas. Pigeons lifted in a cloud, looking on. I have to admit I'm not an outdoor person at heart. I'm always aware that under the spritely twitter of birds, bones are being crunched and ribbons of flesh are being stripped away, all of it the work of bright-eyed creatures without feeling or conscience. I don't look to Nature for comfort or serenity.

Traffic was light. There were no other joggers. I

137

passed the public restrooms, housed in a cinderblock
building painted flesh pink, where two bums huddled
with a shopping cart. One I recognized from two nights
before and he watched me now, indifferently. His friend
was curled up under a cardboard comforter, looking
like a pile of old rags. I reached the turnaround and ran
the mile and a half back. By the time I got home, my
Etonics were soaked, my sweat pants were darkened by
the drizzle, and the mist had beaded in my hair like a net
of seed pearls. I took a long hot shower, optimism
returning now that I was safely home again.

After breakfast, I tidied up and then checked my
automobile insurance policy and determined that the
replacement of my car window was covered, after a fifty-
dollar deductible. At 8:30, I started soliciting estimates
from auto glass shops, trying to persuade someone to
work me in before noon that day. I zipped myself into
my all-purpose dress again, resurrected a decent-
looking black leather shoulder bag that I use for
"formal" wear and filled it with essentials, including the
accursed cashier's check.

I dropped the car off at an auto glass shop not far
from my office and hoofed it the rest of the way to work.
Even with low-heeled pumps, my feet hurt and my
pantyhose made me feel like I was walking around with
a hot, moist hand in my crotch.

I let myself into the office and initiated my usual
morning routines. The phone rang as I was plugging in
the coffeepot.

"Miss Millhone, this is Ramona Westfall."

"Oh hello," I said. "How are you?" Secretly, my
stomach did a little twist and I wondered if Tony Gahan
had told her about his freak-out at the Clockworks the
night before.

"I'm fine," she said. "I'm calling because there's

something I'd like to discuss with you and I hoped you might have some time free this morning."

"Well, my schedule's clear, but I don't have a car. Can you come down here?"

"Yes, of course. I'd prefer that anyway. Is ten convenient? It's short notice, I know."

I glanced at my watch. Twenty minutes. "That's fine," I said. She made some good-bye noises and clicked off. I depressed the line and then put a call through to Barbara Daggett at her mother's house to verify the time of the funeral. She was unavailable to come to the phone, but Eugene Nickerson told me the services were at 2:00 and I said I'd be there.

I took a few minutes to open my mail from the day before, posting a couple of checks to accounts receivable, then made a quick call to my insurance agent, giving her the sketchy details about my car window. I'd no more than put the phone down when it rang again.

"Kinsey, this is Barbara Daggett. Something's come up. When I arrived here this morning, there was some woman sitting on the porch steps who says she's Daddy's wife."

"Oh God. Lovella."

"You know about her?"

"I met her last week when I was down in L.A., trying to get a line on your father's whereabouts."

"And you knew about this claim of hers?"

"I never heard the details, but I gathered they were living in some kind of common-law relationship."

"Kinsey, she has a marriage certificate. I saw it myself. Why didn't you tell me what was going on? I was speechless. She stood out on the front porch, screaming bloody murder until I finally had to call the police. I can't believe you didn't at least *mention* it."

"When was I supposed to do that? At the morgue?

Over at the funeral home with your mother in a state of collapse?"

"You could have called me, Kinsey. Any time. You could have come to my office to discuss it."

"Barbara, I could have done half a dozen things, but I didn't. Frankly, I was feeling protective of your father and I was hoping you wouldn't have to find out about this 'alleged' marriage. That certificate could be a fake. The whole thing could be trumped up, and if not, you've still got problems enough without adding bigamy to his list of personal failings."

"That isn't yours to decide. Now Mother wants to know what the ruckus was about and I have no idea what to say."

"Well, I can see why you're upset, but I'm not sure I'd do it any differently."

"I can't believe you'd take that attitude! I don't appreciate being kept in the dark," she said. "I hired you to investigate and I expect you to pass on whatever comes to light."

"Your father hired me long before you did," I said.

That silenced her for a moment and then she took off again. "To do what? You never did specify."

"Of course I didn't. He talked to me confidentially It was all bullshit, but it's still not mine to flap around. I couldn't stay in business if I blabbed all the information that came my way."

"I'm his daughter. I have a right to know. Especially if my father's a *bigamist*. What else am I paying you for?"

"You might be paying me to exercise a little judgment of my own," I said. "Come on, Barbara. Be reasonable. Suppose I'd told you. What purpose would that have served? If your parents are still legally married, Lovella has no claim whatever and, for all I know, she's perfectly aware of that. Why add to your grief when she might well have slunk away without a word?"

"How did she know he died in the first place?"

"Not from me, I can tell you that. I'm not an idiot. The last thing in the world I wanted was her up here camping out on your doorstep. Maybe she read it in the paper. Maybe she heard it on the news."

She murmured something, temporarily mollified.

"What happened when the cops got there?" I asked.

There was another pause while she debated whether to move on or continue berating me. I sensed that she enjoyed chewing people out and it was hard for her to give up the opportunity. From my point of view, she wasn't paying me enough to take much guff. A little bit, perhaps. I probably should have told her.

"The two officers took her aside and had a talk with her. She left a few minutes ago."

"Well, if she shows up again, I'll take care of it," I said.

"Again? Why would she do that?"

I remembered then that aside from the matter of her father's apparent bigamy, I hadn't told her about the infamous twenty-five thousand dollars, which Billy Polo assumed was part of Daggett's "estate." Maybe Lovella had come up here to collect. "I think we better have a chat soon," I said.

"Why? Is there something *else*?"

I looked up. Ramona Westfall was standing in my doorway. "There's always something else," I said. "That's what makes life so much fun. I've got someone here. I'll talk to you this afternoon."

I hung up and rose to my feet, shaking hands with Mrs. Westfall across the desk. I invited her to take a seat and then poured coffee for us both, using social ritual as a way of setting her at ease, or so I hoped.

She was looking drawn, the fine skin under her

mild eyes smudged with fatigue. She wore a tan poplin
shirtwaist with shoulder epaulets and carried a mesh-
and-canvas handbag that looked like it could be packed
for a quick safari somewhere. Her pale hair had the
sheen of a Breck shampoo ad in a magazine. I tried to
picture her in a raincoat, lurching around the marina
with Daggett's arm draped over her shoulder. Could she
have flipped him, ass over teakettle, right out of that
skiff? Hey, sure. Why not?

She stared at me uneasily, reaching out automatically to straighten some items on my desk. She lined up
three pencils with the points facing me, like little
ground-to-air missiles, and then she cleared her throat.

"Well. We were wondering. Tony never said anything so we thought perhaps we should ask you about it.
Did you tell Tony about the money when you talked to
him last night?"

"Sure," I said. "Not that it did any good. I got
nowhere. He was adamant. He wouldn't even discuss it."

She colored slightly. "We're thinking to take it," she
said. "Ferrin and I talked about it last night while Tony
was out with you and we're beginning to believe we
should put the money in a trustee account for him . . .
at least until he's eighteen and really has a sense of what
he might do with it."

"What brought about the change?"

"Oh everything, I guess. We've been in family
counseling and the therapist keeps hoping we can work
through some of the anger and the grief. He feels Tony's
migraines are stress-related in part, a sort of index of his
unwillingness . . . or maybe inability is a better word
. . . to process his loss. I've been wondering how much
I've contributed to that. I haven't dealt with Abby's
death that well and it can't have helped him." She
paused and then shook her head slightly as though

mbarrassed. "I know it's a reversal. I suppose we've
een unnecessarily rude to you and I'm sorry."

"You don't have to apologize," I said. "Personally,
'd be delighted to have you take the check. At least then
 could feel I'd discharged my responsibilities. If you
 hange your mind later, you can always donate the
 noney to a worthy cause. There are lots of those
 round."

"What about his family? Daggett's. They may feel
 hey're entitled to the money, don't you think? I mean, I
 vouldn't want to take it if there are going to be any legal
 amifications."

"You'd have to talk to an attorney about that," I
aid. "The check is made out to Tony, and Daggett hired
 ne to deliver it to him. I don't think there's any question
 bout his intention. There may be other legal issues I
 lon't know about, but you're certainly welcome to talk to
 omeone first." Secretly, I wanted her to take the damn
 hing and be done with it.

She stared at the floor for a moment. "Tony
 aid . . . last night he mentioned that he might want to
 ;o to the funeral. Do you think he should? I mean, does
 hat seem like a good idea to you?"

"I don't know, Mrs. Westfall. That's way out of my
 ine. Why don't you ask his therapist?"

"I tried, but he's out of town until tomorrow. I don't
 vant Tony any more upset than he is."

"He's going to feel what he feels. You can't control
 hat. Maybe it's something he has to go through."

"That's what Ferrin says, but I'm not sure."

"What's the story on the migraines? How long has
 hat been going on?"

"Since the accident. He had one last night as a
 natter of fact. It's not your fault," she added hastily.
 'His head started bothering him about an hour after he
 ;ot home. He threw up every twenty minutes or so from

midnight until almost four A.M. We finally had to take
him over to the emergency room at St. Terry's. They
gave him a shot and that put him out, but he woke up a
little while ago and he's talking now about going to the
funeral. Did he mention it to you?"

"Not at all. I told him Daggett was dead, but he
didn't react much at the time, except to say he was glad.
Is he well enough to go?"

"He will be, I think. The migraines are odd. One
minute you think he's never going to pull out of it and
the next minute he's on his feet and starving to death. It
happened last Friday night."

"Friday?" I said. The night of Daggett's death.

"That episode wasn't quite as bad. When he came
home from school, he knew he was on the verge of a
headache. We tried to get some medication down him to
head it off, but no luck. Anyway, he pulled out of it after
a while and I ended up fixing him two meatloaf
sandwiches in the kitchen at two A.M. He was fine. Of
course, he had another headache on Tuesday, and then
the one last night. Two the week before that. Ferrin
thinks maybe his going to the funeral will have some
symbolic significance. You know, finish it off for him and
set him free."

"That's always possible."

"Would Barbara Daggett object?"

"I don't see why she would," I said. "I suspect she
feels as guilty as her father did, and she's offered to
help."

"I guess I'll see how he's doing when I get home
then," she said. She glanced at her watch. "I better go."

"Let me give you the check." I pulled my handbag
out of the bottom drawer and took out the check, which
I passed across the desk to her. As her husband had
done the night before, she smoothed out the folds,
looking at it closely as if it might be some preposterous

ake. She folded it up again and slipped it in her bag as
he got to her feet. She hadn't touched her mug of
coffee. I hadn't drunk mine either.

I told her the time and place of the services and
walked her to the door. After she left, I sat down at my
desk again, reviewing everything she'd said. At some
point, I wanted to take Tony Gahan aside and see if he
could verify her presence at the house the night Daggett
died. It was hard to picture her as a killer, but I'd been
fooled before.

17

John Daggett's funeral service took place in the sanctuary of some obscure outpost of the Christian church. The building itself was a one-story yellow stucco, devoid of ornament, located just off the freeway—the sort of chapel you glimpse through the bushes when you're going someplace else. I arrived late. I'd retrieved my VW from the auto glass shop at 1:45 after countless delays, and I confess I'd spent a few contented moments cranking my new car window up and down. The drizzle was beginning to turn serious and I was heartened by the notion that it wouldn't blow straight in on me.

When I reached the gravel parking lot beside the church, there were already fifty cars jammed into space for thirty-five. Some vehicles had nosed out into the vacant lot next door and some hugged the fence along the frontage road. I was forced to pass the place, snag a spot at the end of a long line of cars, and walk back. I could already hear electronic organ music thumping out in a style better suited to a skating rink than a house of God. I noticed from the sign out front that the minister was called a pastor instead of "Reverend" and I wondered if that was significant. Pastor Howard Bowen. The church name was composed of a long string of words and reminded me uneasily of the outfit that

146

stributes pamphlets door-to-door. I hoped they
eren't keen on converts.

Mr. Sharonson, from Wynington-Blake, was stand-
g by himself on the low front steps and he gave me a
ained look as he passed me a mimeographed copy of
e program with a hand-drawn lily on the front. His
anner suggested that the services were spiritually
cond-rate, this being the K mart of churches.

I went in. An usher peeled a metal folding chair
om a stack near the door and flipped it open for me.
he congregation had risen to its feet to sing so I stood
the back row, wedged in among other late arrivals.
he woman on my left offered to share her hymnal and
took my half, my gaze sliding over the page in haste.
hey were on verse four of a ditty that went on and on
out blood and sin. I made some mouth noises which I
ped were being lost in the general din. Aside from the
ct I don't believe in this stuff, I don't sing too good and
was worried I might be denounced on both counts.

Way up at the front, I thought I spotted Barbara
aggett's blonde head, but I didn't see anyone else I
ew. We sat down with a rustle of clothing and the
rape of metal chair legs. While Pastor Bowen, in a
atte black suit, talked about what wretches we were, I
ared at the brown vinyl tile floor and studied the
unch row of stained glass windows which depicted
rms of spiritual torment that made me squirm. Al-
ady, I could feel a burgeoning urge to repent.

I could see Daggett's casket up by the altar, looking
mehow like one of those boxes magicians use when
ey cut folk in half. I checked my program. We'd
ipped through the opening prayer and the invoca-
on, and now that we'd dispensed with the first hymn,
e were apparently settling in for an energetic discourse
the temptations of the flesh, which put me in mind of
e numerous and varied occasions on which I'd suc-
mbed. That was entertaining.

Pastor Bowen was in his sixties, balding, a sm:
man with a tight round face, who looked like he wou
suffer from denture breath. He'd chosen as his subje
matter a passage from Deuteronomy: "The Lord sh:
smite thee in the knees, and in the legs, with a sore bot·
that cannot be healed, from the sole of thy foot unto tl
top of thy head," and I heard more on that subject th:
I thought possible without falling asleep. I was curio
what he could find to say about John Daggett, who
transgressions were many and whose repentances we
few, but he managed to tie Daggett's passing into "l
shall lend to thee, and thou shalt not lend to him; l
shall be the head, and thou shalt be the tail," and sail·
right into an all-encompassing prayer.

When we stood for the final hymn, I felt someon·
eyes on me and I looked over to spot Marilyn Smith tv
rows down, in the company of a man I assumed to l
her husband, Wayne. She was wearing red. I wonder·
if she would leap up and do a tap dance on the coffin li
The congregation by now was really getting into tl
spirit of things and hosannas were being called out on :
sides, accompanied by amens, huzzahs, and much ren
ing and tearing of clothes. I wanted to excuse myse
but I didn't dare. This was beginning to feel like soı
aerobics.

The woman next to me began to sway, her ey
closed, while she hooted out an occasional "Yes, Lord
I'm not given to this sort of orthodox public outbuı
and I commenced to edge my way to the door. I cou
see now that the minister, doing what looked like delto
releases, was leading his merry band of church elders
the equivalent of a canonical conga line with Ess
Daggett bringing up the rear.

At the exit, I came face to face with Billy Polo ar
his sister, Coral. He took me by the arm and pulled n
aside as the service drew to a close behind me ar
people began to crowd through the door. Essie Dagge

was wailing, nearly borne aloft like a football coach after
a big win. Barbara Daggett and Eugene Nickerson had
arranged themselves on either side, giving her what
protection they could. For some reason, the other
mourners were reaching out to touch and pat and grasp
at Essie, as if her grief lent her healing powers.

The pallbearers came last, pulling the coffin along
on a rolling cart instead of toting it. None of the six of
them appeared to be under sixty-five and Wynington-
Blake may have worried that they'd collapse, or topple
their cargo right out into the aisle. As it was, the cart
seemed to have one errant wheel which caused it to
meander, squeaking energetically. The coffin, as though
with a will of its own, headed for the chairs first on one
side and then the other. I could see the pallbearers
struggle to maintain mournful expressions while cor-
recting its course, dragging it up the aisle like a stubborn
dog.

I caught sight of Tony Gahan briefly, but he was
gone again before I could speak to him. The hearse
pulled up in front and the coffin was angled down the
low steps and into the rear. Behind it, the limousine
pulled up and Essie was helped into the back seat. She
was wearing a black suit, with a broad-brimmed black
straw hat, swathed in veiling. She looked more like a
beekeeper than anything else. Stung by the Holy Spirit,
I thought. Barbara Daggett wore a charcoal gray suit
and black pumps, her two-toned eyes looking almost
electric in the pale oval of her face. The rain was falling
steadily and Mr. Sharonson was distributing big black
umbrellas as people ducked off the porch and hurried
to the parking lot.

Cars were being started simultaneously in a rumble
of exhaust fumes, gravel popping as we pulled out onto
the frontage road and began the slow procession to the
cemetery, maybe two miles away. Again, we parked in a
long line, car doors slamming as we crossed the soggy

grass. This was apparently a fairly new cemetery, with
few trees—a wide flat field planted to an odd crop. The
headstones were square cut and low, without any of the
worn beauty of stone angels or granite lambs. The
grounds were well kept, but consisted primarily of
asphalt roadways winding among sections of burial plot
that had apparently been sold "pre-need." I wondered if
cemeteries, like golf courses, had to be designed by
experts for maximum aesthetic effect. This one felt like
a cut-rate country club, low membership fees for the
upstart dead. The rich and respectable were buried
someplace else and John Daggett couldn't possibly
qualify for inclusion among them.

Wynington-Blake had set up a canopy over the
grave itself and, nearby, a second larger one with folding
chairs arranged under it. No one seemed to know who
was supposed to go where and there was a bit of milling
around. Essie and Barbara Daggett were led into the big
tent and placed in the front row, with Eugene Nickerson
on one side and a fat woman on the other in a set of four
folding chairs connected at the base. The back legs were
already beginning to sink into the rain-softened soil,
tilting the four of them backward at a slight angle. I had
a brief image of them trapped like that, staring at the
tent top, legs dangling, unable to right themselves again.
Why is it that grief always seems edged with absurdity?

I eased over to one side, under shelter, but re-
mained standing. Most of the mourners appeared to be
elderly and (perhaps) needed folding chairs more than
I. It looked like the entire church membership had
turned out in Essie Daggett's behalf.

Pastor Bowen had declined a raincoat and he stood
now in the open air, rain collecting on his balding head,
waiting patiently for everyone to get settled. At this
range, I saw evidence of a hearing aid tucked into the
tiny ear cave on his right. Idly, he fiddled with the
device, keeping his expression benign so as not to call

ttention to himself. I wondered if the battery was
horting out from the damp. I could see him tap on the
id with his index finger, flinching then as though it had
uddenly barked to life again.

On the far side of the tent, I saw Marilyn and
Vayne Smith, and behind them Tony Gahan, accom-
anied by his aunt Ramona. He looked like the perfect
rep school gentleman in gray wool slacks, white shirt,
avy blazer, rep tie. As though sensing that he was being
vatched, his eyes strayed to mine, his expression as
mpty as a robot's. If he was expunging raw hate or an
ld sorrow, there was no sign of it. Billy Polo and his
ister stood outside the tent in the rain, sharing an
mbrella. Coral looked miserable. She was apparently
till caught up in the throes of a cold, clutching a fistful
f Kleenex. She belonged in bed with a flannel rag on
er chest reeking of Vick's Vaporub. Billy seemed
estless, scanning the crowd with care. I followed his
aze, wondering if he was looking for someone in
articular.

"Dear friends," the minister said in a powdery
oice. "We are gathered here on the sad occasion of
ohn Daggett's death, to witness his return to the earth
rom which he was formed, to acknowledge his passing,
o celebrate his entry into the presence of our Lord
esus. John Daggett has left us. He is free now of the
ares and worries of this life, free of sin, free of his
urdens, free of blame. . . ."

From somewhere near the back, a woman hollered
ut "Yes, Lord!" and a second woman yelled out
Buullishiit!" in just about the same tone. The minister,
ot hearing that well, apparently took both as spiritual
unctuation marks, Biblical whoopees to incite him to
reater eloquence. He raised his voice, closing his eyes
s he began quoting admonitions against sin, filth,
efiled flesh, lasciviousness, and corruption.

"John Daggett was the biggest asshole who eve
lived so get it straight!" came the jeering voice agair
Heads whipped around. Lovella had gotten to her fee
near the back. The people turned to stare, their face
blank with amazement.

She was drunk. She had the little bitty pink eyes tha
suggest some high-grade marijuana toked up in addi
tion to the booze. Her left eye was still slightly puffy, bu
the bruising had lightened up to a mild yellow on tha
side and she looked more like she was suffering from a
allergy than a rap up the side of the head from the dea
man. Her hair was the same blonde bush I remembered
her mouth a slash of dark red. She'd been weepin
copiously and her mascara was speckled under he
lower lids like soot. Her skin was splotchy, her nose ho
pink and running. For the occasion she'd chosen a blac
sequined cocktail dress, low cut. Her breasts looke
almost transparent and bulged out like condoms in
flated as a joke. I couldn't tell if she was weeping out o
rage or grief and I didn't think this crowd was prepare
to deal with either one.

I was already headed toward the rear. Out of th
corner of my eye, I saw Billy Polo make a beeline towar
her on the far side of the tent. The minister had figure
out by now that she was not on his team and he shot
baffled look at Mr. Sharonson, who motioned the usher
to take charge. We all reached her just about at the sam
time. Billy grabbed her from behind, pinning her arm
back. Lovella flung him off, kicking like a mule, yellin
"Fuck-heads! You scum-sucking hypocrites!" One ushe
snagged her by the hair and the other took her feet. Sh
shrieked and struggled as they carried her toward th
road. I followed, glancing back briefly. Barbara Dagge
was obscured by the mourners who'd stood up for
better look, but I saw that Marilyn Smith was lovin
every trashy minute of Lovella's performance.

By the time I reached Lovella, she was lying in th

front seat of Billy Polo's Chevrolet, hands covering her
face as she wept. The doors were open on both sides of
the car and Billy knelt by her head, shushing and
soothing her, smoothing her rain-tangled hair. The two
ushers exchanged a look, apparently satisfied that she
was under control at that point. Billy bristled at their
intrusion.

"I got her, man. Just bug off. She's cool."

Coral came around the car and stood behind him,
holding the umbrella. She seemed embarrassed by
Billy's behavior, uncomfortable in the presence of Lovella's excess. The three of them formed an odd unit and I
got the distinct impression that the connection between
them was more recent than Billy'd led me to believe.

The graveside service, I gathered, was drawing to a
close. From the tent came the thin, discordant voices of
the mourners as they joined in an a cappella hymn.
Lovella's sobs had taken on the intensity of a child's—
artless, unself-conscious. Was she truly grieving for
Daggett or was something else going on?

"What's the story, Billy?" I said.

"No story," he said gruffly.

"Something's going on. How'd she find out about
his death? From you?"

Billy laid his face against her hair, ignoring me.

Coral shifted her gaze to mine. "He doesn't know
anything."

"How about you, Coral? You want to talk about it?"

Billy shot her a warning look and she shook her
head.

Murmurs and activity from the tent. The crowd was
breaking up and people were beginning to move toward
us.

"Watch your head. I'm closing the car doors," Billy
said to Lovella. He shut the door on the driver's side and
moved around the front to catch the door on the
passenger side. He paused with his hand on the handle,

waiting for her to pull her knees up to make clearance. Idly, he surveyed the mourners still huddled under the cover of the tent. As the crowd shifted, I saw his gaze flicker. "Who's that?"

He was looking at a small group formed by Ramona Westfall, Tony, and the Smiths. The three adults were talking while Tony, his hands in his pockets, passed his shoe over the rung of a folding chair, scraping the mud from the sole. Barbara Daggett was just behind him, in conversation with someone else. I identified everyone by name. I thought Wayne was the one who seemed to hold his attention, but I wasn't positive. It might have been Marilyn.

"How come the Westfalls showed up for this?"

"Maybe the same reason you did."

"You don't know why I came," he said. He was agitated, jingling the car keys, his gaze drifting back to the mourners.

"Maybe you'll tell me one of these days."

His smirk said don't count on it. He signaled to Coral and she got in the back seat. He got in the car and started it, pulling out then without a backwards glance.

18

Barbara Daggett invited me back to her mother's house after the funeral, but I declined. I couldn't handle another emotional circus act. After I've spent a certain amount of time in the company of others, I need an intermission anyway. I retreated to my office and sat here with the lights out. It was only 4:00, but dark clouds were massing again as though for attack. I zipped my shoes off and put my feet up, clutching my jacket around me for warmth. John Daggett was in the ground now and the world was moving on. I wondered what would happen if we left it at that. I didn't think Barbara Daggett gave a damn about seeing justice done, whatever that consisted of. I hadn't come up with much. I thought I was on the right track, but I wasn't sure I really wanted an answer to the question Daggett's death had posed. Maybe it was better to forget this one, turn it under again like top soil, worms and all. The cops didn't consider it a homicide anyway and I knew I could talk Barbara Daggett out of pursuing the point. What was there to be gained? I wasn't in the business of avenging Daggett's death. Then what was I uneasy about? It was the only time in recent memory that I'd wanted to drop a case. Usually I'm dogged, but this time I wanted out. I think I could have talked myself into it if nothing else had occurred. As it happened, my phone rang about ten

minutes later, nudging me into action again. I took m
feet off the desk for form's sake and picked up on th
first ring. "Millhone."

A young-sounding man said hesitantly: "Is this th
office or an answering service?"

"The office."

"Is this Kinsey Millhone?"

"Yes. Can I help you?"

"Yeah, well my boss gave me this number. M
Donagle at the Spindrift Motel? He said you had som
questions about Friday night. I think maybe I saw th
guy you were asking about."

I reached for a lined yellow pad and a pen. "Great.
appreciate your getting in touch. Could you tell me you
name first?"

"Paul Fisk," he said. "I read in the paper some gu
drowned and it just sure seemed like an odd coinc
dence, but I didn't know if I should say anything or not.

"You saw him Friday night?"

"Well, I think it was him. This was about quarter o
two, something like that. I'm on night desk and some
times I step outside for some air, just to keep mysel
awake." He paused and I could hear him shift gear:
"This is confidential, isn't it?"

"Of course. Strictly between us. Why? Did you
girlfriend stop by or something like that?"

His laugh was nervous. "Naw, sometimes I smoke
little weed is all. Place gets boring at two A.M., so that
how I get through. Get loaded and watch old black-and
white movies on this little TV I got. I hope you don
have a problem with that."

"Hey, it's your business, not mine. How long hav
you worked at the Spindrift?"

"Just since March. It's not a great job, but I don
want to get fired. I'm trying to get myself out of deb
and I need the bucks."

"I hear you," I said. "Tell me about Friday night.

"Well, I was on the porch and this drunk went by. It
s raining pretty hard so I didn't get a real good look at
m at the time, but when I saw the news, the age and
ff seemed pretty close."

"Did you see the picture of him by any chance?"

"Just a glimpse on TV, but I wasn't paying much
ention so I couldn't say for sure it was him. I guess I
uld have called the cops, but I didn't have anything
ach to report and I was afraid it'd come out about
... about that other stuff."

"What was he doing, the drunk?"

"Nothing much. It was him and this girl. She had
m by the arm. You know, kind of propped up. They
re laughing like crazy, wandering all over the place on
count of his being so screwed up. Alcohol'll do that,
u know. Bad stuff. Not like weed," he said.

I bypassed the sales pitch. "What about the woman?
d you get a good look at her?"

"Not really. Not to describe."

"What about hair, clothing, things like that?"

"I noticed some. She had these real spiky heels and
aincoat, a skirt, and let's see . . . a shirt with this
eater over it. Like, what do you call 'em, preppies
ar."

"A crewneck?"

"Yeah. Same color green as the skirt."

"You saw all that in the dark?"

"It's not that dark there," he said. "There's a
eetlight right out front. The two of them fell down in
neap they were laughing so hard. She got up first and
ad of looked down to see if her stockings were torn.
: just lay there in a puddle on his back till she helped
m up."

"Did they see you?"

"I don't think so. I was standing in the shadows of
s overhang, keeping out of the wet. I never saw 'em
ok my way."

"What happened after the fall?"

"They just went on toward the marina."

"Did you hear them say anything?"

"Not really. It sounded like she was teasing h
about falling down, but other than that nothing
particular."

"Could they have had a car?"

"I don't think so. Anyway, not that I saw."

"What if they'd parked it in that municipal
across the street?"

"I guess they could have, but I don't know w
they'd walk to the marina in weather like that. See
like if they had a car it'd be easier to drive and then pa
it down there."

"Unless he was too drunk. He'd had his drive
license yanked too."

"She could have driven. She was half sober at leas

"You've got a point there," I said. "What abo
public transportation? Could they have come by bus
cab?"

"I guess, except the buses don't run that late. A c
maybe. That'd make sense."

I was jotting down information as he gave it to n
"This is great. What's your home phone in case I need
get in touch?"

He gave me the number and then said, "I usua
work eleven to seven on weekdays."

I made a quick note. "Do you think you'd recogn
the girl if you saw her again?"

"I don't know. Probably. Do you know who she is

"Not yet. I'm working on that."

"Well, I wish you luck. You think this'll help?"

"I hope so. Thanks for calling. I really apprecia
it."

"Sure thing, and if you catch up with her, let n
know. Maybe you can do like a police lineup or som
thing like that."

"Great and thanks."

He clicked off and I finished making notes, adding
his information to what I had. Dinah had spotted
Daggett and the girl at 2:15 and Paul Fisk's sighting
placed them right on Cabana thirty minutes before. I
wondered where they'd been before that. If they'd
arrived by cab, had she taken one home from the
marina afterward? I didn't get it. Most killers don't take
taxis to and from. It isn't good criminal etiquette.

I hauled out the telephone book and turned to the
Yellow Pages to look up cab companies. Fortunately,
Santa Teresa is a small town and there aren't that many.
Aside from a couple of airport and touring services,
there were six listed. I dialed each in turn, patiently
explaining who I was and inquiring about a 2:00 A.M.
Saturday fare with a Cabana Boulevard drop off. I was
also asking about a pickup anywhere in that vicinity
sometime between 3:00 and 6:00 A.M. According to the
morgue attendant, the watch Daggett had been wearing
was frozen at 2:37, but anybody could have jimmied
that, breaking the watch to pinpoint the time, then
attaching it to his wrist before he was dumped. If she'd
left the boat and swum ashore or rowed to the wharf
and abandoned it there, it was still going to take her a
little time to organize herself for the cab ride home.

All the previous week's trip sheets, of course, had
been filed and there were some heavy sighs and grum-
blings all around at the notion of having to look them
up. Ron Coachella, the dispatcher for Tip Top, was the
only cheerful soul in the lot, primarily because he'd
done a records search for me once before with good
results. I couldn't talk anyone into doing the file check
right then, so I left my name and number and a promise
that I'd call again. "Whoopee-do," said one.

While I was talking, I'd been doodling on the legal
pad, running my pencil around idly so that the line
formed a maze. I circled the note about the green skirt.

Hadn't that old bum pulled a pair of spike heels and
green skirt out of a trash bin at the beach? I remem
bered his shoving discarded clothing into one of th
plastic bags he kept in his shopping cart. Hers? Surel
she hadn't made her way home in the buff. She did hav
the raincoat, but I wondered if she might have had
change of clothes stashed somewhere too. She'd sur
gone to a lot of trouble if she were setting Daggett u
This didn't look like an impulsive act, done in the heat o
the moment. Had she had help? Someone who picke
her up afterward? If the cab companies didn't come u
with a record of a fare, I'd have to consider th
possibility of an accomplice.

In the meantime, I thought I'd better head down t
the beach and look for my scruffy drifter friend. I'
seen him that morning near the public restrooms when
did my run. I tore the sheet off the legal pad and folde
it, shoving it in my pocket as I grabbed up my handba
locked the office, and headed down the back stairs to m
car.

It was now nearly quarter to five, getting chillier b
the minute, but at least it was dry temporarily. I cruise
along Cabana, peering from my car window. Ther
weren't many people at the beach. A couple of powe
walkers. A guy with a dog. The boulevard seeme
deserted. I doubled back, heading toward my plac
passing the wharf on the left and the string of mote
across the street. Just beyond the boat launch and kiddi
pool, I pulled up at a stoplight, scanning the park on th
opposite corner. I could see the band shell where bum
sometimes took refuge, but I didn't see any squatter
Where were all the transients?

I circled back, passing the train station. It occurre
to me that this was probably the bums' dinner hour. I c
over another block and a half and sure enough, ther
they were—fifty or so on a quick count, lined up outsid
the Redemption Mission. The fellow I was looking fo

as near the end of the line, along with his pal. There
as no sign of their shopping carts, which I thought of
a matched set of movable metal luggage, the derelict's
Louis Vuitton. I slowed, looking for a place to park.

The neighborhood is characterized by light indus-
try, factory outlets, welding shops, and quonset huts
here auto body repair work is done. I found a parking
lot in front of a place that made custom surfboards. I
pulled in, watching in my rearview mirror until the
group outside the mission had shuffled in. I locked the
car then and crossed the street.

The Redemption Mission looks like it's made out of
papier-mâché, a two-story oblong of fakey-looking fieldstone, with ivy clinging to one end. The roofline is as
crenellated as a castle's, the "moat" a wide band of
asphalt paving. City fire codes apparently necessitated
the addition of fire escapes that angle down the building
now on all sides, looking somehow more perilous than
the possibility of fire. The property is considered prime
real estate and I wondered who would house the poor if
the bed space were bought out from under them. For
most of the year, the climate in this part of California is
mild enough to allow the drifters to sleep outdoors,
which they seem to prefer. Seasonally, however, there
are weeks of rain . . . even occasionally someone with a
butcher knife intent on slitting their throats. The
mission offers safe sleeping for the night, three hot
meals a day, and a place to roll cigarettes out of the wind.

I picked up cooking odors as I approached—bulk
hamburger with chili seasoning. As usual, I couldn't
remember eating lunch and here it was nearly din-
nertime again. The sign outside indicated prayer services at 7:00 every night and Hot Showers & Shaves on
Mondays, Wednesdays, and Saturdays. I stepped inside.
The walls were painted glossy beige on top and shoe
brown below. Hand-lettered signs pointed me to the

dining room and chapel on the left. I followed the low
murmur of conversation and the clatter of silverware

On the right, through a doorway, I spotted the
dining room—long metal folding tables covered with
paper, metal folding chairs filled with men. Nobody
paid any attention to me. I could see serving plates
stacked high with soft white bread, bowls of applesauce
sprinkled with cinnamon, salads of iceberg lettuce that
glistened with bottled dressing. The table seated twenty
already bent to their evening meal of chili served over
elbow macaroni. Another fifteen or twenty men sat
obediently in the "chapel" to my left, which consisted of
a lectern, an old upright piano, orange molded plastic
chairs, and an imposing cross on the wall.

The scruffy drifter I was looking for sat in the back
row with his friend. Slogans everywhere assured me that
Jesus cared, and that certainly seemed true here. What
impressed me most was the fact that Redemption
Mission (according to the wall signs) was supported by
private donations, with little or no connection to the
government.

"May I help you?"

The man who'd approached me was in his sixties,
heavyset, clean-shaven, wearing a red short-sleeved
cotton shirt and baggy pants. He had one normal arm
and one that ended at the elbow in a twist of flesh like
the curled top of a Mr. Softee ice cream cone. I wanted
to introduce myself, shaking hands, but the stump was
on the right and I didn't have the nerve. I took out a
business card instead, handing it to him.

"I wonder if I might have a word with one of your
clients?"

His beefy brow furrowed. "What's this about?"

"Well, I think he retrieved some articles I'm looking
for from a trash can at the beach. I want to find out if he
still has them in his cart. It will only take a minute"

"You see him in here?"

I indicated the one who interested me.

"You'll have to talk to the both of them," the man ʃid. "Delphi's the fellow you want, but he don't talk. His ɹddy does all the talking. His name is Clare. I'll bring ɹem out if you'll wait out there in the corridor. They ʃt their shopping carts on the back patio. I'd go easy ɹout them carts. They get a might possessive of their ɹasures sometimes."

I thanked him and retraced my steps, lingering in ɹe entranceway until Delphi and Clare appeared. ɹlphi had shed some of his overcoats, but he wore the ɹme dark watch cap and his skin had the same dusky ɹd tone. His friend Clare was tall and gaunt with a very ɹnk tongue that crept out of his mouth through the gap ɹt by his missing front teeth. His hair was a silky white, ɹther sparse, his arms long and stringy, hands huge. ɹlphi made no eye contact at all, but Clare turned out ɹ have some residual charm, left over perhaps from the ɹys before he started to drink.

I explained who I was and what I was looking for. I ɹw Delphi look at Clare with the haunted subservience ɹ a dog accustomed to being hit. Clare may have been ɹe only human being in the world who didn't frighten ɹ abuse him and he evidently depended on Clare to ɹndle interactions of this kind.

"Yep. I know the ones. High heels in black suede. ɹeen wool skirt. Delphi here was pleased. Usually it's ɹm pickin's around that bin. Aluminum cans is about ɹe best you can hope for, but he got lucky, I guess."

"Does he still have the items?"

The tongue crept out with a crafty life of its own, so ɹnk it looked like Clare had been sucking red hots. "I ɹn ask," he said.

"Would you do that?"

Clare turned to Delphi. "What do you think, ɹlphi? Shall we give this little gal what she wants? Up to ɹu."

Delphi gave no evidence whatever of hearin
absorbing, or assenting. Clare waited a decent interv;

"Now that's tough," Clare said to me. "That was l
best day and he likes that green skirt."

"I could reimburse him," I said tentatively. I did
want to insult these guys.

Out came the tongue, like some shy creatu
peering from its lair. Delphi's hearing seemed to in
prove. He shifted slightly. I left Clare to translate tl
movement into dollars and cents.

"A twenty might cover it," Clare said at length

I only had a twenty on me, but I took it out of tl
zippered compartment in my black handbag. I offered
to Delphi. Clare interceded. "Hold that until we've do
our business. Let's step outside."

I filed after them along a short corridor to a ba
exit that opened on a small concrete patio surround
on three sides by an openwork fence made of lathin
Someone had "landscaped" the entire area in annu;
planted in coffee cans and big industrial-sized contai
ers that had held green beans and applesauce. Delp
stood by, looking on anxiously, while Clare paw
through one of the shopping carts. He seemed to kn
exactly where the shoes and skirt were located, whiski
them out in no time flat. He passed them over to me a
I handed him the twenty. It felt somehow like an illi
drug sale and I had visions of them buying a jug of M
Dog 20–20 after I'd left. Clare held the bill up f
Delphi to inspect, then he glanced at me.

"Don't you worry. We'll put this in the collecti
plate," Clare said. "Delphi and me have give up drink.
thought Clare seemed happier about it than Delphi di

19

My dinner that night was cheese and crackers, with
a side of chili peppers just to keep my mouth awake. I'd
changed out of my all-purpose dress into a tee shirt,
jeans, and fuzzy slippers. I ate sitting at my desk, with a
Diet Pepsi on the rocks. I studied the skirt and shoes. I
tried the right shoe on. Too wide for me. The back of
the heel was scuffed, the toe narrowing to a bunion-
producing point. The manufacturer's name on the inner
sole had been blurred by sweat. A pair of Odor-eaters
wouldn't have been out of line here. The skirt was a bit
more informative, size 8, a brand I'd seen at the Village
store and the Post & Rail. Even the lining was in good
shape, though wrinkled in a manner that suggested a
recent soaking. I touched my tongue to the fabric. Salt. I
checked the inseam pockets, which were empty. No
cleaner's marks. I thought about the women connected,
even peripherally, with Daggett's death. The skirt might
fit any one of them, except for Barbara Daggett maybe,
who was big-boned and didn't seem like the type for the
preppy look, especially in green. Ramona Westfall was a
good candidate. Marilyn Smith, perhaps. Lovella Daggett or Billy's sister, Coral, could probably both wear an
8, but the style seemed wrong . . . unless the outfit had
been lifted from a Salvation Army donation box. Maybe
in the morning I'd stop by a couple of clothing stores

and see if any of the salesclerks recognized the skirt. Fa
chance, I thought. A better plan would be to show it
along with the shoes, to all five women and see if anyon
would admit ownership. Unlikely under the circum
stances. Too bad I couldn't do a little breaking an
entering. The matching green sweater might come t
light in someone's dresser drawer.

I padded into the kitchen and rinsed my plate
Eating alone is one of the few drawbacks to single life
I've read those articles that claim you should prepar
food just as carefully for yourself as you would fo
company. Which is why I do cheese and crackers. I don
cook. My notion of setting an elegant table is you don
leave the knife sticking out of the mayonnaise jar. Sinc
I usually work while I eat, there isn't any point i
candlelight. If I'm not working, I have *Time* magazin
propped up against a stack of files and I read it back t
front as I munch, starting with the sections on books an
cinema, losing interest by the time I reach Economy &
Business.

At 9:02, my phone rang. It was the night dispatche
for Tip Top Cab Company, a fellow who identifie
himself as Chuck. I could hear the two-way radi
squawking in the background.

"I got this note from Ron says to call you," said he
"He pulled the trip sheets for last Friday night and sai
to give you the information you were asking about, bu
I'm not really sure what you want."

I filled him in and waited briefly while he ran h
eye down the sheet. "Oh yeah. I guess this is it. He's g
it circled right here. It was my fare. That's probably wh
he asked me to call. Friday night, one twenty-three . .
well, you'd call that early Saturday. I dropped a coupl
off at State and Cabana. Man and a woman. I figure
they were booked into a motel down there."

"I've heard the man was drunk."

"Oh yeah, very. Looked like she'd been drinkin

too, but not like him. He was a mess. I mean, this guy smelled to high heaven. Stunk up the whole back seat and I got a pretty fair tolerance for that kind of thing."

"What about her? Can you tell me anything?"

"Can't help you on that. It was late and dark and raining to beat the band. I just took 'em where they said."

"Did you talk to them?"

"Nope. I'm not the kind of cabbie engages in small talk with a fare. Most people aren't interested and I get sick of repeating myself. Politics, weather, baseball scores. It's all bull. They don't want to talk to me and I don't want to talk to them. I mean, if they ask me something I'm polite, don't get me wrong, but I can't manufacture chitchat to save my neck."

"What about the two of them? They talk to each other?"

"Who knows? I tuned 'em out."

God, this was no help at all. "You remember anything else?"

"Not offhand. I'll give it some thought, but it wasn't any big deal. Sorry I can't be a help."

"Well, at least you've verified a hunch of mine and I appreciate that. Thanks for your time."

"No problem."

"Oh, one more thing. Where'd the fare originate?"

"Now *that* I got. You know that sleazeball bar on Milagro? That place. I picked 'em up at the Hub."

I sat and stared at the phone for a moment after he hung up. I felt like I was running a reel of film backwards, frame by frame. Daggett left the Hub Friday night in the company of a blonde. They apparently had a lot of drinks, a lot of laughs, staggered around in the rain together, fell down, and picked themselves up again. And little by little, block by block, she was steering him toward the marina, herding him toward the boat, guiding him out into the harbor on the last short ride of his life. She must have had a heart of stone and steadier nerves than mine.

I made some quick notes and tossed the index cards in the top drawer of my desk. I kicked off my slippers and laced up my tennies, then pulled on a sweatshirt. I snatched up the skirt and shoes, my handbag, and car keys and locked up, heading out to the VW. I'd start with Coral first. Maybe she'd know if Lovella was still in town. I was remembering now the fragment of conversation I'd overheard the night I eavesdropped on Billy and Coral. She'd been talking to Billy then about some woman. I couldn't remember exactly what she'd said, but I did remember that. Maybe Coral had seen the woman I was looking for.

When I reached the trailer park, I found the trailer dimly lighted, as if someone had gone out and left a lamp burning to keep the burglars at bay. Billy's Chevrolet was in the carport, the hood cold to the touch. I knocked on the door. After a moment, I heard footsteps bumping toward the front.

"Yeah?" Billy's muffled voice came through the door.

"It's Kinsey," I said. "Is Coral here?"

"Uh-uh. She's at work."

"Can I talk to you?"

He hesitated. "About what?"

"Friday night. It won't take long."

There was a pause. "Wait a sec. Let me throw some clothes on."

Moments later, he opened the door and let me in. He had pulled on a pair of jeans. Aside from that, he was barefoot and naked to the waist. His dark hair was tousled. He looked like he hadn't worked out recently, but his arms and chest were still well developed, overlaid by a fine mat of dark hair.

The trailer was disordered—newspapers, magazines, dinner dishes for two still out on the table, the counters covered with canned goods, cracker boxes, bags of flour, sugar, and corn meal. There wasn't a clear surface anywhere and no place to sit. The air was dense, smelling faintly of fresh cigarette smoke.

"Sorry to disturb you," I said. He looked like he'd been screwing his brains out and I wondered who was in the bedroom. "You have company?"

He glanced toward the rear, his dimples surfacing. "No, I don't. Why, are you interested?"

I smiled and shook my head, at the same time caught up in a flash fantasy of me and Billy Polo tangled up in sheets that smelled like him, musky and warm. His skin exuded a masculine perfume that conjured up images of all the trashy things we might do if the barriers went down. I kept my expression neutral, but I could feel my face tint with pink. "I have some questions I was hoping Coral might help me with."

"So you said. Try the Hub. She'll be there till closing time."

I laid the skirt and shoes across the television set, which was the only bare surface I could find. "Do you know if these are hers?"

He glanced at the items, too canny to bite. "Where'd you get 'em?"

"A friend of a friend. I thought you might know whose they were."

"I thought this was supposed to be about Friday night."

"It is. I talked to a cabbie who picked Daggett up at the Hub Friday night and dropped him off down near the wharf."

"I'll bite. So what?"

"A blonde was with him. The cabbie took them both. I figure she met him at the Hub, so I thought Coral might have had a look at her."

Billy knew something. I could see it in his face. He was processing the information, trying to decide what it meant.

I was getting impatient. "Goddamn it, Billy, level with me!"

"I am!"

"No, you're not. You've been lying to me since the first time you ever opened your mouth."

"I have not," he said hotly. "Name one thing."

"Let's start with Doug Polokowski. What's your relation to him? Brother?"

He was silent. I stared at him, waiting him out.

"Half-brother," he said grudgingly.

"Go on."

His tone of voice dropped, apparently with embarrassment. "My mom and dad split up, but they were still legally married when she got pregnant by somebody else. I was ten and I hated the whole idea. I started gettin' in trouble right about then so I spent half my time in Juvenile Hall anyway, which suited me just fine. She finally had me declared a whaddyou call 'em. . . ."

"An out-of-control minor?"

"Yeah, one of them. Big deal. I didn't give a fat rat's ass. Let her dump us. Let her have a bunch more kids. She didn't have any more sense than that, then to hell with her."

"So you and Doug were never close?"

"Hardly. I used to see him now and then when I'd come home but we didn't have much of a relationship."

"What about you and your mother?"

"We're okay. I got over it some. After Doug got killed, we did better. Sometimes it happens that way."

"But you must have known Daggett was responsible."

"Sure I knew. Of course I did. Mom wrote and told me he was bein' sent up to San Luis. At first, I thought I'd get even with him. For her sake, if nothin' else. But it didn't work out like that. He was too pathetic. Know what I mean? Hell, I ended up almost feeling sorry for him. I despised him for the whiny little fucker that he

as, but I couldn't leave him alone. It's like I had to
rment him. I liked to watch him squirm, which maybe
akes me weird but it don't make me a killer. I never
urdered anybody in my life."

"What about Coral? Where was she in all this?"

"Hey, you ask her."

"Could she have been the one with Daggett that
ght? It sounds like Lovella to me, but I can't be sure."

"Why ask me? I wasn't there."

"Did Coral mention it?"

"I don't want to talk about this," he said, irritably.

"Come on. You talked to Daggett Thursday night.
d he mention this woman?"

"We didn't talk about women," Billy said. He began
 snap the fingers of his right hand against his left
alm, making a soft, hollow pop. I could feel myself
ing into a terrier pup mode, worrying the issue like a
whide bone, knotted on both ends.

"He must have known who she was," I said. "She
dn't just materialize out of the blue. She set him up.
he knew what she was doing. It must have been a very
arefully thought-out plan."

The popping sound stopped and Billy's tone took
n a crafty note. "Maybe she was connected to the guys
ho wanted their money back," he said.

I looked at him with interest. That really hadn't
ccurred to me, but it didn't sound bad. "Did you tip
em off?"

"Listen, babe, I'm not a killer and I'm not a snitch.
 Daggett had a beef with somebody, that was his
okout, you know?"

"Then what's the debate? I don't understand what
ou're holding back."

He sighed and ran a hand through his hair. "Lay
ff, okay? I don't know nothin' else so just leave it
lone."

"Come on, Billy. What's the rest of it?" I snapped.

"Oh, shit. It wasn't Thursday," he blurted out. "
met Daggett Tuesday night and that's when he asked m
to help him out."

"So he could hide from the guys at San Luis," I saie
making sure I was following.

"Well, yeah. I mean, they'd called him Monda
morning and that's why he'd hightailed it up here. W
talked on the phone late Monday. He was drunk. I didn
feel like putting myself out. I'd just got home and I wa
bushed so I said I'd meet him the next night."

"At the Hub?"

"Right."

"Which is what you did," I said, easing him along

"Sure, we met and talked some. He was already in
panic so I kind of fanned the flames, just twitting him
There's no harm in that."

"Why lie about it? Why didn't you tell me this t
begin with?" I was crowding him, but I thought it wa
time to persist.

"It didn't look right somehow. I didn't want m
name tied to his. Thursday night sounded better. Like
wasn't all that hot to talk to him. You know, like I didn
rush right out. I can't explain it any better than that."

It was just lame enough to make sense to me. I saic
"All right. I'll buy it for now. Then what?"

"That's all it was. That's the last I saw of him. H
came in again Friday night and Coral spotted him, s
she called me, but by the time I got there, he'd left

"With the woman?"

"Yeah, right."

"So Coral did see her."

"Sure, but she didn't know who she was. Sh
thought it was some babe hittin' on him, like a whore
something like that. The chick was buyin' him all thes
drinks and Daggett was lappin' 'em up. Coral got kind c
worried. Not that either of us really gave a shit, but yo

ow how it is. You don't want to see a guy get taken,
en if you don't like him much."

"Especially if you've heard he's got thirty thousand
llars on him, right?" I said.

"It wasn't thirty. You said so yourself. It was twenty-
e." Billy was apparently feeling churlish now that he'd
ened up. "Anyway, what are you goin' on and on
out? I told you everything I know."

"What about Coral? If you lied, maybe she's been
ng too."

"She wouldn't do that."

"What'd she say when you got there?"

The look on Billy's face altered slightly and I
ught I'd hit on something. I just didn't know what.
mind leapt ahead. "Did Coral *follow* them?" I asked.

"Of course not."

"What'd she say then?"

"Coral wasn't feeling so hot," he replied, uneasily.

"So she'd what, gone home?"

"Not really. She was coming down with this cold and
'd taken a cold cap. She was feeling zonked so she
nt back in the office and lay down on the couch. The
rtender thought she'd left. I get there and I'm pissed
ause I can't find her, I can't find Daggett. I don't
ow what's goin' on. I hang around for a while and
n I come back here, thinking she's home. Only she's
t. It was a fuck-up, that's all. She was at the Hub the
ole time."

"What time did she get home?"

"I don't know. Late. Three o'clock. She had to wait
the owner closed out the register and then he gave
r a lift partway so she had to walk six blocks in the
n. She's been sick as a dog ever since."

I stared at him, blinking, while the wheels went
and and round. I was picturing her at the wharf with
ggett and the fit was nice.

"Why look at me like that?" he said.

"Let me say this. I'm just thinking out loud," I sa
"It could have been Coral, couldn't it? The blonde w
left the Hub with him? That's what's been worrying y
all this time."

"No, uh-uh. No way," he said. His eyes had settl
on me with fascination. He didn't like the line I w
taking, but he'd probably thought about it himself.

"You only have her word for the fact that this oth
woman even exists," I said.

"The cabbie saw her."

"But it could have been Coral. She might have be
the one buying Daggett all those drinks. He knew w
she was and he trusted her too, because of you. S
could have called the cab and then left with him. May
the reason the bartender thought she was gone w
because he saw her leave."

"Get the hell out of here," Billy whispered.

His face had darkened and I saw his muscles ten
I'd been so caught up in my own speculation I had
been paying attention to the effect on him. I picked
the skirt and shoes, keeping an eye on him while I edg
toward the door. He leaned over and opened it for
abruptly.

I had barely cleared the steps when the do
slammed behind me hard. He shoved the curtain asic
staring at me belligerently as I backed out of the carpo
The minute the curtain dropped, I cut around to t
trailer window where I'd spied on him before. T
louvers were closed, but the curtain on that side gap
open enough to allow me a truncated view.

Billy had sunk down on the couch with his head
his hands. He looked up. The woman who'd been in t
back bedroom had now emerged and she leaned agai
the wall while she lit another cigarette. I could see
portion of her heavy thighs and the hem of a shor
nightgown in pale yellow nylon. Like a drowning ma
Billy reached for her and pulled her close, burying

face between her breasts. Lovella. He began to nuzzle at
her nipples through the nylon top, making wet spots.
She stared down at him with that look new mothers have
when they suckle an infant in public. Lazily, she leaned
over and stubbed out her cigarette on a dinner plate,
then wound her fingers into his hair. He grabbed her at
the knees and lowered her to the floor, pushing her
gown up around her waist. Down, down, down, he went.

I headed over to the Hub.

20

It looked like another slow night at the Hub. The rain had picked up again and business was off. The roof was leaking in two places and someone had put out galvanized pails to catch the drips . . . one on the bar, one by the ladies' room. The place, at its best, was populated by neighborhood drinkers—old women with fat ankles in heavy sweaters who started at 2:00 in the afternoon and consumed beer steadily until closing time, men with nasal voices and grating laughs whose noses were bulbous and sunburned from alcohol. The pool players were usually young Mexicans who smoked until their teeth turned yellow and squabbled among themselves like pups. That night the pool room was deserted and the green felt table tops seemed to glow as though lighted from within. I counted four customers in all and one was asleep with his head on his arms. The jukebox was suffering from some mechanical quirk that gave the music a warbling, underwater quality.

I approached the bar, where Coral was perched on a high-backed stool with a Naugahyde top. She was wearing a Western-cut shirt with a silver thread running through the brown plaid, tight jeans rolled up at the ankles, and heels with short white socks. She must have recognized me from the funeral because when I asked if

176

could talk to her, she hopped down without a word
nd went around to the other side of the bar.

"You want something to drink?"

"A wine spritzer. Thanks," I said.

She poured a spritzer for me and pulled a draft
eer for herself. We took a booth at the back so she
uld keep her eye on the clientele in case someone
eeded service. Up close, her hair looked so bushy and
ry I worried about spontaneous combustion. Her
akeup was too harsh for her fair coloring and her
ont teeth were decayed around the edges, as if she'd
een eating Oreo cookies. Her cold must have been at its
orst. Her forehead was lined and her eyes half
quinted, like a magazine ad for sinus medication. Her
ose was so stopped up she was forced to breathe
rough her mouth. In spite of all that, she managed to
noke, lighting up a Virginia Slim the minute we sat
own.

"You should be home in bed," I said, and then
ondered why I'd suggested such a thing. Billy and
ovella were currently back there groveling around on
e floor, probably causing the trailer to thump on its
undations. Who could sleep with that stuff going on?

Coral put her cigarette down and took out a
leenex to blow her nose. I've always wondered where
eople learn their nose-blowing techniques. She favored
e double-digit method, placing a tissue over her
ands, sticking the knuckles on both index fingers up
er nostrils, rotating them vigorously after each honk. I
pt my eyes averted until she was done, wondering idly
she was aware of Lovella's current whereabouts.

"What's the story on Lovella? She seemed dis-
aught at the funeral."

Coral paused in her endeavors and looked at me.
elatedly, I realized she probably didn't know what the

word distraught meant. I could see her put the defini-
tion together.

"She's fine. She had no idea they weren't legall
married to each other. That's why she fell apart. Freaked
her out." She gave her nose a final Roto-rooting and
took up her cigarette again with a sniff.

"You'd think she'd be relieved," I said. "From wha
I hear, he beat the shit out of her."

"Not at first. She was crazy about him when he firs
got out. Still is, actually."

"That's probably why she called him the world
biggest asshole at the funeral," I remarked.

Coral looked at me for a moment and then
shrugged noncommittally. She was smarter than Bill
but not by much. I had the same feeling here that I'
had with him. I was tapping into a matter they'd hope
to bury, but I didn't know enough to pursue the poin

I tried fishing. "I thought Lovella and Billy had
thing at one time."

"Years ago. When she was seventeen. Doesn't cour
for shit."

"She told me Billy set her up with Daggett."

"Yeah, more or less. He talked to Daggett about he
and Daggett wrote and asked if they could be pen pals.

"Too bad he never mentioned his wife," I said. "I d
want to talk to Lovella, so when you see her please te
her to get in touch." I gave her a business card with m
office number on it, which she acknowledged with
shrug.

"I won't see Lovella," she said.

"That's what you think," said I.

Coral's attention strayed to the bartender who wa
holding a finger aloft. "Hang on."

She crossed to the bar where she picked up a coup
of mixed drinks and delivered them to the one oth

able that was occupied. I tried to picture her flipping
Daggett backwards out of a rowboat, but I couldn't quite
make it stick. She fit the description, but there was
something missing.

When she got back to the booth, I held up the high
heels. "These yours?"

"I don't wear suede," she said flatly.

I loved it. Like suede was against her personal dress
code. "What about the skirt?"

She took a final drag of the cigarette and crushed it
in the metal ashtray, blowing out a mouthful of smoke.
"Nope. Whose is it?"

"I think the blonde who killed Daggett wore it
Friday night. Billy says she picked him up in here."

Belatedly, she focused on the skirt. "Yeah, that's
right. I saw her," she said, as if cued.

"Does this look like the skirt she wore?"

"It could be."

"You know who she is?"

"Uh-uh."

"I don't mean to be rude about this, Coral, but I
could use a little help. We're talking murder."

"I've been all tore up about it too," she said, bored.

"Don't you give a shit about any of this?"

"Are you kidding? Why should I care about Daggett? He was scum."

"What about the blonde? Do you remember anything about her?"

Coral shook another cigarette out of the pack.
"Why don't you give it a rest, kid. You don't have the
right to ask us any of this shit. You're not a cop."

"I can ask anything I want," I said, mildly. "I can't
force you to answer, but I can always ask."

She stirred with agitation, shifting in her seat.
"Know what? I don't like you," she said. "People like you
make me sick."

"Oh really. People like what?"

She took her time extracting a paper match from packet, scratching the tip across the striking area until i flared. She lit her cigarette. The match made a tin tinkling sound when she dropped it in the ashtray. She rested her chin on her palm and smiled at me unpleas antly. I wanted her to get her teeth fixed so she'd b prettier. "I bet you've had it real easy, haven't you?" sh said, her voice heavy with sarcasm.

"Extremely."

"Nice white-collar middle-class home. The whol mommy-hubby trip. Bet you had little brothers an sisters. Nice little fluffy white dog . . ."

"This is amazing," I said.

"Two cars. Maybe a cleaning woman once a week. never went to college. I never had a daddy giving me a the advantages."

"Well, that explains it then," I said. "I did meet you mom, you know. She looks like someone who's worke hard all her life. Too bad you don't appreciate the effor she made in your behalf."

"What effort? She works in a supermarket checkou line," Coral said.

"Oh, I see. You think she should do somethin classy like you."

"I'm sure not going to do *this* for life, if that's wha you think."

"What happened to your father? Where was he i all this?"

"Who knows? He bugged out a long time ago."

"Leaving her with kids to raise by herself?"

"Skip it. I don't even know why I brought it u Maybe you should get to the point and let me get back work."

"Tell me about Doug."

"None of your business." She slid out of the booth. "Time's up," she said, and walked away. God, and here I was being friendly.

I picked up the shoes and skirt and dropped a couple of bucks on the table. I moved to the entranceway, pausing in the shelter of the doorway before I stepped out into the rain. It was 10:17 and there was no traffic on Milagro. The street was shiny black and the rain, as it struck the pavement, made a noise like bacon sizzling in a pan. A mist drifted up from the manhole covers that dotted the block, and the gutters gushed in a widening stream where water boiled back out of the storm drains.

I was restless, not ready to pack it in for the night. I thought about stopping by Rosie's, but it would probably look just like the Hub—smoky, drab, depressing. At least the air outside, though chilly, had the sweet, flowery scent of wet concrete. I started the car and did a U-turn, heading toward the beach, my windshield stippled with rain.

At Cabana, I turned right, driving along the boulevard. On my left, even without a moon visible, the surf churned with a dull gray glow, folding back on itself with a thundering monotony. Out in the ocean, I could see the lights on the oil derricks winking through the mist. I'd pulled up at a stoplight when I heard a car horn toot behind me. I checked my rearview mirror. A little red Honda was pulling over into the lane to my right. It was Jonah, apparently heading home just as I was. He made a cranking motion. I leaned over and rolled the window down on the passenger side.

"Can I buy you a drink?"

"Sure. Where?"

He pointed at the Crow's Nest to his right, a restaurant with exterior lights still burning. The light

changed and he took off. I followed, pulling into the lot
behind him. We parked side by side. He got out first,
hunching against the rain while he opened an umbrella
and came around to my door. We huddled together and
puddle hopped our way to the front entrance. He held
the door and I ducked inside, holding it for him then
while he lowered the umbrella and gave it a quick shake.

The interior of the Crow's Nest was done in a
halfhearted nautical theme which consisted primarily of
fishing nets and rigging draped along the rafters and
mariner's charts sealed into the table tops under a half
inch of polyurethane. The restaurant section was closed
but the bar seemed to be doing all right. I could see
maybe ten tables occupied. The level of conversation
was low and the lighting was discreet, augmented by fat
round jars where candles glowed through orange glass.
Jonah steered us past a small dance floor toward a table
in the corner. The place had an aura of edgy excite-
ment. We were protected by the weather, drawn together like the random souls stranded in an airport
between flights.

The waitress appeared and Jonah glanced at me.

"You decide," I said.

"Two margaritas. Cuervo Gold, Grand Marnier,
shaken, no salt," he said. She nodded and moved off.

"Very impressive," I said.

"I thought you'd like that. What brings you out?"

"Daggett, of course." I filled him in, realizing as I
summed it up that I'd had just about as much of Bill
Polo and his ilk as I could take for one night.

"Let's don't talk about him," I said when I was done.
"Tell me what you're working on."

"Hey, no way. I'm here to relax."

The waitress brought our drinks and we paused
briefly while she dipped neatly, knees together, and

aced a cocktail napkin in front of each of us, along
th our drinks. She was dressed like a boatswain except
at her high-cut white pants were spandex and her
ins hung out the back. I wondered how long uniforms
e that would last if the night manager was required to
ueeze his hairy fanny into one.

When the waitress left, Jonah touched his glass to
ine. "To rainy nights," he said. We drank. The tequila
d a little "wow" effect as it went down and I had to pat
yself on the chest. Jonah smiled, enjoying my discom-
ure.

"What brings you out so late?" I asked.

"Catching up on paperwork. Also, avoiding the
use. Camilla's sister came down from Idaho for a
ek. The two of them are probably drinking wine and
rving me up like a roast."

"Her sister doesn't like you, I take it."

"She thinks I'm a dud. Camilla came from money.
irdre doesn't think either one of them should take up
th guys on salary, for God's sake. And a cop? It's all too
urgeois. God, I gotta watch myself here. All I do is
mplain about life on the home front. I'm beginning to
und like Dempsey."

I smiled. Lieutenant Dempsey had worked Narcot-
for years, a miserably married man whose days were
ent complaining about his lot. His wife had finally
ed and he'd turned around and married a woman just
e her. He'd taken early retirement and the two of
em had gone off in an RV. His postcards to the
partment were amusing, but left people uncomfort-
le, like a stand-up comic making mean-spirited jokes
a spouse's expense.

Conversation dwindled. The background music was
tape of old Johnny Mathis tunes and the lyrics
ggested an era when falling in love wasn't complicated

by herpes, fear of AIDS, multiple marriages, spous
support, feminism, the sexual revolution, the Bomb, t
Pill, approval of one's therapist, or the specter
children on alternate weekends.

Jonah was looking good. The combination
shadow and candlelight washed the lines out of his fac
and heightened the blue of his eyes. His hair look
very dark and the rain had made it look silkier. He wo
a white shirt, opened at the neck, sleeves rolled up, l
forearms crosshatched with dark hair. There's usually
current running between us, generated I suppose
whatever primal urges keep the human race reprodu
ing itself. Most of the time, the chemistry is kept in che
by a bone-deep caution on my part, ambivalence abo
his marital status, by circumstance, by his own u
easiness, by the knowledge on both our parts that on
certain lines are crossed, there's no going back and
way to predict the consequences.

We ordered a second round of drinks, and then
third. We slow danced, not saying a word. Jonah smell
of soap and his jaw line was smooth and sometimes
hummed with a rumbling I hadn't heard since I sat
my father's lap as a very young child, listening to h
read to me before I knew what words meant. I thoug
about Billy Polo lowering Lovella to the trailer floo
The image was haunting because it spoke so eloquen
of his need. I was always such a stoic, so careful not
make mistakes. Sometimes I wonder what the differen
is between being cautious and being dead. I thoug
about rain and how nice it is to sink down on cle
sheets. I pulled my head back and Jonah looked down
me quizzically.

"This is all Billy Polo's fault," I said.

He smiled. "What is?"

I studied him for a moment. "What would Cami
do if you didn't come home tonight?"

His smile faded and his eyes got that look. "She's
the one who's talking about an open relationship," he
said.

I laughed. "I'll bet that applies to her, not you."

"Not anymore," he said.

His kiss seemed familiar.

We left soon afterward.

21

I drove to the office at 9:00. The rain clouds wer
hunched above the mountains moving north, whil
above, the sky was the blue white of bleached denim
The city seemed to be in sharp focus, as if seen throug
new prescription lenses. I opened the French doors an
stood on the balcony, raising my arms and doing one c
those little butt wiggles so favored by the football se
That for you, Camilla Robb, I thought, and then
laughed and went and had a look at myself in th
mirror, mugging shamelessly. Amazing Grace. I looke
just like myself. Where tears erase the self, good se
transforms and I was feeling energized.

I put the coffee on and got to work, typing up m
case notes, detailing the conversations I'd had with Bil
and Coral. Cops and private eyes are always caught u
in paperwork. Written records have to be kept c
everything, with events set out so that anyone wh
comes along afterward will have a clear and compreher
sive résumé of the investigation to that point. Since
private eye also bills for services, I have to keep track c
my hours and expenses, submitting statements period
cally so I can make sure I get paid. I prefer fieldwork;
suspect we all do. If I'd wanted to spend my days in a
office, I'd have studied to be an underwriter for th

isurance company next door. Their work seems boring
0 percent of the time while mine only bores me about
ne hour out of every ten.

At 9:30, I touched base with Barbara Daggett by
hone, giving her a verbal update to match the written
ccount I was putting in the mail to her. The duplication
f effort wasn't really necessary, but I did it anyway.
Vhat the hell, it was her money. She was entitled to the
est service she could get. After that, I did some filing,
ien locked up again, taking the green skirt and heels
ith me down the back stairs to my car, heading out to
Aarilyn Smith's. I was beginning to feel like the prince
1 search of Cinderella, shoe in hand.

I took the highway north, driving in the newly
ashed air. Colgate is only a fifteen-minute drive, but it
ave me a chance to think about events of the night
efore. Jonah had turned out to be a clown in bed . . .
inny and inventive. We'd behaved like bad kids, eating
iacks, telling ghost stories, returning now and then to a
vemaking which was, at the same time, intense and
omfortable. I wondered if I'd known him in another
fe. I wondered if I'd know him again. He was so
enerous and affectionate, so amazed at being with
imeone who didn't criticize or withhold, who didn't
ithdraw from his touch as though from a slug's. I
ouldn't imagine where we'd go from here and I didn't
ant to start worrying. I'm capable of screwing things
o by trying to solve all the problems in advance instead
' simply taking care of issues as they surface.

I missed my off-ramp, of course. I caught sight of it
I sped by, cursing good-naturedly as I took the next
xit and circled back.

By the time I reached Wayne and Marilyn Smith's
ouse, it was nearly 10:00. The bicycles that had been
irked on the porch were gone. The orange trees,

though nearly leafless with age, still carried the aura o
ripe fruit, a faint perfume spilling out of the surround
ing groves. I parked my car in the gravel drive behind
compact station wagon I assumed belonged to her. .
peek into the rear, as I passed, revealed a gumm
detritus of fast-food containers, softball equipmen
school papers, and dog hair.

I cranked the bell. The entrance hall was deserted
but a golden retriever bounded toward the front doo
toenails ticking against the bare floors as it skittered to
stop, barking joyfully. The dog's entire body waggle
like a fish on a hook.

"Can I help you?"

Startled, I glanced to my right. Marilyn Smith w:
standing at the bottom of the porch steps in a tee shir
drenched jeans, and a straw hat. She wore goatski
gardening gloves and bright yellow plastic clogs th.
were spattered with mud. When she realized it was m
her expression changed from pleasant inquiry to
barely disguised distaste.

"I'm working in the garden," she said, as if I hadr
guessed. "If you want to talk you'll have to come o
there."

I followed her across the rain-saturated lawn. Sh
tapped a muddy trowel against her thigh, distracted

"I saw you at the funeral," I remarked.

"Wayne insisted," she said tersely, then looked ov
her shoulder at me. "Who was the drunk woman? I lik
her."

"Lovella Daggett. She thought she was married
him, but it turned out the warranty hadn't run out on l
first wife."

When we reached the vegetable patch, she wade
between two dripping rows of vines. The garden was
its winter phase—broccoli, cauliflower, dark squash

cked into a spray of wide leaves. She'd been weeding. I
uld see the trampled-looking spikes scattered here
d there. Farther down the row, there was evidence
at the earth had been turned, heavy clods piled up
ear a shallow excavation site.

"Too wet for weeding, isn't it?"

"The soil here has a high clay content. Once it dries
t, it's impossible," she said.

She shucked the gardening gloves and began to tear
dths from an old pillow case, tying back the masses
‾ sweet pea plants that had drooped in the rain. The
rips of white rag contrasted brightly with the lime
‾een of the plants. I held up the skirt and shoes I'd
ought.

"Recognize these?"

She scarcely looked at the articles, but the chilly
nile appeared. "Is that what the killer wore?"

"Could be."

"You've made progress since I saw you last. Three
ys ago, you weren't even certain it was murder."

"That's how I earn my pay," I said.

"Maybe Lovella killed him when she found out he
as a bigamist."

"Always possible," I said, "though you still haven't
id for sure where you were that night."

"Oh, but I did. I was here. Wayne was at the office
d neither of us has corroborating witnesses." She was
ing that bantering tone again, mild and mocking.

"I'd like to talk to him."

"Make an appointment. He's in the book. Go down
the office. The Granger Building on State."

"Marilyn, I'm not your enemy."

"You are if I killed him," she replied.

"Ah, yes. In that case, I would be."

She tore off another strip of pillow case, the width

of cotton dangling from her hand like something lin
with death. "Sounds like you have suspects. Too b
you're short on proof."

"But I do have someone who saw her and th
should help, don't you think? This is just prelimina
work, narrowing the field," I said. It was bullshit,
course. I wasn't sure the motel clerk could identi
anybody in the dark.

Her smile dimmed by a watt. "I don't want to talk
you anymore," she whispered.

I raised my hands, as if she'd pulled a gun. "I'
gone," I said, "but I have to warn you, I'm persister
You'll find it unsettling, I suspect."

I kept my eyes on her as I moved away. I'd seen t
muddy hoe she was using and I thought it best not
turn my back.

I cruised by the Westfalls on my way into town.
was going to have to show the skirt to Barbara Daggett
some point, but the Close was on my way. The lc
fieldstone wall surrounding the place was still a da
gray from the passing rain. I drove through the gat
and parked along the road as I had before, pulling ov
into dense ivy. By day, the eight Victorian houses we
enveloped in shade, sunlight scarcely penetrating t
branches of the trees. I locked the car and picked n
way up the path to the front steps. In the yard, t
trunks of the live oak were frosted with a fungus
green as the oxidized copper on a roof. Tall palr
punctuated the corners of the house. The air felt co
and moist in the wake of the storm.

The front door was ajar. The view from the hallw
was a straight shot through to the kitchen and I cou
see that the back door was open too, the screen do
unlatched. A portable radio sat on the counter a
music blasted out, the *1812 Overture.* I rang the bell, b

₁e sound was lost against the booming of cannons as
₁e last movement rose to a thunder pitch.

I left the front porch and walked around to the
₁ck, peering in. Like the rest of the house, the kitchen
₁d been redone, the owners opting here to modernize,
₁ough the Victorian character had been retained.
here was a small floral print paper on the walls, lots of
icker, oak, and fern. The cabinet doors had been
ˑplaced with leaded glass, but the appliances were all
rictly up-to-date.

There was no one in the room. A door on the left
₁as open, the oblong of shadow suggesting that the
₁sement stairs must be located just beyond. Two brown
ˑocery bags sat on the kitchen table and it looked like
₁meone had been interrupted in the course of unload-
g them. There was an electric percolator plugged into
₁e outlet on the stove. While I was watching, the ready-
₁ht went on. Belatedly, I picked up the smell of hot
₁ffee.

The music ended and the FM announcer made his
ˑncluding remarks about the piece, then introduced a
rahms concerto in E minor. I knocked on the frame of
.e screen door, hoping someone would hear me before
ˑe music started up again. Ramona appeared from the
ˑpths of the basement. She was wearing a six-gore wool
irt in a muted gray plaid, with a line of dark maroon
₁nning through it. Her pullover sweater was dark
₁aroon, with a white blouse under it, the collar pinned
₁dately at the throat by an antique brooch. For effect, I
ˑcided not to mention the heels and wool skirt I'd
₁ought.

"Tony?" she said. "Oh, it's you."

She had an armload of ragged blue bath towels
₁ich she dumped on a chair. "I thought I heard
₁meone knock. I couldn't see who it was through the

screen." She turned the radio off as she passed and the
she opened the screen door to admit me.

"Tony's bringing groceries in from the garage. W
just got back from the market. Have a seat. Would y
like a cup of coffee? The pot's fresh."

"Yes, please. That's nice." I moved the pile of ra
out of the chair and sat down, putting the skirt an
shoes on the table in front of me. I saw her eyes stray
them, but she made no comment.

"Isn't this a school day for him?" I asked.

"They're giving the sophomores some sort of a
ademic placement tests. He finished early so they let hi
go. He's got an appointment with his therapist short
anyway."

I watched her move about the kitchen, fetchin
cups and saucers. She had one of those hairstyles th
settle into perfect shape with a flick of the head.
butcher my own at six-week intervals with a pair of n;
scissors and a two-way mirror, causing salon stylists
pale when they see me. "Who *did* that to you?" th
always ask. I wanted perfect waves like hers, but I did
think I could achieve the effect.

Ramona poured two cups of coffee. "There's som
thing I probably should have mentioned before," s
said. She took a ceramic pitcher from the cupboard ar
filled it with milk, realizing then that I was waiting f
her to continue. Her smile was thin. "John Dagg
called here Monday night, asking to talk to Tony. I to
his number, but Ferrin and I decided it wasn't a go
idea. It might not matter much at this point, but
thought you should be aware."

"What made you think of it?"

She hesitated. "I came across the number on t
pad by the phone. I'd forgotten all about it."

I could feel a tingle at the back of my neck—th

ammy feeling you get when your body overloads on
ugar. Something was off here, but I wasn't sure what it
was.

"Why bring it up now?" I asked.

"I thought you were tracking his activities early in
he week."

"I wasn't aware that I'd told you that."

Her cheeks tinted. "Marilyn Smith called me. She
mentioned it."

"How'd Daggett know where to reach you? When I
alked to him on Saturday, he had no idea where Tony
was and he certainly didn't have your name or number."

"I don't know how he got it," she said. "What
difference does it make?"

"How do I know you didn't make a date to meet him
Friday night?"

"Why would I do that?" she said.

I stared at her. A millisecond later she realized what
I was getting at.

"But I was here Friday night."

"I haven't heard that verified so far."

"That's ridiculous! Ask Tony. He knows I was here.
You can check it out yourself."

"I intend to," I said.

Tony thumped up the wooden porch steps, armed
with two more grocery bags, his attention diverted as he
groped for the screen door handle, missing twice. "Aunt
Ramona, can you give me a hand with this?"

She crossed to the door and held it open. Tony
spotted me and the green skirt at just about the same
time and I saw his gaze jump to his aunt's face
quizzically. Her expression was neutral, but she busied
herself right away, pushing canned goods aside so he
could set one bag on the table top. The second bag she
took herself and placed on the counter. She sorted

through and lifted out a carton of ice cream. "I bett‹
get this put away," she murmured. She crossed to t‹
freezer.

"What are you doing here?" Tony said to me.

"I was curious how you were feeling. Your au‹
mentioned that you had a migraine Monday night.'

"I feel okay."

"What'd you think about the funeral?"

"Bunch of freaks," he said.

"Let's get these unloaded, dear," his aunt said. T‹
two of them began to put groceries away while I sippe
my coffee. I couldn't tell if she was deliberately distra‹
ing him or not, but that was the effect.

"You need some help?" I asked.

"We can manage," she murmured.

"Who was that lady who went nuts?" Tony ask‹
Lovella had made a big impression on everyone.

Ramona held up a soft drink in a big plastic bott‹
"Stick this in the refrigerator while you're there," s‹
said.

She released the bottle an instant before he'd gott‹
a good grip on it and he had to scramble to catch
before it toppled to the floor. Had she done th
deliberately? He was waiting for my reply so I gave hi
a brief rendition of the tale. It was gossip, in some wa‹
but he was as animated as I'd seen him and I hoped
keep his attention.

"I don't mean to interrupt, but Tony does ha
homework to take care of. Finish your coffee,
course," she said. Her tone suggested that I suck it rig
down and scram.

"I'm due back at the office anyway," I said, getti‹
up. I looked at Tony. "Could you walk me to my car

He glanced at Ramona, whose gaze dropped aw
from his. She didn't protest. He ducked his head
assent.

He held the door for me while I gathered the skirt
d shoes and turned back to her. "I nearly forgot. Are
se yours, by any chance?"

"I'm sure not," she said to me, and then to him,
on't be long."

He looked like he was on the verge of saying
nething, but he shrugged instead. He followed me
t on the porch and down the steps. I led the way as we
:led the house. The path to the street was paved with
pping-stones spaced oddly, so that I had to watch my
t to gauge the distances.

"I have a question," I said as we reached the car.

He was watching me warily by then, interested but
guard.

"I was curious about the migraine you had Friday
ht. Do you remember how long that one lasted?"

"Friday night?" His voice had a croak in it from
prise.

"That's right. Didn't you have a migraine that
ht?"

"I guess."

"Think back," I said. "Take your time."

He seemed uncomfortable, casting about for some
ual clue. I'd seen him do this before, reading body
guage so he could adjust his response to whatever
s expected of him. I waited in silence, letting his
:iety accumulate.

"I think that's the day I got one. When I came home
m school," he said, "but then it cleared."

"What time was that?"

"Real late. After midnight. Maybe two . . . two-
-ty, something like that."

"How'd you happen to notice the time?"

"Aunt Ramona made me a couple of sandwiches in
kitchen. It was a real bad headache and I'd been
owing up for hours so I never had dinner. I was
rving. I must have looked at the kitchen clock."

"What kind of sandwiches?"

"What?"

"I was wondering what kind she made."

His gaze hung on mine. The seconds ticked aw

"Meatloaf," he said.

"Thanks," I said. "That helps."

I opened the VW on the driver's side, tossing sh and shoes on the passenger seat as I got in. His vers was roughly the same as his aunt's, but I could h sworn the "meatloaf" was a wild guess.

I started the car and did a U-turn, heading tow: the gates. I caught a glimpse of him in the rearvi mirror, already moving toward the house.

22

It's a fact of life that when a case won't break, you
have to go through the motions anyway, stirring up the
waters, rattling all the cages at the zoo. To that end, on
my way into town I did a long detour that included a
stop at the trailer park, in hopes that Lovella would still
be there. It was obvious to me, as I'm not a fool, that
toting a green wool skirt and a pair of black suede heels
all over town was a pointless enterprise. No one was
going to claim them and if someone did, so what? The
articles proved nothing. No one was going to break
down sobbing and confess at the mere sight of them.
The pop quiz was simply my way of putting them all on
notice, making the rounds one more time to announce
that I was still on the job and making progress, however
insignificant it might appear.

I knocked at the trailer door, but got no response. I
jotted a note on the back of a business card, indicating
that Lovella should call. I tucked it in the doorjam, went
back to my car, and headed for town.

Wayne Smith's office was located on the seventh
floor of the Granger Building in downtown Santa
Teresa. Aside from the clock tower on the courthouse,
the Granger is just about the only structure on State
Street that's more than two stories high. Part of the
charm of the downtown area is its low-slung look. The

flavor, for the most part, is Spanish. Even the trash
containers are faced with stucco and rimmed with
decorative tile. The telephone booths look like small
adobe huts and if you can ignore the fact that the bums
use them for urinals, the effect is quaint. There are
flowering shrubs along the walk, jacaranda trees, and
palms. Low ornamental stucco walls widen in places to
form benches for weary shoppers. Everything is clean,
well kept, pleasing to the eye.

The Granger Building looks just like hundreds of
office buildings constructed in the twenties—yellow
brick, symmetrical narrow windows banded with granite
friezes, topped by a steeply pitched roof with matching
gables. Along the roofline, just below the cornice, there
are decorative marble torches affixed to the wall with
inexplicable half shells mounted underneath. The style
is an anomaly in this town, falling as it does between the
Spanish, the Victorian, and the pointless. Still, the
building is a landmark, housing a movie theater, a
jeweler's, and seven stories of office space.

I checked the wall directory in the marble foyer for
Wayne Smith's suite number, which turned out to be
702. Two elevators serviced the building and one was
out of order, the doors standing open, the housing
mechanism in plain view. It's not a good idea to
scrutinize such things. When you see how elevators
actually work, you realize how improbable the whole
scheme is . . . raising and lowering a roomful of people on a few long wires. Ridiculous.

A fellow in coveralls stood there, mopping his face
with a red bandanna.

"How's it going?" I asked, while I waited for the
other elevator doors to open.

He shook his head. "Always something, isn't it? Last
week it was that one wouldn't work."

The doors slid open and I stepped in, pressing
seven. The doors closed and nothing happened for

hile. Finally, with a jolt, the elevator began its ascent,
opping at the seventh floor. There was another inter-
inable delay. I pressed the "DOOR OPEN" button. No
ce. I tried to guess how long I could survive on just
at one ratty piece of chewing gum at the bottom of my
indbag. I banged the button with the flat of my hand
d the doors slid open.

The corridor was narrow and dimly illuminated, as
ere was only one exterior window, located at the far
d of the hall. Four dark, wood-paneled doors opened
each side, with the names of the professional tenants
gold-leaf lettering that looked as if it had been there
ice the building went up. There was no activity that I
uld perceive, no sounds, no muffled telephones ring-
g. Wayne Smith, C.P.A., was the first door on the right.
pictured a receptionist in a small waiting area, so I
iply turned the knob and walked in without knock-
g. There was only one large room, tawny daylight
tering in through drawn window shades. Wayne Smith
is lying on the floor with his legs propped up on the
at of his swivel chair. He turned and looked at me.

"Oh sorry! I thought there'd be a waiting room," I
d. "Are you okay?"

"Sure. Come on in," he said. "I was resting my
ck." He removed his legs from the chair, apparently in
me pain. He rolled over on his side and eased himself
o an upright position, wincing as he did. "You're
nsey Millhone. Marilyn pointed you out at the funeral
sterday."

I watched him, wondering if I should lend him a
nd. "What'd you do to yourself?"

"My back went out on me. Hurts like a son of a
ch," he said. Once he was on his feet, he dug a fist into
small of his back, twisting one shoulder slightly as if
ease a cramp. He had a runner's body—lean, stringy
iscles, narrow through the chest. He looked older
in his wife, maybe late forties while I pegged her in

her early thirties. His hair was light, worn in a crewcu
like something out of a 1950s high school annual.
wondered if he'd been in the military at some point. Th
hairstyle suggested that he was hung up in the past, h
persona fixed perhaps by some significant event. H
eyes were pale and his face was very lined. He moved
the windows and raised all three shades. The roo
became unbearably bright.

"Have a seat," he said.

I had a choice between a daybed and a molde
plastic chair with a bucket seat. I took the chair, doing
surreptitious visual survey while he lowered himself in
his swivel chair as though into a steaming sitz bath. H
had six metal bookcases that looked like they were mad
of Erector sets, loosely bolted and sagging slightly fro
the weight of all the manuals. Brown accordion file cas
were stacked up everywhere, his desk top virtual
invisible. Correspondence was piled on the floor ne
his chair, government pamphlets and tax law updat
stacked on the window sill. This was not a man you
want to depend on if you were facing an I.R.S. audit. H
looked like the sort who might put you there.

"I just talked to Marilyn. She said you came by t
house. We're puzzled by your interest in us."

"Barbara Daggett hired me to investigate h
father's death. I'm interested in everyone."

"But why talk to us? We haven't seen the man
years."

"He didn't get in touch last week?"

"Why would he do that?"

"He was looking for Tony Gahan. I thought
might have tried to get a line on him through you

The phone rang and he reached for it, conductin
business-related conversation while I studied him. H
wore chinos, just a wee bit too short, and his socks we
the clinging nylon sort that probably went up to h
knees. He switched to his good-bye tone, trying to clo

ut his conversation. "Uh-huh, uh-huh. Okay, great.
'hat's fine. We'll do that. I got the forms right here.
)eadline is the end of the month. Swell."

He hung up with an exasperated shake of his head.

"Anyway," he said, as a way of getting back to the
ubject at hand.

"Yeah, right. Anyway," I said, "I don't suppose you
emember where you were Friday night."

"I was here, doing quarterly reports."

"And Marilyn was home with the kids?"

He sat and stared at me, a smile flickering off and
n. "Are you implying that we might have had a hand in
ohn Daggett's death?"

"Someone did," I said.

He laughed, running a hand across his crewcut as if
hecking to see if he needed a trim. "Miss Millhone,
ou've got a hell of a nerve," he said. "The newscast said
 was an accident."

I smiled. "The cops still think so. I disagree. I think
 lot of people wanted Daggett dead. You and Marilyn
re among them."

"But we wouldn't do a thing like that. You can't be
erious. I despised the man, no doubt about that, but
e're not going to go out and track a man down and kill
im. Good God."

I kept my tone light. "But you did have the motive
nd you had the opportunity."

"You can't hang anything on that. We're decent
eople. We don't even get parking tickets. John Daggett
ust have had a lot of enemies."

I shrugged by way of agreement. "The Westfalls," I
id. "Billy Polo and his sister, Coral. Apparently, some
rison thugs."

"What about that woman who set up such a howl at
e funeral?" he said. "She looked like a pretty good
ndidate to me."

"I've talked to her."

"Well, you better go back and talk to her again. You're wasting time with us. Nobody's going to be arrested on the basis of 'motive' and 'opportunity.'"

"Then you don't have anything to worry about."

He shook his head, his skepticism evident. "Well, can see you have your work cut out for you. I'd appreciate it if you'd lay off Marilyn in this. She's had trouble enough."

"I gathered as much." I got up. "Thanks for you time. I hope I won't have to bother you again." I moved toward the door.

"I hope so too."

"You know, if you did kill him, or if you know who killed him, I'll find out. Another few days and I'm going to the cops anyway. They'll scrutinize that alibi of yours like you wouldn't believe."

He held his hands out, palms up. "We're innocent until proven otherwise," he said, smiling boyishly.

23

Waiting for the elevator, I replayed the conversation, trying to figure out what I'd missed. On the surface, there was nothing wrong with his response, but I felt irritated and uneasy, maybe just because I wasn't getting anyplace. I banged on the DOWN button. "Come on," I said. The elevator door opened partway. Impatiently, I shoved it back and got on. The doors closed and the elevator descended one floor before it stopped again. The doors opened. Tony Gahan was standing in the corridor, a shopping bag in hand. He seemed as surprised to see me as I was to see him.

"What are you doing here?" he said. He got on the elevator and we descended.

"I had to see someone upstairs," I said. "What about you?"

"A shrink appointment. He's been out of town and now his return flight was delayed. His secretary's supposed to pick him up in an hour so she said to come back at five."

We reached the lobby.

"How are you getting home? Need a ride?" I asked.

He shook his head. "I'm going to hang around down here." He gestured vaguely at the video arcade across the street where some high school kids were horsing around.

"See you later then," I said.

We parted company and I returned to the parking lot behind the building. I got in my car and circled the four blocks to the lot behind my office where I parked. For the time being, I left the skirt and shoes in the backseat.

There were no messages on my answering machine but the mail was in and I sorted through that, wondering what else to do with myself. Actually, I realized I was exhausted, the emotional charge from Jonah having drained away. I'm not used to drinking that much, for starters, and I tend, being single, to get a lot more sleep. He'd left at 5:00, before it was light, and I'd managed maybe an hour's worth of shut-eye before I'd finally gotten up, jogged, showered, and fixed myself a bite to eat.

I tilted back in my swivel chair and propped my feet up on the desk, hoping no one would begrudge me a snooze. The next time I was aware of anything, the clock hands had dissolved magically from 12:10 to 2:50 and my head was pounding. I staggered to my feet and trotted down the hall to the ladies' room. I peed, washed my hands and face, rinsed my mouth out, and stared at myself in the mirror. My hair was mashed flat in the back and standing straight up everywhere else. The flourescent light in the room made my skin look sickly. Was this the consequence of illicit sex with a married man? "Well, I soitonly hope so," I said. I ducked my head under the faucet and then dried my hair with eight rounds of hot air from a wall-mounted machine that had been installed (the sign said) to help protect me from the dangers of diseases that might be transmitted through paper towel litter. Idly, I wondered what diseases they were worried about. Typhus? Diphtheria?

I could hear my office phone from halfway down the hall and I started to run. I snagged it on the sixth ring, snatching up the receiver with a winded hello.

"This is Lovella," the glum voice said. "I got this note to call you."

I took a deep breath, inventing as I went along. "Right," I said. "I thought we should touch base. We really haven't talked since I saw you in L.A." I sidled round my desk and sat down, still trying to catch my breath.

"I'm mad at you, Kinsey," she said. "Why didn't you tell me you had Daggett's money?"

"To what end? I had a cashier's check, but it wasn't made out to you. So why mention it?"

"Because I'm standing around telling you I'm married to a guy who'd just as soon kill me as look at me and you're telling me to call the rape crisis center, some bullshit like that. And all the time, Daggett had thousands of dollars."

"But he stole the money. Didn't Billy tell you that?"

"I don't care where it came from. I'd just like to have a little something for myself. Now he's dead and she gets everything."

"Who, Essie?"

"Her and that daughter."

"Oh come on, Lovella. He couldn't have left them enough to worry about."

"More than he left me," she said. "If I'd known about the money, I might have talked him out of some."

"Yeah, right. As generous as he was," I said drily. "If you'd gotten your hands on it, you might be dead now instead of him. Unless Billy's been lying to me about the hunks from San Luis who were after him." I'd never really taken that story seriously, but maybe it was time I did.

She was silent. I could practically hear her shifting gears. "All I know is I think you're a shit and he was too."

"I'm sorry you feel that way, Lovella. John hired me, and my first loyalty was to him . . . misguided, as it

turned out, but that's where I was coming from. Yo
want to vent a little more on the subject before we tur
to something else?"

"Yeah. I should have got the money, not someon
else. I was the one who got banged around. I still got tw
cracked ribs and an eye looks like it's all sunk in on on
side from the bruise."

"Is that why you freaked out at the funeral?"

Her tone of voice became tempered with sheepish
ness. "I'm sorry I did that, but I couldn't help myself. I'
been sittin' in some bar drinkin' Bloody Marys since te
o'clock and I guess I got outta hand. But it bugged m
all that Bible talk. Daggett never went to church a day i
his life and it didn't seem right. And that old fat-a
claimed she was married to him? I couldn't believe m
eyes. She looked like a bulldog."

I had to laugh. "Maybe he didn't marry her for he
looks," I said.

"Well, I hope not."

"When did you see him last?"

"At the funeral home, where else?"

"Before that, I mean."

"Day he left L.A.," she said. "Week ago Monday.
never saw him after he took off."

"I thought maybe you hopped a bus on Thursd
after I left."

"Well, I didn't."

"But you could have, couldn't you?"

"What for? I didn't even know where he went.'

"But Billy did. You could have come up to Cora
last week. You might have met him at the Hub Frid
night and bought him a couple of drinks."

Her laugh was sour. "You can't pin that on me.
that was me, how come Coral didn't recognize me, huh

"For all I know, she did. You're friends. Maybe sl
just kept her mouth shut."

"Why would she do that?"

"Maybe she wanted to help you out."

"Coral doesn't even like me. She thinks I'm a slut so why would she help me?"

"She might've had reasons of her own."

"I didn't kill him, Kinsey, if that's what you're getting at."

"That's what everyone says. You're all wide-eyed and innocent. Daggett was murdered and nobody's guilty. Amazing."

"You don't have to take my word for it. Ask Billy. Once he gets back, he can tell you who it was for sure, anyway."

"Oh hey, sounds great. How's he going to manage that?"

There was a pause, as if she'd said something she really wasn't authorized to say. "He thought he recognized somebody at the funeral and then he figured out where he'd seen 'em before," she said reluctantly.

I blinked at the telephone receiver. In a quick flash, I remembered Billy's staring at the little group formed by the Westfalls, Barbara Daggett, and the Smiths. "I don't understand. What's he up to?"

"He set up a meeting," she said. "He wants to find out if his theory's right and then he said he'd call you."

"He's going to *meet* with her?"

"That's what I said, isn't it?"

"He shouldn't be doing that by himself. Why didn't he notify the police?"

"Because he doesn't want to make a fool of himself in front of them. Suppose he's wrong? He doesn't have any proof, anyway. Just a hunch is all and even that's not hundred percent."

"Do you have any idea who he was talking about?"

"Uh-uh. He wouldn't tell, but he was pretty happy with himself. He said we might get some money after all."

Oh God, I thought, not blackmail. I could feel my

heart sink. Billy Polo wasn't smart enough to pull that off. He'd blow it like he did every other crime he tried. "Where's the meeting taking place?"

"What makes you ask?" she said, turning cagey.

"Because I want to go!"

"I don't think I should tell."

"Lovella, don't do this to me."

"Well, he didn't say I could."

"You've told me this much. Why not the rest? He could be in trouble."

She hesitated, mulling it over. "Down at the beach somewhere. He's not dumb, you know. He made sure it was public. He figured in broad daylight, there wouldn't be any problem, especially with other people around."

"Which beach?"

"What if he gets mad at me?"

"I'll square it with him myself," I said. "I will *swear* I forced the information out of you."

"He's not going to like it if you show up and spoil everything."

"I won't spoil it. I'll lurk in the background and make sure he's okay. That's all I'm talking about."

Silence. She was so slow I thought I'd scream. "Look at it this way," I said. "He might be happy for the help. What if he needs backup?"

"Billy wouldn't need back up from a *woman*."

I closed my eyes, trying to keep my temper in check. "Just give me a hint, Lovella, or I'll come over to the trailer and rip your heart out by the roots." That, she heard.

"You better never tell him I told," she warned.

"Cross my heart and hope to die. Now come on."

"I think it's that parking lot near the boat launch. . . ."

I banged the phone down and snagged my hand bag. I locked the office in haste and ran down the hall going down the back stairs two and three at a time. I'

ad to park my car at the far end of the lot and once I
ot to the pay booth, there were three other cars in front
f mine. "Come on, come on," I murmured, banging on
he steering wheel.

Finally, it was my turn. I showed the attendant my
arking permit and shot through the gate as soon as the
ar went up.

Chapel is one way, heading up from the beach, so I
ad to turn right, take a left, and hit the one-way street
oing down again. I caught the light wrong at 101 so
nat delayed me. I didn't want to miss this one. I didn't
ant to show up two minutes late and miss the only
hance I might have. I pictured a citizen's arrest . . .
ne and Billy Polo saving the day.

The light turned green and I crossed the highway.
wo blocks more and I reached Cabana where I took a
ight turn. The entrance to the lot I wanted was all the
ay around the bend near Santa Teresa City College. I
ot a ticket from the machine and threaded my way
long the perimeter of the lot. I scanned the parked
ars, hoping for a glimpse of Billy's white Chevy. The
narina was on my right, the sun reflecting starkly from
ne white sails of a stately boat as it glided out of the
arbor. The boat launch itself was at the very end of the
arking lot, through a second parking gate. I pulled a
econd ticket and the arm went up. I found a slot and
ft my car, proceeding on foot.

Four joggers passed me. There were people on the
oat dock, people on the walk, people by the snack shop
nd the public restrooms. I broke into a trot, searching
ne landscape ahead of me for some sign of Billy or the
londe. I heard three hollow pops in quick succession
ead ahead. I ran. No one else was reacting, but I could
ave sworn it was the sound of shots.

I reached the boat launch, where the parking lot
ants down into the water. There was no one in sight.
o one running, no one leaving the scene in haste. The

air was still, the water lapping softly at the asphalt. Tw
pontoon piers extend into the water about thirty fee
but both were empty, no boats or pedestrians in sight.
did a three-sixty turn, surveying every foot of the area
And then I spotted him. He was lying on his side by
boat trailer, one arm caught under him awkwardly. H
struggled, gasping, and turned himself over on his back
I crossed the macadam rapidly.

A man in cutoffs had come out of a snack shop an
he peered at me as I went past. "Is that guy okay?"

"Call the cops. Get an ambulance," I snapped.

I knelt beside Billy, angling so he could see me. "I
me," I said. "Don't panic. You'll be fine. We'll have hel
here in a second."

Billy's eyes strayed to mine. His face was gray an
there was a widening puddle of quite red blood spread
ing out under him. I took his hand and held it. A crow
was beginning to collect, people running from a
directions. I could hear them buzzing at my back.

Somebody handed me a beach towel. "You want t
cover him with this?"

I grabbed the towel. I let go of him long enough t
unbutton his shirt, opening it so I could see what I wa
dealing with. There was a hole in his belly. He must hav
been shot from behind, because what I was looking a
was an exit wound, ragged, welling with blood. The slu
must have severed the abdominal aorta. A coil of h
lower intestine was visible, gray and glistening, bulgin
through the hole. I could feel my hands start to shake
but I kept my expression neutral. He was watching me
trying to read my face. I made a pad of the towe
pressing it against the wound to staunch the flow c
blood.

He groaned, breathing rapidly. He had one han
resting on his chest and his fingers fluttered. I took hi
hand again, squeezing hard.

He tilted his head. "Where's . . . my leg? I can't
el nothin' down there."

I glanced down at his right knee. The pantleg
oked like it had caught on a nail. Blood and bone
emed to blossom through the tear.

"Don't sweat it. They can fix that. You'll be fine," I
id. I didn't mention the blood soaking through the
wel. I thought he probably knew about that.

"I'm gut-shot."

"I know. Relax. It's not bad. The ambulance is on its
ay."

The hand I held was icy, his fingers pale. There
ere questions I should have asked, but I didn't. I
uldn't. You don't intrude on someone's dying with a
illshit interrogation like you're some kind of pro. This
as just me and him and nothing else entered into it.

I studied his face, sending love through my eyes,
lling him to live. His hair looked curlier than I
membered it. With my free hand, I moved it away
om his forehead. Sweat beaded on his upper lip.

"I'm goin' . . . I can feel myself goin' out . . ." He
itched my hand convulsively, bucking against a surge
pain.

"Take it easy. You'll be fine."

He began to hyperventilate and then his struggle
bsided. I could see the life drain away, see it all fade—
lor, energy, awareness, pain. Death comes in a gather-
g cloud that settles like a veil. Billy Polo sighed, his
ze still pinned on my face. His hand relaxed in mine,
t I held on.

24

I sat on the curb near the snack shop and stared
the asphalt. The proprietor had brought me a can
Coke and I held the cold metal against my temple. I fe
sick, but there wasn't anything wrong with me. Lieuten
ant Feldman had appeared and he was hunkered ov
Billy's body, talking to the lab guys, who were baggin
his hands. The ambulance had backed around an
waited with its doors open, as if to shield the body fro
the public view. Two black-and-whites were parke
nearby, radios providing a squawking counterpoint
the murmurs of the gathering crowd. Violent death is
spectator sport and I could hear them trading con
ments about the way the final quarter had been playe
They weren't being cruel, just curious. Maybe it w
good for them to see how grotesque homicide really i
The beat officers, Gutierrez and Pettigrew, ha
arrived within minutes of Billy's demise and they
radioed for the CSI unit. The two of them wou
probably drive over to the trailer park to break the ne
to Coral and Lovella. I felt I should ride along, but
couldn't bring myself to volunteer yet. I'd go, but for t
moment, I was having trouble coping with the fact
Billy's death. It had happened so fast. It was so irrevoc
ble. I found it hard to accept that we couldn't rewind t
tape and play the last fifteen minutes differently.

would arrive earlier. I would warn him off and he could walk away unharmed. He'd tell me his theory and then 'd buy him the beer I'd promised him that first night at he Hub.

Feldman appeared. I found myself staring at his pantlegs, unable to look up. He lit a cigarette and came down to my level, perching on the curb. I hugged my knees, feeling numb. I barely know the man, but what 've seen of him I've always liked. He looks like a cross between a Jew and an Indian—a large flat face, high cheekbones, a big hooked nose. He's a big man, probably forty-five, with a cop haircut, cop clothes, a deep rumbling voice. "You want to bring me up to speed on his?" he said.

It was the act of opening my mouth to speak that brought the tears. I held myself in check, willing them back. I shook my head, struggling with the nearly overwhelming rush of regret. He handed me a handkerchief and I pressed it to my eyes, then folded it, addressing my remarks to the oblong of white cotton. There was an "F" embroidered in one corner with a thread coming loose.

"Sorry," I murmured.

"That's okay. Take your time."

"He was such a screw-up," I said. "I guess that's that gets me. He thought he was so smart and so tough."

I paused. "I guess you never know which people ill affect your life," I said.

"He never said who shot him?"

I shook my head. "I didn't ask. I didn't want the last minutes of his life taken up with that stuff. I'm sorry."

"Well, he might not have said anyway. What was the setup?"

I started talking, saying anything that came to mind. He let me ramble till I finally took control of myself and began to lay it out systematically. After

hundreds of reports, I know the drill. I cited chapte
and verse while he nodded, making notes in a battere
black notebook.

When I finished, he tucked his ballpoint pen awa
and shoved the notebook back into the inside pocket o
his suitcoat. He got up and I rose with him, automati
cally.

"What next?" I asked.

"Actually, I got Daggett's file sitting on my desk," h
said. "Robb told me you tagged it a homicide and
thought I'd take a look. We had a double killing, one c
those execution-style shootings, up on the Bluffs lat
yesterday and we've had to put a lot of manpower o
that one, so I haven't had a chance as yet. It'd help if yo
came down to the station and talked to Lieutenar
Dolan yourself."

"Let me see Billy's sister first," I said. "This is th
second brother she's lost in the whole Daggett mess.

"You don't think there's any chance she's the on
who plugged him?"

I shook my head. "I thought she might connect t
Daggett's death, but I can't picture her involved in thi
Unless I'm missing something big. For one thing, h
wouldn't have to meet her out in public like this. It wa
someone at the funeral, I'm almost sure."

"Make a list and we'll take it from there," he saic

I nodded. "I can also stop by the office and mak
some copies of my file reports. And Lovella may kno
more than she's told us so far." It felt good, turnin
everything over to him. He could have it all. Essie an
Lovella and the Smiths.

Pettigrew approached, holding a small plastic Zi
loc bag by one corner. In it were three empty bra
casings. "We found these over by that pickup truc
We're sealing off the whole parking lot until the gu
have a chance to go over it."

I said, "You might check the trash bins. Tha

ere I found the skirt and shoes after Daggett was
led."

Feldman nodded, then gave the shells a cursory
ok. "Thirty-twos," he remarked.

I felt a cold arrow shoot up my spine. My mouth
nt dry. "My thirty-two was stolen from my car a few
ys ago," I said. "Gutierrez took the report."

"A lot of thirty-twos around, but we'll keep that in
ind," Feldman said to me, and then to Pettigrew, "Let's
stle these folk out of here. And be polite."

Pettigrew moved away and Feldman turned to
dy me. "Are you all right?"

I nodded, wishing I could sit down again, afraid
ce I did I'd be stuck.

"Anything you want to add before I let you go?"

I closed my eyes for a moment, thinking back. I
ow the snapping sound a .32 makes when fired and
e shots I'd heard weren't like that. "The shots," I said.
hey sounded odd to me. Hollow. More like a pop than
bang."

"A silencer?"

"I've never heard one except on TV," I said,
eepishly.

"I'll have the lab take a look at the slugs, though I
n't know where anybody'd get a silencer in this town."
e made another quick note in his book.

"You can probably order one from the back of a
agazine," I said.

"Ain't that the truth."

The photographer was snapping pictures and I
uld see Feldman's gaze flick in that direction. "Let me
nd to this guy. He's new. I want to make sure he covers
erything I need."

He excused himself and crossed to Billy's body
ere he engaged in a conversation with the forensic
otographer, using gestures to describe the various
gles he wanted.

Maria Gutierrez came up to me. "We're going out
the trailer park. Gerry said you might want to come

"I'll follow in my car," I said. "You know where
is?"

"We know the park. We can meet you there if y
want."

"I'm going to see if Billy's car is here in the lot. I'll
along shortly, but don't wait on my account."

"Right," she said.

I watched them pull out and then I worked my w
through the lot, checking the vehicles in the ar
adjacent to the boat launch. I spotted the Chevy thr
rows from the entrance, tucked between two RV's. T
temporary sticker was still on the windshield. T
windows were down. I stuck my head in witho
touching anything. The car looked clean to me. Nothi
in the front seat. Nothing in the back. I went around
the passenger window and peered in, checking t
floorboards from that side. I don't even know what I w
hoping for. A hint, some suggestion of where we mig
go from here. It looked as if Feldman might initiate
formal investigation after all, and glad as I was to turn
over to him, I still couldn't quite let go.

I stopped by my car and picked up the skirt a
shoes, which I handed over to Lieutenant Feldman
told him where to find Billy's car and then I finally g
back in mine and took off. In my heart, I knew I'd be
stalling to allow Pettigrew and Gutierrez a chance
deliver the news of Billy's death. That has to be the wo
moment in anybody's life, finding two uniformed cops
your door, their expressions somber, voices grave.

By the time I got to the trailer park, the word h
apparently spread. By some telepathic process, peo
were collecting in twos and threes, all staring at t
trailer uncomfortably, chatting in low tones. The trai
door was closed and I heard nothing as I approache

ut my appearance had generated conversation at my
ack.

A fellow stepped forward. "You a family friend?
ecause she's had bad news. I wasn't sure if you were
ware," he said.

"I was there," I said. "She knows me. How long ago
id the officers leave?"

"Two minutes. They were real good about it . . .
lked to her a long time, making sure she was all right.
m Fritzy Roderick. I manage the park," he said,
ffering me his hand.

"Kinsey Millhone," I said. "Is anybody with her
ow?"

"I don't believe so, and we haven't heard a peep. We
ere just talking among ourselves here . . . the neigh-
ors and all . . . wondering if someone ought to sit
ith her."

"Is Lovella in there?"

"I don't know the name. Is she a relative?"

"Billy's ex-girlfriend," I said. "Let me see if I can
nd out what's going on. If she needs anything, I'll let
ou know."

"I'd appreciate that. We'd like to help any way we
n."

I knocked at the trailer door, uncertain what to
xpect. Coral opened it a crack and when she saw it was
e, she let me in. Her eyes were reddened, but she
emed in control. She sat down on a kitchen chair and
cked up her cigarette, giving the ash a flick. I sat down
the banquette.

"I'm sorry about Billy," I said.

She glanced at me briefly. "Did he know?"

"I think so. When I found him, he was already in
ock and fading fast. I don't think he suffered much if
at's what you're asking."

"I'll have to tell Mom. The two cops who came said
ey'd do it, but I said no." Her voice trailed off, hoarse

from grief or the head cold. "He always knew he'd d
young, you know? Like when we'd see old people on th
street, crippled or feeble. He said he'd never end up lik
them. I used to beg him to straighten up his act, but h
had to do everything his way." She lapsed into silenc

"Where's Lovella?"

"I don't know," Coral said. "The trailer was emp
when I got here."

"Coral, I wish you'd fill me in. I need to know wh
was going on. Billy told me three different versions o
the same tale."

"Why look at me? I don't know anything."

"But you know more than I do."

"That wouldn't take much."

"Level with me. Please. Billy's dead now. There
nothing left to protect. Is there?"

She stared at the floor for a moment and then sh
sighed and stubbed out her cigarette. She got up an
started clearing the table, running water in the tir
stainless steel kitchen sink. She squirted in Ivory Liqui
dropping silverware and plates into the mounting sud
talking in a low monotone as she worked. "Billy w
already up at San Luis when Daggett got there. Dagge
had no idea Doug was related to us, so Billy struck up a
acquaintance. We were both of us bitter as hell."

"Billy told me he and Doug were never close."

"Bullshit. He just told you that so you wouldr
suspect him. The three of us were always thick
thieves."

"So you did intend to kill him," I said.

"I don't know. We just wanted to make him pay. W
wanted to punish him. We figured we'd find a way onc
we got close. Then Daggett's cellmate died and he got
that money."

"And you thought that would compensate?"

"Not me. I knew I'd never be happy till the da
Daggett died, but I couldn't do it myself. I mean, k

neone in cold blood. Billy was the one who said the
ney would help. We couldn't bring Doug back, but at
st we'd have something. He always knew Daggett
ed the cash, but he didn't think he'd get away with it.
ggett gets out of prison and sure enough, he's home
e. He starts throwin' money around. Lovella calls
ly and we decide to go for it."

"So the guys up at San Luis never did figure it out,"
aid.

"Nope. Once Billy saw Daggett was in the clear, we
:ided to rip him off."

"And Lovella was part of it?"

Coral nodded, rinsing a plate, which she placed in
 dish rack. "They got married the same week he got
, which suited us just fine. We figured if she didn't
 him out of it, she could steal it. . . ."

"And failing that, what?"

"We never meant to kill anyone," she said. "We just
ited the money. We didn't have much time anyway
ause he'd already spent part of it. He went through
 grand before we could bat an eye and we knew if we
n't move fast, he'd blow the whole wad."

"You didn't realize he intended to give the rest of it
Tony Gahan?"

"Of course not," she said with energy. "Billy
ldn't believe it when you told him about that. We
ught most of it was still around somewhere. We
ught we could still get our hands on it."

I watched her face, trying to compute the informa-
 she was giving me. "You mean you set Daggett up
h Lovella so you could con him out of twenty-five
usand bucks?"

"That's right," she said.

"You were splitting it three ways! That's a little over
ht grand apiece."

"So?"

"Coral, eight grand is nothing."

"Bullshit, it's nothing! Do you know what I could
with eight grand? How much do you have? Do you ha
eight grand?"

"No."

"So, all right. Don't tell me it's nothing."

"All right. It's a fortune," I said. "What we
wrong?"

"Nothing at first. Billy called him up and said
guys at San Luis heard about the money and th
wanted it back. He told Daggett they were coming af
him, so that's when Daggett split."

"How'd you know he'd hightail it up here?"

"Billy told Daggett he'd help him out," she said w
a shrug. "And then when Daggett got into town, B
started working on him, trying to get him to fork it o
to us. He said he'd act as a go-between, smooth it all o
and get him off the hook."

"He'd already given it to me at that point, righ

"Sure, but we didn't know that. He acted like he s
had it handy. He acted like he might turn it over to Bi
but that was all crap. Of course, he was drunk all
time by then."

"So he was conning you while you conned hir

"He was just stringing us along!" she said indigna
ly. "Billy met him Tuesday night and Daggett was r
cagey. Said he needed time to get his hands on it.
said he'd bring it in Thursday night, so Billy met him
the Hub again, only Daggett said he needed one m
day. Billy really laid into him. He said these guys w
getting very pissed and might kill Daggett anyw
whether he gave 'em the money or not. Daggett got r
nervous and swore he'd have it the next night, wh
was Friday."

"The night he died."

"Right. I was working that night, and I was su
posed to keep an eye on him, which I did. Billy decid
to come late, just to make him sweat, and before I kn

at was happening this woman showed up and started
ing him drinks. You know the rest."

"Billy told me you took some kind of cold cap and
shed in the back room. Was that true?"

"I was just laying low," she said. "When I saw
ggett leave, I knew Billy'd have a fit. I already felt bad
ugh without putting up with his bullshit."

"And Billy finally figured out who she was?"

"I don't know. I guess. I wasn't here this morning,
I don't know what he was up to."

"Look. I have to go down to the police station and
Lieutenant Dolan what's been going on. If Lovella
les back, please tell her it's urgent that she get in
ch. Will you do that?"

Coral wedged the last clean dish against the pile in
rack. She filled a glass with water and poured it over
lot of them, rinsing off the few remaining suds. She
ned to look at me with a gaze that chilled. "Do you
lk she killed Billy?"

"I don't know."

"Will you tell me if you find out it's her?"

"Coral, if she did it, she's dangerous. I don't want
in the middle of this."

"But will you tell me?"

I hesitated. "Yes."

"Thank you."

25

I had a brief chat with the manager of the tra
park. I gave him my card and asked him to call m
Lovella came back. I didn't really trust Coral to do
The last I saw of him, he was tapping at her door. I
in my car and headed over to the police station. I as
for Lieutenant Dolan at the desk, but he and Feldm
were in a section meeting. The clerk buzzed Jonah
me and he came as far as the locked door, admitting
into the corridor beyond. Both of us were circumspe
pleasant, noncommittal. No one observing us could h
guessed that mere hours ago, we'd been cavorting s
naked on my Wonder Woman sheets.

"What happened when you got home?" I ask
"Nothing. Everybody was asleep," he said. "We h
something in the lab you might want to see." He mo
down the hall to the right and I followed. He loo
back at me. "Feldman had the guys check the trash
at your suggestion. We think we found the silence

"You did?" I said, startled.

He opened the half-door into the crime lab, hol
it for me as I passed in front of him. The lab tech
out, but I could see Billy's bloody shirt, tagged, on
counter, along with an object I couldn't at first iden

"What's that," I said. "Is *that* it?" What I was loo

222

was a large plastic soft drink bottle, painted black,
ng on its side with a hole visible in the bottom.

"A disposable silencer. Handmade. A sound sup-
essor, in effect. It's been wiped clean of prints," Jonah
id.

"I don't understand how it works."

"I had to have Krueger explain it to me. The bottle's
ed with rags. Take a look. The barrel of the gun is
ually wrapped with tape and the bottle affixed to it
th a one-inch hose clamp. The soda bottle has a
nforced bottom, but it's only effective for a few shots
cause the noise level increases each time as the exit
le gets larger. Obviously, the device works best at close
nge."

"God, Jonah. How do people know about these
ngs? I never heard of it."

He picked up a paperbound booklet from the
unter behind me, flipping through it carelessly so I
uld see. Every page was filled with diagrams and
otographs, illustrating how disposable silencers could
made out of common household objects. "This is
m a gun shop down in Los Angeles," he said. "You
ght to see what you can do with a length of window
een or a pile of old bottle caps."

"Jesus."

Lieutenant Becker stuck his head in the door. "Line
e for you," he said to Jonah and then disappeared.
ah glanced at the lab phone, but the call hadn't been
nsferred.

"Let me take this and I'll be right back," Jonah said.
ang on."

"Right," I murmured. I leaned toward the silencer,
ing to remember where I'd seen something similar.
rough the hole in the bottom, I caught a glimpse of
: blue terrycloth filling the interior. When I realized
at it was, my mental process clicked in, and the
erior machinery fired up. I knew.

I straightened up and crossed to the door, checkin
the corridor, which was empty. I headed for my car.
could still see Ramona Westfall coming up the baseme
stairs with an armload of ragged blue bath towels, whi
she'd dumped on the chair. The plastic bottle had be
filled with a soft drink which she nearly dropped as s
passed it to Tony to refrigerate.

I stopped by the office long enough to try t
Westfall's number. The phone rang four times and th
the machine clicked in.

"Hello. This is Ramona Westfall. Neither Ferrin n
I can come to the phone right now, but if you'll lea
your name, telephone number, and a brief messa
we'll get back to you as soon as possible. Thank you.'
hung up at the sound of the tone.

I checked my watch. It was 4:45. I had no id
where Ramona was, but Tony had a 5:00 appointme
just a few blocks away. If I could intercept him, I cou
lean on him some about her alibi since he represent
the only confirmation she had. How had she pulled
off? He had to be on heavy medication for the migrai
so she might have slipped out while he was sleepin
adjusting the kitchen clock when she got back so sh
be covered for the time of Daggett's death. Once she v
home again, Tony had wakened—she'd probably ma
sure of that so she'd have someone to corroborate
time. She'd fixed the sandwiches, chatting pleasan
while he ate, and as soon as he went back to bed, :
changed the clock again. Or maybe it wasn't even
complicated as that. Maybe the watch Daggett wore h
been set for 2:37 and then submerged. She could ha
killed him earlier and been home by 2:00. Tony m
have realized what she'd done and tried to shield h
when he understood how close my investigation v
bringing me. It was also possible that he was in caho
with her, but I hoped that wasn't the case.

I locked my office and went down the front sta

tting up State Street on foot. The Granger Building
s only three blocks up and it made more sense than
pping in my car and driving all the way around to the
rking lot behind the building. Tony might still be
nging out at the arcade across the street. I had to get
m before she had a chance to intercept. I didn't want
m going home. She had to realize things were getting
t, especially since I'd shown up at the house with the
oes and skirt. All I needed from him was an indication
was on the right track and then I'd call Feldman. I
ought about the Close, which I knew would be gloomy
th the gathering twilight. I didn't want to go back
re unless I had to.

I checked the arcade. Tony was at the rear, on the
ht-hand side, playing a video game. He was concen-
ting fully and I didn't think he was aware of me. I
ited, watching small creatures being blasted off the
een. His scores weren't that good and I was tempted
have a try at it myself. The creatures suddenly froze
o place, random weapons firing off here and there
hout regard to his manipulations. He looked up. "Oh
"

"I need to talk to you," I said.

His eyes moved to the clock. "I got an appointment
five minutes. Can it wait?"

"I'll walk you over. We can talk on the way."

He picked up his package and we moved out to the
eet. The fading afternoon sun seemed bright after
darkness of the arcade. Even so, the fog was rolling
November twilight beginning to descend. I punched
button at the crosswalk and we waited for the light to
nge. "Last Friday . . . the night Daggett died, do
remember where your uncle was?"

"Sure. Milwaukee, on a business trip."

"Are you on medication for the migraines?"

"Well, yeah. Tylenol with codeine. Compazine if I'm
owing up. How come?"

"Is it possible your aunt went out while you slept

"No. I don't know. I don't understand what you'
getting at," he said.

I thought he was stalling, but I kept my mouth shu
We'd reached the Granger Building and Tony move
into the lobby ahead of me.

The elevator that had been out of order was now
operation, but the other one was immobilized, doo
open, the housing visible, two sawhorses in front of tl
opening with a warning sign.

Tony was watching me warily. "Did she say she we
out?"

"She claims she was home with you."

"So?"

"Come on, Tony. You're the only alibi she has.
you were zonked on medication, how do you kne
where she was?"

He pressed the elevator button.

The doors opened and we got on. The doors clos
without incident and we went up to six. I checked l
face as we stepped into the hallway. He was clea
conflicted, but I didn't want to press just yet. We head
down the corridor toward the suite his psychiatr
apparently occupied.

"Is there anything you want to talk about?" I aske

"No," he said, his voice breaking with indignatic
"You're crazy if you think she had anything to do w
it."

"Maybe you can explain that to Feldman. He's
charge of the case."

"I'm not talking to the cops about her," Tony sa
He tried the office door and found it locked. "Shit, l
not here."

There was a note taped to the door. He reached
to snatch the piece of paper, turning the movement i
an abrupt shove. Next thing I knew, I was on my har
and knees and he'd taken off. He banged on the eleva

tton and then veered right. I was up and running
en I heard the door leading to the stairway slam back
ainst the wall. I ran, banging into the stairwell only
conds after he did. He was already heading up.

"Tony! Come on. Don't do this."

He was moving fast, his footsteps scratching on the
ncrete stairs. His labored breathing echoed against
e walls as he went up. I don't keep fit for nothin', folks.
e had youth on me, but I was in good shape. I flung
y bag aside and grabbed the rail, starting up after him,
ounting the steps two at a time. I peered upward as I
n, trying to catch sight of him. He reached the seventh
or and kept on going. How many floors did this
ilding have?

"Tony. Goddamn it! Wait up! What are you doing?"

I heard another door bang up there. I stepped up
pace.

I reached the landing at the top. The elevator
pairman had apparently left the door to the attic
locked and Tony had shot through the gap, slamming
e door behind him. I snatched the handle, half expect-
g to find it locked. The door flew open and I pushed
ough, pausing on the threshold. The space was dim
d hot and dry, largely empty except for a small door
ening off to my right where the elevator brake,
ave, and drive motors were located. I ducked my
ad into the cramped space briefly, but it appeared to
empty. I pulled out and peered around. The roof was
other twenty feet up, the rafters steeply pitched,
bers forming a ninety-degree angle where they met.

Silence. I could see a square of light on the floor
I looked up. A wooden ladder was affixed to the
l to my right. At the top, a trap door was open and
ning daylight filtered down. I scanned the attic.
ere was an electrical panel sitting on some boxes. It
ked like some kind of old light board from the
ater on the ground floor. For some reason, there was

a massive papier-mâché bird standing to one side . . .
blue jay, wearing a painted business suit. Wooden cha
were stacked, seat to seat, to my left.

"Tony?"

I put a hand on one of the ladder rungs. He mig
well be hiding somewhere, waiting for me to head up
the roof so he could ease out and down the steps agair
started up, climbing maybe ten feet so I could survey t
attic from a better vantage point. There was no mo
ment, no sound of breathing. I looked up again a
started climbing cautiously. I'm not afraid of heigh
but I'm not fond of them either. Still, the ladder seem
secure and I couldn't figure out where else he might l

When I got to the top, I pulled myself into a sitti
position and peered around. The trap came out ir
small alcove, hidden behind an ornamental pedime
with a matching pediment halfway down the length
the roof. From the ground, the two of them had alwa
looked strictly decorative, but I could see now that c
disguised a brace of air vents. There was only a v
narrow walkway around the perimeter of the ro
protected by a short parapet. The steep pitch of the ro
would make navigating hazardous.

I peered down into the attic, hoping to see To
dart out of hiding and into the stairwell. There was
sign of him up here, unless he'd eased around to the
side. Gingerly, I got to my feet, positioning mys
between the nearly vertical roofline on my left and
ankle-high parapet on my right. I was actually walk
in a metal rain gutter that popped and creaked un
my weight. I didn't like the sound. It suggested that a
minute now the metal would buckle, toppling me off
side.

I glanced down eight floors to the street, wh
didn't seem that far away. The buildings across from
were two stories high and lent a comforting illusion
proximity, but pedestrians still seemed dwarfed by

eight. The streetlights had come on, and the traffic below was thinning. To my right, half a block away, the bell tower at the Axminster Theater was lighted from within, the arches bathed in tawny gold and warm blue. The drop had to be eighty feet. I tried to remember the velocity of a falling object. Something-something per foot per second was as close as I could come, but I knew the end result would be an incredible splat. I paused where I was and raised my voice. "Tony!"

I caught a flash of movement out of the corner of my eye and my heart flew into my throat. The plastic bag he'd been carrying was eddying downward, floating lazily. Coming from where? I peered over the parapet. I could see one of the niches that cut into the wall just below the cornice molding. The frieze that banded the building had always looked like marble from the street, but I could see now that it was molded plaster, the niche itself down about four feet and to the left. A half shell extended out maybe fifteen inches at the bottom edge and it held what was probably meant to be some sort of lamp with a torch flame, all molded plaster like the frieze. Tony was sitting there, his face turned up to mine. He'd climbed over the edge and he was now perched in the shallow ornamental niche, his arm locked around the torch, legs dangling. He'd taken a wig out of the bag he carried, donning it, looking up at me with a curious light in his eyes.

I was looking at the blonde who'd killed Daggett.

For a moment, we stared at each other, saying nothing. He had the cocky look of a ten-year-old defying his mom, but under the bravado I sensed a kid who was hoping someone would step in and save him from himself.

I put a hand on the pediment to steady myself. "You coming up or shall I come down?" I kept my tone matter-of-fact, but my mouth was dry.

"I'll be going down in a minute."

"Maybe we could talk about that," I said.

"It's too late," he said, smiling impishly. "I'm poise for flight."

"Will you wait there until I reach you?"

"No grabbing," he warned.

"I won't grab."

My palms were damp and I wiped them on n jeans.

I squatted, turning to face the roof, extending foot tentatively down along the frieze. I glanced dow trying to find some purchase. Garlands of pineappl grapes, and fig leaves formed a bas relief design th wound across the face of the building. "How'd you c this?" I asked.

"I didn't think about it. I just did it. You don't ha to come down. It won't help."

"I just don't want to talk to you hanging over th edge," I said, lying through my teeth. I was hoping get close enough to nab him, ignoring visions grappling with him at that height. I steadied myse tucking a toe into the shallow crevice formed by curling vine. The niche was only four feet away. ground level, I wouldn't have given it a thought.

I sensed that he was watching me, but I didn't da look. I held onto the parapet, lowering my left foo

He said, "You're not going to talk me out of this

"I just want to hear your side of it," I said.

"Okay."

"You won't try to kill me, will you?" I asked.

"Why would I? You never did anything to me."

"I'm glad you recognize that. Now I feel rea confident." I heard him laugh lightly at my tone.

I've seen magazine pictures of a man who can clin a vertical cliff face in a pair of tennis shoes, holdi himself with the tips of his fingers tucked into sm cracks that he discovers as he ascends. This has alwa seemed like a ludicrous pursuit and I usually flip to

rticle that makes more sense. The sight of the photo-
raphs makes me hyperventilate, especially the ones
ken from his vantage point, staring down into some
awning crevasse. Maybe, if the truth be known, I'm
nore anxious about heights than I let on.

I allowed my right foot to inch down again as far as
he lip of the niche. I found a handhold, down and to
he right. Felt like a pineapple, but I wasn't sure.
inning my safety to a phony piece of fruit. I had to be
uts.

The hardest part was actually letting go of the
oping once my foot was resting safely in the recess. I
ad to bend my knees, turning slightly to the right,
nking little by little until I could take a seat. Tony, ever
allant, actually gave me a hand, steadying me until I
ased down next to him. I'm not a brave soul. I'm really
ot. I just didn't want him flying off the side of that
uilding while I looked on. I locked my left arm around
he torch, just below his, holding onto my wrist with my
ght hand. I could feel sweat trickle down my sides.

"I hate this," I said. I was winded, not from effort
ut from apprehension.

"It's not bad. Just don't look down."

Of course I did. The minute he said that I had an
resistible desire to peek. I was hoping somebody would
oot us, like they always do on TV. Then the cops would
me with nets and the fire engines would arrive and
mebody would talk him out of this. I'm an organism of
e earth, a Taurus. I was never born of air, of water, or
fire. I'm a creature of gravity and I could feel the
ound whisper. The same thing happens to me in old
otels when I'm staying on the twenty-second floor. I
en a window and want to fling myself out.

"Oh, Jesus. This is such a bad idea," I said.

"For you maybe. Not for me."

I tried to think back to my short life as a cop and the
andard procedure for dealing with potential suicides.

Stall for time was the first rule. I didn't recall anythin
about hanging your ass off the side of a building, bu
here I was. I said, "What's the story, babe. You want t
tell me what's been going on?"

"There's not much to it. Daggett called the house o
Monday. Aunt Ramona made a note of the number so
called him back. I dreamed about killing him. I couldn
wait. I had fantasies for months, every night before
went to sleep. I wanted to catch him with a wire aroun
his neck and twist till it bit into his windpipe and hi
tongue bugged out. It doesn't take that long. I forge
what that's called now . . ."

"Garroting," I supplied.

"Yeah, I would have liked that, but then I figured
was better if it looked like an accident because that way
could get away with it."

"Why'd he call?"

"I don't know," Tony said uncomfortably. "He wa
drunk and blubbering, said he was sorry and wanted t
make it up to me for what he did. I go, 'Fine. Why don
we meet and talk?' And he goes, 'It would mean so muc
to me, son.'" Tony was acting out the parts, using
quavering falsetto for Daggett. "So then I tell him I'
meet him the next night at this bar he's calling from, th
Hub, which didn't give me much time to put togethe
this getup."

"Was that Ramona's skirt?"

"Nah, I got it at the Salvation Army thrift store for
buck. The sweater was another fifty cents and the sho
were two bucks."

"Where'd the sweater go?"

"I tossed it in another trash can a block away fro
the first. I thought it would all end up at the dump

"What about the wig?"

"That was Aunt Ramona's from years ago. Sh
didn't even know it was gone."

"Why'd you keep it?"

"I don't know. I was going to put it back in her closet where I got it, in case I needed it again. I had it on at the beach, but then I remembered Billy already knew who I was." He broke off, obviously confused. "I might have told my shrink about the whole thing if he'd been here. Anyway, the wig's expensive. This is real hair."

"The color's nice too," I said. I mean, where else could I go with this? Even Tony recognized the absurdity and he flashed me a look.

"You're humoring me, right?"

"Of course I'm humoring you!" I snapped. "I didn't come down here so we could have an argument."

He did a half shrug, smiling sheepishly.

I said, "Did you actually meet him there Tuesday night?"

"Not really. I went. I had it all worked out by then, only when I walk in, he's sittin' at this table talking to some guy. Turned out to be Billy Polo, but I didn't know it at the time. Billy was sitting in this booth with his back to the door. I saw Daggett, but I didn't realize he had company till I was right there in front of him. I veer off the minute I spot Billy, but by then he's had a good look at me. I'm not worried. I figure I'll never see him again anyway. I hang around for a while but they're really into it. I can tell Billy's leaning all over him and isn't likely to get up so I take a hike and go home."

"Was this one of the nights you had a migraine?"

"Yeah," he said. "I mean, some are real and some are fake, but I have to have a pattern, know what I mean? So I can come and go as I please."

"How'd you get down to the Hub, by cab?"

"My bike. The night I killed him, I rode down and left it at the marina and then I called a cab from a pay phone and took it over to the Hub."

"How'd you know he'd show up?"

"Because he called again and I said I'd be there."

"He never twigged to the fact that you'd showed up
the first time in drag?"

"How was he going to know? He hadn't seen me
since way before the trial. I was twelve, thirteen
something like that, a fat boy back then. I figured even i
he guessed, I'd do it anyway, kill his ass . . . and once
he was dead, who would know?"

"What went wrong?"

His brow furrowed. "I don't know. Well, I do. The
plan went fine. It was something else." His eyes met
mine and he looked every bit of fifteen, the blonde wig
adding softness and dimension to a face that was nearl
formless with youth. I could see how he'd pass as a
woman, slim, with a clear complexion, sweet smile on hi
wide mouth. He looked down at the street and for a
moment I thought he meant to swing out into space.

"When I was eight, I had these pet mice," he said.
"Really sweet. I kept 'em in this cage with a wheel and a
water bottle hanging upside down. Mom didn't think I'd
take care of 'em but I did. I'd cut up strips of paper i
the bottom of the cage so they could nest. Anyway, th
girl mouse had these babies. They couldn't have been as
long as this." He was indicating the end of his littl
finger. "Bald," he went on. "Just little bitty old things
We had to go out of town one weekend and when we go
back the cat had tried to get in the cage. Knocked it of
the desk and everything. The mice were gone. Probabl
the cat got 'em except for this one that had been layin
in all these paper shreds. Well, the water had spilled s
the paper was damp and the little thing must have ha
pneumonia or something because it was panting, like
couldn't breathe good. I tried to keep it warm. I watche
it for hours and it just kept getting worse and worse so
decided I better . . . you know, do away with it. So
wouldn't suffer anymore."

He leaned forward, swinging his feet back an
forth.

"Don't do that," I murmured anxiously. "Finish the
y. I want to know what happened next."

He looked over at me then, his tone of voice mild. "I
ed it in the toilet. That's the only way I could think of
ill it. I couldn't crush it, so I just figured I'd flush it
y. The little thing was half dead anyway and I
ught I'd be doing it a favor, putting it out of its
ery. But before I could do it, that little tiny hairless
y started struggling. You could tell it was in a total
ic, trying to get out of there, like it knew what was
pening . . ." He paused, dashing at his eyes. "Dag-
did that and now I can't get away from the look on
face, you know? I see it all day long. He knew. Which
fine with me. I wanted that. I wanted him to know it
me and his life wasn't worth two cents. I just didn't
ik he'd care. He was a drunk and a bum and he killed
hose people. He should have died. He shoulda been
1 to go. I was putting him out of his misery, you
w? So why'd he have to make it so hard?"

He fell silent and then he let out a deep breath.
iyway, that's how that went. I can't sleep anymore. I
am about that stuff. Makes me sick."

"What about Billy? I assume he figured it out when
saw you at the funeral."

"Yeah. That was weird. He didn't give a shit about
gett, but he felt like he should get part of the money
e kept his mouth shut. I would have given him all of
ut I didn't believe him. You should have seen him.
iggering around, making all these threats. I figured
1 start bragging one night about what he knew and
re I'd be."

The edge of the niche was beginning to cut into my
r end. I was hanging on so tightly that my arm was
ing numb, but I didn't dare ease up. I couldn't figure
how to get us out of this, but I knew I'd better start
ing fast.

"I killed a man once," I said. I meant to say more,

but that's all I could get out. I clamped my tee
together, trying to force the feelings back down whe
I'd been keeping them. It surprised me that after all t
time, it was still so painful to think about.

"On purpose?"

I shook my head. "Self-defense, but dead is dea

His smile was sweet. "You can always come w
me."

"Don't say that. I'm not going to jump and I do
want you to either. You're fifteen years old. There a
lots of other ways out."

"I don't think so."

"Your parents have money. They could hire Mel
Belli if they wanted to."

"My parents are dead."

"Well, the Westfalls, then. You know what I mea

"But Kinsey, I murdered two people and it's f
degree because I looked it up. How'm I gonna get av
with that?"

"The way half the killers in this country do," I s
with energy. "Hell, if Ted Bundy's still alive, v
shouldn't you be?"

"Who's he?"

"Never mind. Someone who did a lot worse th
you."

He thought for a moment. "I don't think it wo
work. I hurt too bad and I don't see the point."

"There isn't a point. That's the part you inver

"Could you do me a favor."

"All right. What's that?"

"Could you tell my aunt I said good-bye? I mean
write her a note, but I didn't have a chance."

"Goddamn it, Tony! Don't do this. She's had enou
pain."

"I know," he said, "but she's got my Uncle Fe
and they'll be okay. They never really knew what to
with me anyway."

"Oh, I see. You've got this all worked out."

"Well, yeah, I do. I've been reading up on this stuff [ ] it's no big deal. Kids kill themselves all the time."

I hung my head, almost incapable of framing a [re]ponse. "Tony, listen," I said finally. "What you're [tal]king about is dumb and it doesn't make any sense. Do [you] have any idea how crummy life seemed when I was [you]r age? I cried all the time and I felt like shit. I was [ugl]y. I was skinny. I was lonely. I was mad. I never [tho]ught I'd pull out of it, but I did. Life is hard. Life [hur]ts. So what? You tough it out. You get through and [the]n you'll feel good again, I swear to God."

He tilted his head, watching me intently. "I don't [thin]k so. Not for me. I'm in too deep. I can't bear any [mo]re. It's too much."

"Tony, there are days when none of us can bear it, [but] the good comes around again. Happiness is season[al l]ike anything else. Wait it out. There are people who [lov]e you. People who can help."

He shook his head. "I can't do that. It's kind of like I [mad]e a deal with myself to go through with this. She'll [und]erstand."

I could feel my temper snapping. "You want me to [tell] her that? You took a flying leap because you made a [fuc]king *deal* with yourself?" His face clouded with [unc]ertainty. I pressed on in a softer tone. "You want me [to te]ll her we sat up here like this and I couldn't talk you [out] of it? I can't let you do it. You'll break her heart."

He looked down at his lap, his eyes remote, face [puck]ering up the way boys do in lieu of tears. "It doesn't [hav]e anything to do with her. Tell her it was me and she [is] just great. I love her a lot, but it's my life, you know?"

I was silent for a moment, trying to figure out [whe]re to go next.

His face brightened and he held up an index finger. [I n]early forgot. I have a present for you." He shifted, [letti]ng go of the torch with a move that made me snatch

at him instinctively. He laughed at that. "Take it easy.
just reaching in the waistband of my jeans."

I looked to see what he'd produced. My .32
across his palm. He held his hand out so I could take
realizing belatedly that I couldn't free up a hand
reach for it.

"That's okay. I'll put it right here," he said kin
He set it in the niche, behind the ornamental torch I
clinging to.

"How'd you get it?" Stalling, stalling.

"Same way I did everything else. I used my he
You put your home address on that business card
gave Aunt Ramona, so I rode over on my bike
waited till you got home. I was going to introd
myself, you know, and act like this real polite kid w
good manners and a nifty haircut and stuff like th
Real innocent. I wasn't sure how much you knew an
thought maybe I could steer you off. I saw the car
you almost stopped, but then you took off again. I
to pedal my ass off to keep up with you and then
parked at the beach and I saw a chance to go thro
your stuff."

"You killed Billy with that?"

"Yeah. It was handy and I needed someth
quick."

"How'd you know about disposable silencers?"

"Some kid at school. I can make a pipe bomb to
he said. Then he sighed. "I gotta go soon. Time's ne
up."

I glanced down at the street. It was really get
dark up here, but the sidewalk was bright, the arc
across the way lit up like a movie house. Two people
the far side of the street had spotted us, but I could
they hadn't figured out what was going on. A stunt
movie being shot? I looked at Tony, but he didn't s
to be aware. My heart began to bang again and it m
my chest feel tight and hot.

"I'm getting tired," I said casually. "I may go back up, but I need some help. Can you give me a hand?"

"Sure," he said. And then he paused, his whole body alert. "This isn't a trick, is it?"

"No," I said, but I could hear my voice shake and the lie cut my tongue like a razor blade. I've always lied with ease and grace, with ingenuity and conviction and I couldn't get this one out. I saw him make a move. I grabbed him, hanging on for dear life, but all he had to do was give his arm a quick twist and my hand came loose. I reached again, but it was too late. I saw him push out, lifting off. For a moment, he seemed to hover there, like a leaf, and then he disappeared from my line of sight. I didn't look down again after that.

I thought I heard a siren wailing, but the sound was mine.

I billed Barbara Daggett for $1,040.00, which she
paid by return mail. It's nearly Christmas now and I
haven't slept well for six weeks. I've thought a lot about
Daggett and I've changed my mind about one thing. I
suspect he knew what was going on. From a distance,
Tony might have passed for a woman, but up close, he
looked exactly what he was . . . a young kid playing
dress-up, smart beyond his years, but not wise enough
by half. I don't think Daggett was fooled. Why he went
along with the game, I'm not sure. If he believed what
Billy'd told him, he must have figured he was dead
either way. Maybe he felt he owed Tony that last
sacrifice. I'll never know, but it makes more sense to me
that way. Some debts of the human soul are so enormous
only life itself is sufficient forfeit. Perhaps in this case, all
of the accounts are now paid in full . . . except mine.

—Respectfully submitted,
Kinsey Millhone

ABOUT THE AUTHOR

SUE GRAFTON has written novels, articles, short fiction, a screenplay, and numerous teleplays. She has also lectured on writing at colleges and conferences in Southern California and the Midwest. Her first mystery, 'A' IS FOR ALIBI, won an award from the Cloak and Clue Society of Wisconsin. 'B' IS FOR BURGLAR won both the Anthony and the Shamus awards for best novel of 1985, and 'C' IS FOR CORPSE won the Anthony Award for Best Novel in 1986. "The Parker Shotgun" won a Macavity Award from the Mystery Readers of America and an Anthony for Best Short Story of 1986. Grafton, who was born in Louisville, Kentucky, now lives in Southern California with her husband, Steven Humphrey.

BANTAM MYSTERY COLLECTION

S U E   G R A F T O N
has written novels, articles, short fiction, a screenplay, and numerous teleplays. She has also lectured on writing at colleges and conferences in Southern California and the Midwest. Her first mystery, 'A' IS FOR ALIBI, won an award from the Cloak and Clue Society of Wisconsin. 'B' IS FOR BURGLAR won both the Anthony and the Shamus awards for best novel of 1985, and 'C' IS FOR CORPSE won the Anthony Award for Best Novel in 1987. "The Parker Shotgun" won a Macavity Award from the Mystery Readers of America and an Anthony for Best Short Story of 1986. Grafton, who was born in Louisville, Kentucky, now lives in Southern California with her husband, Steven Humphrey.

The client came to Kinsey Millhone with an
job—just deliver $25,000 to a fifteen-yea
kid. A little odd, and a little too easy,
Kinsey took Alvin Limardo's retainer c
anyway. It turned out to be as phony as he
In real life, his name was John Dagge
chronic drunk with a record as long as you
and a reputation for sleazy deals. B
wasn't just a deadbeat. By the time K
caught up with him, he was a dead bo
with a whole host of people who
delighted to hear the news. But how do
make a stiff pay up what he owes you?

ISBN 0-553-27163-6

27163

0 76783 00599 0